W9-BSU-278

WITHDRAWN

THE LADY HAS A PAST

3 1526 05523792 6

THE LADY HAS A PAST

AMANDA QUICK

THORNDIKE PRESS
A part of Gale, a Cengage Company

GALE
A Cengage Company

Copyright © 2021 by Jayne Ann Krentz.
Thorndike Press, a part of Gale, a Cengage Company.

ALL RIGHTS RESERVED
This is a work of fiction. Names, characters, places, and incidents either are the product of the author's imagination or are used fictitiously, and any resemblance to actual persons, living or dead, business establishments, events, or locales is entirely coincidental.
Thorndike Press® Large Print Core.
The text of this Large Print edition is unabridged.
Other aspects of the book may vary from the original edition.
Set in 16 pt. Plantin.

LIBRARY OF CONGRESS CIP DATA ON FILE.
CATALOGUING IN PUBLICATION FOR THIS BOOK
IS AVAILABLE FROM THE LIBRARY OF CONGRESS.

ISBN-13: 978-1-4328-8679-0 (hardcover alk. paper)

Published in 2021 by arrangement with Berkley, an imprint of Penguin Publishing Group, a division of Penguin Random House LLC.

Printed in Mexico
Print Number: 01   Print Year: 2021

For Frank, as always, with love

CHAPTER 1

Charles Adlington was in the process of trying to drown his wife in the pool when Lyra Brazier walked into the walled garden behind the mansion.

At least that's what it looked like.

Lyra froze, trying to process the surreal scene. Everything appeared so *normal* — the California sun dancing on the water, the umbrella-shaded lounge chairs, the pitcher of martinis on the table, the bag of golf clubs leaning against a garden bench. Just another postcard-perfect day in the seaside paradise that was Burning Cove.

Except that Adlington was attempting to murder his wife.

Lyra told herself the Adlingtons might be playing some kind of boisterous game. The violent splashing made it difficult to be sure what was going on. She couldn't even be absolutely certain that Marcella and Charles Adlington were the two people in the pool.

She had never met the couple. That seemed the most logical conclusion, however, given that the villa belonged to them and there was no one else around, not even a housekeeper or gardener.

But the husband was supposed to be playing golf. That left another horrifying possibility — that Marcella was being attacked by a stranger.

The woman in the pool managed to surface long enough to scream.

"Help me. My husband is trying to kill me."

So much for the assaulted-by-a-stranger theory.

Charles looked up from his task of trying to hold Marcella's head underwater, saw Lyra, and immediately released his victim. He splashed frantically toward the pool steps.

"You're next, you interfering bitch. How dare you try to put me away? Do you know who I am?"

He moved with surprising speed for such a big man. He reached the top step just as Lyra overcame the shock that had bolted her to the ground. She was not imagining things. She really had walked in on a murder in progress. The smart thing to do was run. But Adlington was a strong, athletic man and he was wearing only a pair of belted

8

swim shorts. He could move fast.

She, on the other hand, was dressed for what was supposed to have been an interview with a wealthy client. Her fashionable stacked-heel sandals, stockings, and snug-fitting, calf-length skirted suit were not designed for running.

There was another factor as well. She could not leave the woman in the pool alone to deal with a violent man who was apparently in a killing mood.

Adlington was closing in fast. There was madness and rage in his eyes.

She rushed toward the golf bag and grabbed an iron. Adlington was almost upon her now.

Using the proper two-handed grip, she swung the club with all the strength she could muster. The years of being captain of the golf team at the elite women's college she had attended paid off. She aimed for Adlington's head. The club slammed into the side of his skull with a stomach-churning thud. Blood spurted.

Adlington toppled to the side and went down hard. He landed on the tiled patio and did not move. A crimson lake began to form around his head.

Lyra stared at him, shocked at her own act of violence, unnerved by the possibility that she might have just killed a man, and light-headed with the certainty that she had almost been murdered. Her pulse was skittering and she could not catch her breath.

"Thank God you arrived when you did." The woman in the pool staggered through the water to the steps. "Charles was trying to murder me. The doctors at the asylum told me they had cured him. I was a fool to believe them."

Lyra finally managed to breathe. "Marcella Adlington?"

"Yes." Marcella made it out of the pool and grabbed a towel from a nearby table. "I'm Marcella Adlington."

She was in her late thirties or very early forties, an attractive blonde who had probably been nothing short of ravishing when she was in her twenties. She had the kind of bone structure that would ensure she aged well. Her fashionable frock was soaking wet and clung to her elegantly curved body like a second skin. Her shoulder-length hair hung in wet tendrils. Mascara ran down her cheeks. Her maroon red lipstick was smeared.

She blotted her face and peered at Lyra. "You're not Raina Kirk, are you? I was told she was an older, more experienced woman."

"Miss Kirk couldn't make the appointment," Lyra said. "She sent me instead. I'm Lyra Brazier."

"I see." Marcella collapsed onto a bench, clutching the towel. "Forgive me. I feel a little shaky." She stared at the unmoving body of her husband. "Is he —"

Lyra glanced at the man crumpled on the patio. "I don't know. We must call the police."

"Yes, of course." Marcella wrapped her arms around herself and started to rock gently back and forth. "I hope he's dead. I was absolutely terrified of him."

Lyra pulled herself together, dropped the golf club, and hurried around the edge of the pool. She stopped close to Marcella. The woman was trembling violently.

"Please let him be dead," Marcella whispered. "He was going to kill me. They said he was cured, but he intended to murder me. He said it would look like an accidental drowning. He said the police would assume I got drunk on martinis, fell into the pool, and died. He had it all planned out, you see."

Lyra grabbed two thick towels from the stack on a nearby bench. A heavy object that had been tucked between the towels tumbled out and landed on the tiles with a clat-

11

ter. Startled, she looked down and saw a pistol.

Marcella stiffened. "I bought it a while ago. I was so afraid of him. But in the end it didn't do me any good. He caught me by surprise. Said he knew I was waiting for a private investigator. He realized I intended to try to find evidence to have him committed again."

Lyra did not respond, for the simple reason that she could not sort out her own feelings. On the one hand, she hoped that Charles Adlington was never again going to be a threat. But the possibility that she might have killed a man, even in self-defense, was too much to deal with in that moment. She reminded herself that she was a professional. She had to remain calm, cool, and collected.

She wrapped a dry towel around Marcella's shoulders. "Wait here."

Skirting the pool, she went back across the patio and approached the body warily. The bleeding appeared to have slowed. She hoped that was a good sign. But when she got closer it occurred to her that it might indicate that Adlington's heart had stopped beating.

She glanced at the golf club. There was blood and hair and possibly other matter on it. She did not want to examine it too closely. Adlington showed no obvious signs of life, but maybe he was faking unconsciousness. If she tried to check for a pulse, he might grab her and overpower her.

She turned to look at Marcella. "I'm going to call the police. Where's the nearest phone?"

"What?" Marcella blinked a couple of times and jerked her attention away from the body. "Oh. The phone. Yes, of course. Inside the conservatory."

"Keep an eye on him," Lyra said. "I'll be right back. Whatever you do, don't get too close to him. He may still be conscious."

"Wait." Marcella sprang to her feet. "Don't leave me out here with him. What if he's not dead?"

"I have to call the police."

"I'll come with you."

Marcella made her way around the pool. Lyra waited for her. Together they went into the glass-walled conservatory. The phone was on a small table. Lyra picked up the receiver and dialed the operator.

"Burning Cove police, please," she said. "Homicide." She tightened her grip on the phone to try to still the trembling in her fingers. She was a private investigator. She had to look good in front of the client.

Competent.

"One moment, I'll connect you," the operator said.

A moment later a gruff, male voice came on the line. "Homicide. Brandon."

"This is Lyra Brazier. I'm an investigator for Kirk Investigations."

"Yeah? Didn't know Miss Kirk had hired another investigator. Business is picking up, huh?"

Lyra decided this was not the time to explain that she was technically an apprentice investigator.

"I'm calling from the Adlington residence on Harborview Drive, Detective," she said. "There's been an incident involving Mrs. Adlington's husband. We need the police and an ambulance."

"Mrs. Adlington is hurt?" Brandon's voice sharpened abruptly. "How bad?"

Lyra studied the unmoving figure on the patio. "Mrs. Adlington is fine. It's Mr. Adlington who has been injured. I don't know how badly. He appears to be . . . unconscious." She cleared her throat. "Possibly dead."

"Are you and Mrs. Adlington safe?"

"Yes."

"Stay where you are. I'm on my way."

There was a click on the other end of the

line. Brandon had hung up. Lyra dropped the receiver into the cradle and looked at Marcella, who was staring at her husband through the glass panes of the conservatory.

"I knew he was becoming increasingly unbalanced again," she said. "But I also knew no one would believe me. When there were other people around he always managed to appear perfectly normal. He even fooled the doctors at the asylum. I had to have proof."

"You wanted to hire Kirk Investigations to try to find credible evidence that your husband was a danger to you and that he should be locked up in a mental hospital," Lyra said.

There was a short pause before Marcella answered. Lyra got a ghostly frisson of intuitive awareness. Something was off. She was almost certain that Marcella was rapidly rewriting a script.

"Yes," Marcella said, speaking a little too quickly now. "Yes, that was why I made an appointment with a private investigator today. But Charles showed up a short time ago. He was supposed to be playing golf. That's his bag of clubs out there."

Sirens sounded in the distance.

"I'll go around to the front of the house and escort Detective Brandon and the

15

ambulance crew back here," Lyra said. She glanced at Charles, who still had not moved. "Do you want to come with me?"

"No." Marcella took a deep breath. "I'll stay in here. If he moves, I'll lock the door. He's not much of a threat now, is he? Not with that head wound. Assuming he's even alive."

"Assuming that," Lyra said. "No, he's not a threat. Not at the moment, at any rate."

Lyra walked quickly out of the conservatory and followed the flagstone path around the big house. A police car and an ambulance were pulling into the circular driveway.

The passenger-side door of the car opened. A man in a rumpled suit and a battered fedora climbed out. She recognized him. She had met Brandon recently when her sister, Vivian, had become the target of an assassin.

The sight of his hat made her realize that the fashionably feminine version of a fedora she'd had on when she arrived at the villa was no longer perched at a smart angle on her carefully pinned-up hair. It had come off during the short, brutal fight with Adlington.

Detective Brandon had the tough, world-weary look of a good cop who has seen human nature at its worst but who is determined to do his job. He gave Lyra a short, crisp nod.

"Miss Brazier," he said. "Where's Adlington?"

"On the patio behind the house," Lyra said. "I'll show you."

Brandon didn't wait for her. He took off along the flagstone path. Two ambulance attendants hauled a stretcher out of their vehicle and followed. Lyra had to trot to keep up with them.

"Talk to me," Brandon ordered over his shoulder.

"I had an appointment with Mrs. Adlington this afternoon," Lyra said. "Well, Raina had the appointment, but she thought it would be good experience for me to interview the client, so I came here instead. Mrs. Adlington expressed interest in hiring Kirk Investigations, but she didn't say why. When I got here I found Mr. and Mrs. Adlington in the pool. It looked like Mr. Adlington was trying to drown his wife. When he saw me he climbed out of the pool and came after me."

"Yeah? What did you —" Brandon went through the garden gate, saw the body, the blood, and the three iron, and came to a sudden stop. "You hit him with a *golf club*?"

"It was the closest thing at hand."

Brandon whistled appreciatively. "You must have a hell of a swing."

"It's actually a pretty boring game, but my parents both play and so did my ex-fiancé and, well, it was expected, if you know what I mean."

Brandon shot her an unreadable look. "Right. We didn't have any golf courses or country clubs in my neighborhood. We played baseball in the middle of the street."

"Sounds more interesting than golf, but then, almost anything is."

She wasn't paying close attention to the conversation, because she was watching the ambulance attendants. They had positioned the stretcher beside Adlington's unmoving form.

"Hold on," Brandon called to the two men. "I want to take a look before you move him."

He strode across the patio and crouched beside Adlington. Lyra stayed where she was. She had no desire to take a closer look.

"Is he alive?" she whispered.

Brandon looked surprised by the question. "Hell no. Several whacks to the head with a golf club would probably take down a small elephant."

"Several whacks?" Lyra forgot to breathe. "But I only hit him once."

18

Brandon shrugged. "It's hard to keep track of stuff like that when you're scared and fighting for your life."

"I know exactly how many times I hit him," Lyra said.

But the three iron was not on the patio where she had left it. The club had been moved. It was now a few feet from the original position. She looked at Marcella Adlington.

Marcella moved to stand next to her. She raked her fingers through her wet hair. There was a plea for understanding in her eyes. She lowered her voice.

"I had to be sure," she said.

CHAPTER 2

"Marcella Adlington set me up," Lyra said. She walked to the window of the office and contemplated the view of the palm-shaded street through the wooden blinds. "I can't prove it, but I'm certain of it. At the last minute everything went off script. She had to improvise."

"She wanted to be certain her husband really was dead," Raina Kirk said.

"Yes."

Raina leaned back in the big chair and tapped one elegantly polished nail on the gleaming desk. She was not sure how to deal with the situation. She had no intention of telling Lyra that she understood Marcella Adlington's panic and determination all too well.

Nevertheless, she got the nagging feeling that it was her responsibility to offer some words of comfort. Lyra was, after all, very new in the investigation business. She had been on the job for only three days.

But Raina had no idea what to say. Until now Kirk Investigations had been a one-woman business, *her* business. In her other life back in New York she had worked as a secretary for a couple of professional killers. Neither that role nor her new one here in Burning Cove had prepared her for dealing with an employee who had been subjected to a major emotional shock. Maybe she wasn't cut out for management.

In hindsight it had probably been a mistake to take Lyra Brazier on as an apprentice. Was there even such a thing as an apprentice in the investigation business? That had been Lyra's description of the position she sought at the firm when she had walked through the door and announced she wanted to work for Kirk Investigations.

One thing had quickly become clear: When Lyra started talking, it was astonishingly difficult to resist her. Raina had sat politely through the pitch, fully intending to say no, but somehow she had ended up agreeing to give Lyra a trial run as an apprentice.

Today it was starting to look as if she might not last long in the job she had so convincingly talked her way into. Lyra came from a wealthy, privileged background. Her father owned an international shipping company. She was smart, well-educated, stylish, and determined, but she had led a very sheltered life. She lacked experience of the real world.

Lyra had been born and raised to be a socialite — to marry an upper-class man from a good family, to host charity luncheons, to throw lavish parties and attend the opera. She had definitely not been brought up to risk her neck trying to uncover other people's secrets. And now, three days into the job, she had nearly gotten herself murdered on her very first assignment.

I should let her go, Raina thought. *For her own good.* There was an unmistakable aura of naïveté and cheerful innocence about Lyra. The private investigation business was not a good career choice for the naïve and the innocent.

But one thing stopped her from firing Lyra on the spot. Yes, a madman had tried to murder her that day, but she had fought off her attacker with a golf club and she had saved herself and the client. She also understood that she had been used. She was no longer quite so naïve or so innocent. She was learning fast.

"You're right," Raina said. "Marcella Adlington was certainly very specific about the time of the appointment this afternoon. She was not dressed for swimming or sunbathing, yet she insisted you meet her poolside."

Lyra swung around, her hazel eyes sharp and clear. "She had a gun hidden in a stack of towels. The fact that Charles Adlington was dressed for swimming indicates that his presence at the scene was not a surprise to his wife."

"I agree."

"I found out later that his car was parked in the garage. He had been there for a while. She must have told him she planned to hire a private investigator to try to get him committed again, because when he realized I was there, he stopped trying to drown her and came after me."

"If Marcella had shot her husband without any obvious reason, she would have been arrested for murder. She needed a witness and a believable explanation for pulling the trigger. She told him she was expecting an investigator because she knew he would fly into a rage when he saw you. That would give her the excuse to kill him. She would be the heroine of the situation because she stopped her husband from murdering you. She certainly would not have been arrested

23

in those circumstances, and her terrifying husband would be safely dead."

Lyra began to pace the room. "But things went wrong. He turned on her first."

"If you hadn't arrived when you did, she would have died. You saved her life when you used that golf club on Adlington."

Lyra stopped in the middle of the room. "But suddenly Marcella was faced with an unplanned scenario. The whole point was to make sure she got rid of her husband, but she wasn't sure that Adlington was dead. Neither of us could tell if he was alive, and we didn't dare get close enough to check for a pulse."

"So when you went around the house to greet Detective Brandon, Marcella picked up the golf club and made certain that her husband would not survive."

Lyra nodded slowly. "Yes, that is exactly what happened. I don't believe Marcella ever intended to hire Kirk Investigations. She just wanted her husband dead."

Raina sighed. "Welcome to my world. Rule number one is always assume the client is lying or, at the very least, not telling you the whole truth. Everyone has secrets to protect."

"Right. I'll remember that."

Raina sat forward and clasped her hands

on the desktop. "Are you sure you want to be a private investigator?"

"Please don't fire me because of what happened today."

Raina raised her brows. "I'm not going to let you go because of that. After all, you saved the client —"

"Non-client."

"You saved the non-client and yourself. You exhibited remarkably sharp thinking under extraordinarily dangerous circumstances. I am very impressed with your golf swing, by the way."

Lyra's jaw tightened. Shadows veiled her eyes. She turned away and went back to the window.

"What bothers me is that I'll never know," she said quietly.

"Never know what?" Raina asked.

"If I'm the one who killed Charles Adlington. I only struck him once, Raina, but I hit him very hard. There was a lot of blood. But Marcella Adlington hit him several more times."

Raina tried and failed to come up with a comforting response. She said the only words she knew to be true.

"You did what you had to do to save yourself and Marcella Adlington," she said. "That's all that matters. There are always unanswered questions in this business. Fact of life. You have the makings of a good investigator, but I believe you should give your career plans some serious thought before you decide if you want to stay with this firm."

Lyra folded her arms. "Okay."

"And now we are going to follow a long-standing tradition in this business."

Lyra gave her a wan smile. "What's that?"

"We're going to celebrate."

Lyra looked bemused. "What are we celebrating?"

"How about the fact that you and Marcella Adlington both survived?"

Lyra took a deep breath. "You're right. That is definitely something worth celebrating."

"This evening you and I will go out on the town. We will start with cocktails and dinner at the Burning Cove Hotel and then we will catch a cab to the hottest nightclub in town, the Paradise."

CHAPTER 3

"I'm afraid you have become a problem, Mr. Cage." Erling Lennox took a pistol out from inside his hand-tailored coat. "You have served your purpose. I am delighted with the Milton you found for me. But I'm afraid that in the process of tracking it down you learned too much about my collection and my business. I regret I won't have the opportunity to make use of your expertise in the future. You came highly recommended."

"I appreciate the compliment," Simon Cage said, "but I won't be able to return it. In the course of my work I have encountered any number of murderers, blackmailers, and embezzlers who were a hell of a lot smarter than you are. On a scale of one to ten, I'd put you at about a three."

It took a couple of beats for the insult to register. When it did, Lennox reddened with fury. Like so many men born into a world

27

of wealth, privilege, and power, he assumed he was vastly more intelligent than those he considered his social inferiors. Simon never ceased to be amazed by the fact that people who got away with blackmail or murder once or twice came to the conclusion they were superior beings. Men like Lennox experienced an intoxicating sense of power when they discovered they could manipulate others or take a human life.

"Who are you, Simon Cage?" Lennox asked. "You aren't a real book dealer, are you?" The flash of rage was fading from his eyes now. A trace of wariness, perhaps even outright alarm, was taking its place. "What is going on here?"

"I'm exactly who it says I am on my business card. Simon Cage, Antiquarian Book Dealer. The Milton is a forgery, by the way. You were conned. Nothing personal. Just part of the job."

Lennox moved out from behind his desk. He kept the pistol leveled at Simon's chest.

"Who are you working for?" he rasped.

They were in Lennox's private library, an elegantly paneled room in an impressively furnished mansion located on a hillside overlooking Los Angeles.

Simon was standing in the narrow aisle formed by two long wooden bookcases that reached almost to the ceiling. He gripped his heavy leather briefcase in one hand, aware that he was an easy target for Lennox, who had moved to stand at the front of the aisle. Simon could move backward or forward but he could not dodge left or right.

They were the only two people in the big house. Lennox's wife was visiting friends on the East Coast. The housekeeper and butler-chauffeur had been given the evening off. The realization that neither of them was present had been Simon's first indication that he was not meant to leave the mansion alive that night.

He leaned one shoulder against a bookcase and used his free hand to push his gold-rimmed spectacles higher on his nose. "What makes you think I'm working for anyone other than myself?"

"You conned me into hiring you," Lennox said, jaw clenching. "You wanted access to my library because you were hoping to discover certain information."

"I wasn't *hoping* to find the records of the transactions involving your embezzlement activities. It would be more accurate to say I was sure the evidence that you have been systematically defrauding your investors would be here in your library." Simon plucked a book off the shelf. "And here it is."

Lennox stared at the book in Simon's hand. For a few seconds he was speechless.

"Impossible," he finally blurted out. "How in hell did you find that one book among the hundreds in this room? Someone must have told you it was here. Who betrayed me? Was it my housekeeper? My wife? I can't believe either of them knows anything about my business affairs. I've been so damned careful."

"What you've been is damned careless." Simon dropped the book into the open briefcase. "Your mistake was in murdering your business associate. You staged that fatal crash on Mulholland to get rid of Haywood because you wanted to control the whole business. But you left your prints all over that Bugatti of his."

Lennox's mouth fell open. "That's impossible. There was a fire."

"The kind of prints you left behind aren't erased by fire."

"What the hell are you talking about?"

"I don't have time for this. It's getting late and I've got a long drive ahead of me tomorrow."

"You're right. You don't have much time left at all. I can guarantee that you won't be

30

driving anywhere tomorrow." Lennox hesitated. "Tell me who you're working for, damn it. Is it one of my investors?"

"My client is only concerned with the blackmail materials." Simon patted the heavy briefcase. "I've got those, too. It's the FBI that's interested in the embezzlement and fraud side of your business. Ever since they took down Al Capone on tax evasion charges, the Bureau has had a lot of respect for financial records. The special agents are waiting in the garden, by the way. I'll give them your very informative ledger on my way out."

Lennox's eyes narrowed. "Do you really think I'm going to fall for that story?"

"Why not? I used to work for one of the slickest con men in the business, and if there's one thing I learned, it's that the easiest person to con is another con artist."

Lennox's eyes tightened at the corners. "Tell me how you know that I sabotaged Haywood's Bugatti."

"Now, why would I give you that information if it's the only thing that's keeping me alive?"

"Because I will put a bullet in your guts, Mr. Cage. I'm told it takes a long time to die that way and that the process is exceedingly painful. Sooner or later you will beg me to end the agony."

"I should apologize for implying you aren't very intelligent. Hiding your files in your library was a sound idea. After all, who would ever think to search for them here?" Simon gestured to indicate the large collection of books. "Any serious thief would look for a hidden safe before he thought about these shelves. After all, it would take days to go through every volume in this room."

"And yet you found my records after a single walk-through of my collection?"

Simon smiled. "While you accompanied me. It's the prints you left behind, you see."

"That makes no sense. Every book in here has my prints on it. I handled all of them at one time or another."

"I'm talking about a different kind of prints — like those on the Bugatti," Simon said. "The kind you leave when you get very excited. Nervous. Enraged. Prints like that are very, very hot."

"Stop lying. Someone talked. *Who was it?*"

"I doubt if you would believe me if I tried to explain. People rarely do. Now, I would appreciate it if you would get out of the way. It's late, and as I said, I've got a long drive ahead of me in the morning. I'd like to get some sleep."

"Don't move."

Simon raised the large briefcase and cradled it in front of his chest. At the same time he leaned one shoulder against a big bookcase, putting his body weight into it.

The heavy bookcase rocked a little. Simon leaned harder.

"Stop," Lennox shouted. "What are you doing?"

He took a hasty step back, trying to get out of the aisle. He raised his pistol and fired.

Simon was braced for the impact; nevertheless, the bullet struck the steel-lined briefcase with enough force to spin him backward and sideways. He came up hard against the rocking bookshelf. His glasses flew off.

The long bookshelf shuddered and slowly toppled into the neighboring aisle. Rows of heavy volumes were jarred loose and tumbled to the floor.

Startled, confused, and distracted, Lennox hastily retreated a couple of steps.

"You should be dead," he shouted.

"Not yet."

Simon charged forward down the aisle, using the briefcase as a shield.

Lennox got off another shot but was scrambling backward so quickly he lost his balance. This time the bullet thudded into a bookcase.

In the next instant Simon slammed into him with the briefcase. Both men went down, but Lennox was on the bottom. He lay still, mouth opening and closing, the breath knocked out of him.

Meanwhile the rows of bookcases fell in a cascading wave. There was a dull rumble. Volumes flew off the shelves.

Simon leaped to his feet, thought briefly about trying to retrieve his glasses, and immediately concluded it was a lost cause.

He kicked Lennox's pistol under the desk and headed for the door of the library. Behind him the roar of the toppling bookcases ceased.

The special agents from the Bureau pounded down the hall.

"Sounded like gunshots and an explosion," one of the agents said. "You okay?"

"I'm fine," Simon said. Automatically he started to adjust his glasses and then realized he was no longer wearing them. "The bookcases weren't anchored to the floor. You'd think Lennox would have known better. This is earthquake country, after all."

"He's from back East." The agent shrugged. "Probably never considered earthquakes when he furnished this place. Is he alive in there?"

"Yes. I left him on the floor. Pistol is under the desk."

"We'll take it from here." The agent waved the other agents toward the library. "What about the fraud evidence?"

Simon set the briefcase on the floor and reached down to unlatch it. He took out the book and handed it to the agent. "It's all in there. The details of every fraudulent transaction. Lennox was very, very thorough when it came to keeping two sets of books. This one has all the evidence you'll need to get a conviction."

The agent examined the cover of the book, mystified. And then he chuckled. "Dale Carnegie's *How to Win Friends and Influence People*. Well, what do you know? My wife gave me a copy of this book a couple of months ago. She said it would help me advance in the Bureau. Never got around to reading it."

"Trust me, the details inside that particular copy will guarantee you a promotion," Simon said.

He went on down the hall and out into the night. The custom-built Cord was parked in the drive. He got behind the wheel and opened the glove box to take out his spare pair of eyeglasses. His vision was excellent, but he had learned early on that

35

people expected antiquarian book dealers to wear spectacles.

He tucked the glasses into the pocket of his jacket. The scars on the back of his right hand burned a little. The doctor had warned him he might experience some itching or irritation from time to time. Acid burns often took a long time to heal. He was told it had something to do with nerve damage. But he suspected that his other senses had been affected, too. He was more acutely aware of the energy laid down in objects than he had been before the McGruder case.

He massaged the roughened skin for a moment and then fired up the powerful engine. A glass of whiskey would calm things down.

He drove away from the mansion and headed toward Santa Monica. The familiar rush of energy that came with the successful closing of a case hit his veins like a powerful drug. It would inevitably be followed by the crash, but for now he could savor the satisfaction.

It would have been nice to share the victory with someone, preferably an interesting woman, but there was no one waiting for him at the house. He was well aware that was his own fault.

He enjoyed the company of women but

he had learned the hard way to keep things superficial. His relationships always ended badly. Either the lady realized there was no future with him and left to pursue other options or she discovered his secrets and fled.

It occurred to him that he was reflecting on the past. That was not good. The thrill of success was wearing off already, and he hadn't even had a chance to enjoy some whiskey. Maybe he needed a vacation.

In the morning he had to drive to Burning Cove to deliver the contents of the briefcase to Luther Pell. Why not stay there for a while? He would book a room at a nice hotel. Spend his mornings relaxing in a lounge chair while reading the latest Cooper Boone mystery. In the afternoons he would take long walks on the beach. In the evenings he would drink ice-cold martinis in Pell's nightclub.

And maybe, with a little luck, he would meet the perfect woman — a sophisticated, reckless, experienced divorcée who was fresh off the train from Reno and eager to celebrate her newfound freedom, no strings attached. The kind of woman high-minded people labeled *fast*. He got a pleasant little frisson of anticipation at the thought.

A short time later he pulled into the garage attached to the house that served as his home and his business. There was no sign out front. He worked by referral only.

He would have a drink and get some sleep. In the morning he would pack and head for Burning Cove.

He collected the mail from the box, used his key to open the front door, and let himself into the darkened house. He turned on the hall light and paused to drop the contents of the mailbox onto the small table. There were the usual assortment of advertising circulars and bills. There was also a letter.

Most of the letters he received were from potential clients requesting his assistance in tracking down and authenticating a rare volume. Occasionally he got complaints because he had not provided the answers that the client wanted. It wasn't his fault there were a lot of forgeries in the world of antiquarian books.

But the letter on the table tonight was different. The stationery was cheap, for one thing. Most clients used good-quality paper. If they couldn't afford quality paper, they couldn't afford him.

He picked up the letter. There was no return address. Cautiously he heightened his senses.

A whisper of anxiety. Desperation. Excitement.

He opened the envelope and took out the single sheet inside. The note was short.

Dear Simon:
I write with wonderful news. A prestigious academic institution in California is offering me a position in its new parapsychology laboratory. It is a fully equipped and well-funded facility designed to rival the parapsychology lab that Rhine and McDougall established a few years ago at Dukc University. There is one small condition that must be satisfied before the appointment is final, namely a demonstration of my paranormal energy–sensing machine. A simple matter, of course, but I would appreciate your assistance. I promise you it will not take much of your time.

I am currently finishing my East Coast tour. As soon as I am free I will take the train to Los Angeles.

I look forward to seeing you soon.

Yours truly,
Otto

Simon crushed the letter in his fist and tossed it into the waste basket. He had been struggling to close the door on his past for nearly five years, ever since he had walked away from Dr. Otto Tinsley and his Institute of Parapsychology road show.

The memory of learning a hard truth while standing in the pouring rain in a Seattle graveyard rose up to haunt him, as it always did when he thought about Tinsley. Predictably, it was accompanied by another memory.

He was twelve years old and he was in the hallway outside the office of the director of the orphanage. He was straining to overhear the conversation taking place on the other side of the closed door because he knew his future hinged on the outcome.

It was not the first time he had eavesdropped on Elaine Marsden's conversation with a doctor. Marsden was the director of the orphanage, and this was not the first consultation she had sought. There had been two previous occasions. Each one had ended with a terrifying recommendation: "The boy is hopelessly delusional. He should be committed to an asylum for the insane."

Director Marsden had insisted on obtaining one more opinion. Dr. Otto Tinsley was now about to deliver it. If this ended with the same diagnosis, Simon had plans to run away that night.

40

"I am convinced that I can cure the boy's delusions, but it will take time," Tinsley said. "He will have to accompany me."

"The only way I can allow him to leave with you is if you adopt him."

"Certainly," Tinsley said.

"Sign here," Marsden said.

There was relief and hope in her voice. She did not know what the future held for Simon, but she had managed to save him from an asylum. She had given him a chance.

Out in the hall Simon decided he would not be running away that night after all. He was going home with Dr. Otto Tinsley, who had promised to cure him of the delusions; make him normal.

Things hadn't quite worked out that way, of course. Home had turned out to be a life on the road and Tinsley hadn't even tried to cure him of his delusions, but the two of them had formed a family of sorts.

Until Seattle.

He went into the bathroom, took out the cream he kept in a drawer, and massaged it into the scars on his right hand. Then he headed into the kitchen, opened a cupboard, and took down the whiskey bottle.

No question about it — a vacation in Burning Cove and some long, hot nights with a fast, reckless divorcée who wouldn't

41

ask a lot of questions were exactly what he needed.

CHAPTER 4

Raina took a sip of her martini and set the stemmed glass on the pristine white tablecloth. "I didn't know what else to say to her."

"You told her the truth," Luther Pell said. "She did what she had to do to survive and now she will have to learn to live with that knowledge."

Raina looked at the man she had never expected to meet, the one man in the world who knew some of her secrets and understood that she concealed others, but who accepted her without judgment. In the flickering light of the candle that sat in the middle of the table, Luther's eyes were as cold and unflinching as those of a leopard. You had to look deeper to see the wounded artist under the sleek and rather dangerous exterior.

Luther Pell played the part he had crafted for himself with cool ease and a great deal of style. Raina suspected that was because on one level it was the truth. He actually was the sophisticated, successful owner of a glamorous nightclub. He really did have connections in the criminal underworld and equally murky links to a certain clandestine government agency. He allowed very few people to get close enough to him to catch glimpses of the complicated man beneath the surface.

Luther Pell had secrets. So did she. Over the course of the past couple of months they had begun to share some of those secrets, but in many ways they were still mysteries to each other. Lately she had allowed a little flame of hope to ignite. For the first time in a very long while she was beginning to imagine a future that involved love, a future with Luther.

At the moment they were seated in one of the star booths that ringed the dance floor. Normally, she and Luther occupied the private booth on the mezzanine. The discreetly concealed table upstairs provided Luther with a full view of his nightclub. But tonight Raina had requested a booth near the dance floor for herself and Lyra because she had concluded that the best tonic for her new apprentice investigator was a night of champagne and dancing. Luther had joined them at the table, which had made certain that everyone in the Paradise was aware of his guests.

"Your plan is working," Luther said. He angled his head toward Lyra, who was whirling around the floor with the well-dressed scion of a wealthy family that was vacationing at the Burning Cove Hotel. "Your apprentice has been dancing ever since the two of you arrived."

Raina watched Lyra for a moment. Luther was right; the plan to take Lyra's mind off the events at the Adlington house was working — maybe a little too well. Tonight Lyra radiated a nervy, glamorous energy that struck Raina as almost feverish.

Lyra was attractive but she was certainly not the most beautiful woman in the room. The competition was always stiff at the Paradise because the nightclub drew every Hollywood star and aspiring actor and actress who happened to be in town. Nevertheless, Lyra could hold her own. She was endowed with a natural presence that would make most people — male and female — look twice. But it was her spirited enthusiasm, her curiosity, and her interest in other people that gave her that magic ingredient — charm. People were attracted to her. They wanted to talk to her. They wanted to tell her their secrets. That ability would make her an excellent investigator if she chose to remain in the profession.

Tonight Lyra was a blaze of shimmering moonlight in a silver lamé gown. The bias-cut skirt flared out around her ankles whenever she went into a turn. Her amber-brown hair was caught back behind her ears with a pair of silver clips and fell in deep waves to her shoulders. Her lipstick was the latest shade of red. The young man she was dancing with was enchanted. Maybe it was the way she looked at him — as if he were the only man in the room. Raina smiled. The next man would get the same treatment.

"I agreed to take her on as an apprentice because she was so determined to become an investigator," Raina said. "She told me she feels she has a calling for the work."

Luther raised his brows. "A calling? For the private investigation business?"

"Don't laugh. I realize it's not exactly a religious vocation, but I know what she means, and so do you."

Luther shrugged. "A need to find answers?"

"For people who need those answers. Kirk Investigations may have to do some divorce work to pay the bills, but my goal is to attract clients who are desperate to close a hole in their lives. I think Lyra has the heart for the job, and the right instincts, too. She certainly handled herself well this afternoon."

Luther's mouth kicked up a little with approval. "I read about her impressive golf swing in the evening edition of the *Burning Cove Herald.*"

"Lyra only took one swing. It knocked him down and out, but he wasn't necessarily dead at that point. Marcella Adlington was evidently afraid that her husband might survive. She took a few extra whacks at his head with the golf club while Lyra and the police were out of sight at the front of the house."

"Interesting." Luther's brows rose. "That wasn't mentioned in the paper."

"Only because Lyra kept quiet about it. She knew it might have gone badly for Mrs. Adlington."

"Juries frown on wives who murder their husbands, regardless of the justification."

"Exactly. As it stands, Lyra was simply defending herself from a homicidal maniac."

"And protecting her client at the same time," Luther mused.

"Mrs. Adlington never got the opportunity to become a client of Kirk Investigations.

You could say the firm took care of her problem pro bono. Not a habit I want to encourage."

"Understandable."

"Unfortunately, the upshot of what happened today is that Lyra will never know if she killed a man or not."

Luther stopped smiling. "That will be hard to get past."

"Yes, and it gets worse. It became obvious afterward that Marcella Adlington planned the whole thing."

"Meaning?"

"She set up the appointment with Kirk Investigations knowing that her husband would fly into a rage and attack whoever showed up at the house. Marcella had a gun ready to shoot him and play the heroine. But things did not go exactly according to plan."

"So she improvised with the golf club."

"Yes." Raina took another sip of her martini and lowered the glass. "I expect Lyra will have a few nightmares for a while. Cocktails, champagne, and a night of dancing won't prevent the bad dreams."

"No," Luther said. "They won't."

He spoke with the certainty of a man who had already experimented with that particular therapy.

"I'm going to have a few nightmares, myself," Raina said.

Luther's eyes were shadowed with grim understanding. "Because you sent her into harm's way."

Raina knew he understood those kinds of nightmares, too. He had sent people into harm's way. He had also been in deadly danger himself on more than one occasion. He had run a clandestine government intelligence agency in the Great War and for several years afterward. Now, in addition to his nightclub, which provided excellent cover, he operated a very discreet private consulting firm, Failure Analysis, Inc. It handled delicate, off-the-books investigations for a certain government agency, the FBI, and the occasional private client.

"I assumed the Adlington case was just another take-some-photos-that-will-prove-my-husband-is-cheating-so-I-will-have-grounds-for-a-divorce job," Raina said. "I thought it would be a good way to introduce Lyra to the business. She actually knows a lot about photography, because she has frequently assisted her sister, Vivian, with her studio photography. Next time I'll insist the potential client come into the office for the first interview."

"Don't set any hard-and-fast r~~s,~~"

Luther advised. "In the future there may be clients who desperately need your help who can't risk being seen in a private investigator's office."

Raina contemplated that for a moment. "I suppose you're right. I told Lyra to think long and hard about whether she really wants to be a private investigator. I wonder if she will show up at the office tomorrow morning?"

"It will be her choice. She has a right to make it. Don't try to decide her future for her."

Raina sighed. "I'm afraid she may have based her career decision on Nancy Drew and Nick and Nora Charles. If nothing else, today's experience will teach her not to romanticize the investigation business."

CHAPTER 5

Luther left her bed shortly after three that morning. He never spent the night. They had not discussed the fact that he did not stay for breakfast. There was no need to talk about it. Raina understood. The decision had been made by mutual, albeit silent agreement.

It wasn't about her reputation. True, she and Luther were reasonably discreet, but their relationship was hardly a secret in Burning Cove, a town that was famous as a destination for those seeking illicit trysts and liaisons. Given Luther's notorious image and the fact that she was a woman of a certain age who was engaged in a business many viewed as slightly shady, rumors that his speedster had been parked outside her house until breakfast would not raise many eyebrows.

They both had their reasons for the way they chose to conduct the affair. She sensed

51

that Luther did not stay for breakfast because he was afraid of falling asleep beside her; afraid of waking up in a nightmare that had its origins in the war. She knew something about his nightmares, because she had seen his paintings. The dark, stormy landscapes that hung in his office and in his private quarters above the Paradise were straight from his dreams. Painting was his therapy, his way of surviving the memories.

Her reasons for not inviting him to stay until morning were similar. She did not want to wake up in the middle of a nightmare about a home that had become a prison.

"Now that you've got an apprentice who can watch the office, what do you say to taking off from work early tomorrow?" Luther said, fastening his white shirt. "I can order a picnic lunch from one of the local restaurants. We could drive out to Smuggler's Cove and take a walk on the beach."

"That sounds like a lovely idea," Raina said. "Assuming I've still got an apprentice."

"Something tells me Lyra will show up at the office," Luther said.

Raina smiled, amused by his certainty. "You sound very confident of that."

Luther leaned over the bed and planted a

palm on either side of her. "She may be feeling the effects of all that champagne she drank tonight, but I'll bet she shows up. Get some sleep."

He kissed her, straightened, collected his jacket, and headed for the door.

"Good night," she said. "Drive carefully."

She wanted to say, *Good night, Luther, my love,* but she didn't. Neither of them had used the word *love;* not yet. Maybe never.

"Don't worry," Luther said. "At this hour there won't be anyone else on the road."

A moment later she heard the front door open and close. She waited for the distinct click that told her he had used the key she had given him to lock it.

She settled back into the pillows, taking comfort in the faint, lingering trace of his scent. She was not surprised when sleep eluded her. She lay quietly gazing up at the shadowed ceiling and wondered if Lyra was able to sleep. Probably not.

Luther had sent her home in the Paradise limo with instructions to the driver to see her safely inside her beachfront cottage. She had been flushed and giddy from the champagne and the dancing, but the nervy energy unleashed by what had happened at the Adlington residence had not yet burned itself out.

At five o'clock Raina abandoned the effort to get some sleep. She got up, took a shower, put on a floral dressing gown, made a pot of coffee, and opened the front door. The early edition of the *Burning Cove Herald* was on the doorstep.

She took the paper inside and settled down at the kitchen table to read the headlines. Not surprisingly, Lyra was on the front page again. This time there was a photo of her glamorously dressed in her silver evening gown arriving at the Paradise. The headline said it all: LADY PRIVATE EYE WHO DISPATCHED CRAZED KILLER WITH GOLF CLUB CELEBRATES AT LOCAL NIGHTCLUB.

If Lyra did show up for work today, she was likely to be inundated with clients, probably of the male variety. Last night the men in the Paradise had lined up to take her out onto the dance floor.

A woman who radiated an aura of danger and glamour fascinated a certain kind of man. Those same men would be terrified by the prospect of marrying such a woman, of course. But the possibility of going to bed with one would be an irresistible challenge to a lot of males who assumed that an affair with a *fast woman* came with no strings attached.

Raina was quite certain that Lyra could handle any man who thought it might be exciting to seduce — or be seduced by — an attractive woman with a killer golf swing. She had been raised in the hothouse of San Francisco's high society. She had been taught from childhood to navigate the treacherous social waters of that world. She could deal with the male of the species.

The question was whether she would change her mind about her newfound calling. Raina hoped she didn't. *Yesterday I was ready to fire her for her own good, and today I want her to stay.*

Lyra might be naïve and inexperienced when it came to the harsh realities of life, but she radiated positive energy the way a light bulb chases off the shadows when you flip the switch. It would be nice to have that sort of energy around the office. Lyra could put the clients at ease. People would open up and talk to her.

There were a number of logical reasons for employing her at Kirk Investigations, but was it the right thing to do? Maybe it would be better to offer Lyra a job as the firm's secretary. That way she could deal with the clients, but in a much safer capacity.

On the other hand, my last job as a secretary

nearly got me killed.

It was a moot question, because Lyra had no secretarial skills. She had not been trained to type or take shorthand. In any event, although she was happy to do anything asked of her, she had made it quite clear she wanted to become a full-fledged investigator.

Raina put down the paper and got to her feet to pour herself a second cup of coffee. For a moment she stood at the kitchen counter, contemplating the bright California dawn.

Luther was right, she decided. She should let Lyra make her own decision.

She went back to the kitchen table and turned the page to read the list of celebrities who had been seen checking into the Burning Cove Hotel. It was always good to know who was in town. Sometimes film stars who wished to have discreet investigations conducted preferred to hire someone who was not connected to the powerful studios. There were no secrets in Hollywood.

Things were different in Burning Cove. The studio fixers had very little power here. If you wanted something hushed up or discreetly buried in this town, you went to Luther Pell or Oliver Ward, the owner of the Burning Cove Hotel.

The phone rang at seven. Raina turned cold. Her palms tingled. No good news ever came over the phone at that hour of the day.

She got to her feet and plucked the receiver off the wall phone.

"Yes?"

The voice on the other end of the line belonged to a ghost, and as was the case with specters, it brought a warning. A body that had been safely buried had come out of the grave and wanted revenge. Raina forced herself to listen carefully.

"I understand," she said.

The ghost hung up.

A wave of panic slammed through Raina.

Unthinking, driven by force of habit — secretarial training ran deep — she made a note on the small pad of paper that hung on the wall beside the phone. She certainly didn't need the reminder. The ghost's instructions were seared into her consciousness. But seeing the words written down made her realize she was not in the middle of an old nightmare. She was wide awake, and this was real.

She took a deep breath and fought back the wave of terror that threatened to choke her. She would not run, not this time. But one thing was blazingly clear. She could not put everyone she cared about in Burning Cove in danger. This threat came from her past. She would deal with it.

She collected her nerves and forced herself to think. When she felt she had the bare bones of a plan, she went upstairs to pack.

She started with the necessities — her pistol and an extra box of ammunition.

CHAPTER 6

Raina walked through the front door of the office dressed in stylish trousers, a long-sleeved shirt, and a pair of lace-up sport shoes. Her hair was covered in a triangle silk scarf knotted under her chin. It was the sort of scarf a woman used when she went for a drive with the top down.

Lyra, seated at her desk, her aching head propped in her hands, struggled to hide her astonishment. Raina always came to work in fashionable, crisply tailored business suits and heels.

"Good morning," Lyra said, trying to sound somewhat normal. "Coffee? I just made a pot."

She was on her third cup that morning — the first two had been consumed at her kitchen table an hour ago. The caffeine combined with a hearty dose of aspirin was just starting to take the edge off the headache that had awakened her at dawn. She had not dared to risk breakfast. On the way to the office she had made a mental note to go easy on the champagne the next time she barely avoided getting murdered.

Raina appeared both startled and relieved to see her. "No coffee, thanks. I had a couple of cups at breakfast. So, you decided to come into the office today?"

"Of course."

The fact that she had been seriously contemplating handing in her resignation was another matter entirely. She had not yet made the decision, which meant that, for the moment, she was a dedicated employee of Kirk Investigations.

Raina glanced at the elegant Bakelite pen tray, the green leather blotter, and the other stylish desk accessories that Lyra had purchased for her position as an apprentice investigator.

"I hope you didn't come in just to pack up your things," Raina said.

"Not unless you're letting me go." Lyra used one finger to nudge the copy of the *Burning Cove Herald* on her desk. "I suppose you've seen the morning headlines?"

"Yes. Read the paper at breakfast. We're fortunate that Irene Ward covered the story. She's an excellent journalist. Got the facts right. She even managed to put in a nice mention of Kirk Investigations."

"Why did you think I might not show up today, Raina?"

"I told you to think seriously about whether you really wanted to be an investigator. I was afraid you would decide this line of work wasn't for you."

Lyra cleared her throat. "I admit there are some aspects of the job that I did not anticipate."

"That's true of all careers, isn't it?" Raina said. She went briskly toward her desk. "I certainly ran into a few surprises in my previous position at a law firm."

"You're a lawyer?"

"No. I was a secretary." Raina opened a drawer and took out a sheet of paper. "I'm very glad you've decided to remain on the job, because I need you to take charge of Kirk Investigations while I'm out of town."

"You're going away?"

"I have been asked to do a favor for an old . . . acquaintance. It's a very urgent, very personal matter."

"I understand," Lyra said.

She didn't understand — not at all. Something was wrong. The little frissons on the back of her neck warned her that whatever was going on, it was anything but normal. Her curiosity was stirring in spite of the headache. It was all she could do not to press Raina for more information. This wasn't any of her business.

Raina picked up a pen and began to write on the notepaper. "I hope to be back by the end of the week."

Lyra set her cup down so hard it clanged against the saucer. "You want me to take charge of Kirk Investigations for the rest of the *week*? But I've only been on the job for three — make that four — days. I have no idea what I'm doing."

"You've got what it takes." Raina finished her note. "You'll be fine."

She slipped the note into an envelope, wrote a name on the front, and put it squarely in the middle of her desk blotter. She jumped to her feet and headed for the door.

"See you in a few days," she said over her shoulder.

A rush of anxiety brought Lyra up out of her chair. She could no longer contain herself.

"Raina, what's wrong?"

"I told you, something has come up. It's a personal matter. Nothing to worry about, but I really can't discuss it." Raina paused at the door. "Oh, by the way, Luther will stop in later today. We had plans for this afternoon. Please give him that note on my desk."

"You haven't told Mr. Pell that you're leaving town?"

"He would demand to know where I'm going, and I'd rather not waste time on a quarrel that will change nothing."

Raina went outside onto the sidewalk. Lyra hurried after her.

"Wait a second," she said. "What if Mr. Pell thinks I know where you're going but I won't tell him? He'll get mad at me. I do not want Luther Pell mad at me. He's got mob connections, among other things."

"Why do you think I'm not giving you any details?" Raina said. She opened the door of her flashy little convertible and got behind the wheel. "This way you won't have to lie to him. And, more importantly, neither will I. I doubt if either of us would be successful."

"What if some new clients walk through the door this week?"

"You're in charge," Raina said. "You decide which cases to take. Just be sure to get a retainer up front and try not to get killed."

"Right," Lyra said, trying to sound at least semicompetent and professional.

Raina turned the key in the ignition,

pulled away from the curb, and drove off down the street.

Lyra waited until the speedster disappeared around the corner before she went back into the office. She closed the glass-paned door and leaned back against it, both hands wrapped around the brass knob.

She was in charge of Kirk Investigations. For the rest of the week.

It was a staggering thought. A huge responsibility.

She had awakened that morning with a lot of serious questions about her future in the private investigation business. It was obvious now that it was not always going to be the thrilling, rewarding career she had envisioned. As recently as yesterday she had seen herself as an agent of justice for those who had nowhere else to turn; an investigator dedicated to seeking answers for desperate people. She would find those who defrauded others. She would track down long-lost heirs and missing relatives. Maybe she would help the police track down a murderer or two.

She would be a grown-up, real-life Nancy Drew. She even had the car for the job. And a stylish trench coat. And a very fashionable fedora.

Yesterday the Adlingtons had dramatically

changed her view of the profession.

The champagne and the dancing had been a fine tonic, but like all such remedies, the effects had been short-lived. By morning they had worn off, leaving behind the memory of the sickening thud of the golf club striking Charles Adlington's skull. Her dreams had been filled with the disturbing images of the three iron lying in the wrong position on the patio and the additional damage that had been done to Adlington's head. She would never forget Marcella Adlington's words. *I had to be sure.*

She had arrived at work this morning intending to have a long talk with Raina. She had planned to explain that she had some doubts about what she had been convinced was her calling. She had wanted to discuss the realities of what lay ahead.

But it was clear now that she would have to rethink her career options at some point in the future because Raina had left her in charge of Kirk Investigations. She could not just walk out the door and close down the office. She had to stick around until Raina returned. She had responsibilities.

She pushed herself away from the door, straightened her shoulders, and started across the room to her desk. It was Tuesday. She could handle the office until Friday.

What could possibly go wrong between now and the end of the week?

What was really starting to worry her was the growing conviction that her boss was in serious trouble.

Rule number one is always assume the client is lying or, at the very least, not telling you the whole truth. Everyone has secrets to protect.

CHAPTER 7

Simon set the briefcase on the massive wooden desk. He unlatched it and started to open it.

Luther leaned forward and eyed the hole in the leather on the side of the briefcase. Light glinted on the bit of steel that could be seen underneath.

"Looks like a bullet hole," he said.

"The book business can get rough at times," Simon said. He reached into the briefcase, pulled out an envelope, and handed it to Luther. "I think this packet contains the items you asked me to find."

Luther ripped open the envelope and dumped a small diary and a couple of letters onto the desk. "Yes. Thank you. My friend will be extremely grateful. His son's career is at stake. Why people write down potentially damaging information about their personal lives is a mystery to me. You'd think they would figure out how disastrous that kind of stuff can be."

Simon looked at a couple of the paintings hanging on the paneled walls of Luther's office. The pictures were landscapes that depicted the coast around Burning Cove during violent storms. There were no figures in the scenes, but the images seethed with violence and rage and anguish.

Simon had once made the mistake of getting too close to one of Luther's paintings. The energy infused into it was so fierce he had not even had to touch it to sense that the scene came straight out of Pell's nightmares. Luther might not make the mistake of writing letters or keeping a diary, but he sure as hell had found a way to exorcise a few of his personal demons.

"It can be extremely difficult to conceal strong emotions," Simon said. "Your friend's son apparently believed himself to be deeply in love."

"With another man. This diary and these letters would have destroyed both of their careers." Luther glanced at the heap of envelopes, papers, and photographs that remained inside the briefcase. "Did you find all of these items in Lennox's library?"

"Yes. I decided I might as well take them, too. No sense letting the Bureau get hold of a lot of material that could ruin the lives of so many people."

Luther smiled a cold smile. "J. Edgar Hoover would love to get his hands on this stuff. Nothing he enjoys more than having leverage over other people."

"The Bureau's special agents were happy enough with the records of Lennox's financial dealings. They'll never miss these items because they weren't aware they exist."

"I'll see to it that these materials are returned to their rightful owners," Luther said. "Anonymously, of course."

Simon closed and latched the briefcase.

Luther watched him. "How's the burn doing?"

"It's fine," Simon said. "It gets a little irritated from time to time but I'm told that's normal."

"I owe you," Luther said.

"No, you don't. If we're finished here, I'll be on my way."

"Heading back to Los Angeles so soon?" Luther asked.

"No, thought I'd check into a local hotel and take a short vacation."

"I can get you a room at the Burning Cove."

"I've heard that hotel is booked solid for months in advance."

"I've got connections."

Simon smiled. "Imagine that. Thanks. I'll take you up on the offer."

"By the way, why don't you join me for drinks at the Paradise this evening? I'll introduce you to a friend. Raina Kirk. She owns the only private investigation agency in town."

"A lady private investigator? Sounds interesting."

"I'll ask her to bring along her new apprentice. I think you'll find Miss Brazier interesting, too. She's single. Attractive. Smart."

"I didn't know there was such a thing as an apprentice private investigator."

"Lyra learns fast," Luther said. "Got a hunch she'll be promoted soon."

"What makes you say that?"

Luther picked up the phone. "She was attacked by a madman yesterday when she walked in on a murder in progress. She defended herself with a three iron."

"Huh." Simon felt a stirring of interest. "What happened to the guy who tried to kill her?"

"Died of severe injuries to the head. A three iron can do a lot of damage if you know how to handle it."

"And Miss Brazier?"

"Knows how to handle a three iron."

Luther pushed a copy of the *Burning Cove Herald* across the desk. "Afterward she spent the night drinking champagne and dancing in my club."

Simon studied the picture of a stylish woman in a pale gown and high heels getting out of a cab in front of the Paradise Club. He could not take his eyes off her. Even in a newspaper photo she was a compelling fusion of mystery and glamour. Anticipation heated his blood. A lady PI who had taken down an insane killer and then partied all night at a hot nightclub was just the kind of woman he had hoped to find in Burning Cove. A reckless, free-spirited, modern woman. The sort who came with no strings attached.

"Is Miss Brazier divorced by any chance?" he asked.

"No," Luther said.

"Well, no one is perfect."

CHAPTER 8

"What do you mean, Raina left town?"
Luther said. "That's impossible. She would
have told me if she had a reason to travel."

Lyra got to her feet, moving with caution.
It was noon. The headache she had awakened with had finally disappeared beneath
the onslaught of aspirin and coffee, but she
was still feeling a bit fragile. The last thing
she needed was a major confrontation with
one of the most powerful men in Burning
Cove.

*Thanks for leaving me to face him, Raina.
You owe me, Boss.*

Lyra reminded herself that, thanks to her
family's social standing and her father's
shipping business, she had met a lot of
powerful men, including tycoons and important politicians. She knew how to handle
them.

Luther Pell, however, was definitely in a
different category. The curriculum at the

exclusive women's college she had attended had not included a course on how to handle men who operated nightclubs and were rumored to have mob connections.

She composed herself. She might not possess a lot of useful job skills, but she was very good when it came to talking her way out of trouble.

"All I can tell you is that Raina stopped in at the office long enough to see if I had come to work this morning," she said. She crossed to Raina's desk and picked up the sealed envelope. "She told me she had a case that required her to leave town for a few days. Something about an old acquaintance who needed her help. She left this note for you."

"A note?" Luther glanced at the letter, disbelief etched on his stern features. "No. She wouldn't do that. She wouldn't just take off and leave a damned note."

"Please don't look at me as if I made her disappear, Mr. Pell," Lyra said. "I assure you I don't know anything more about this than you do." She handed Luther the envelope. "I'm just the messenger."

Luther gave her a considering look. His eyes narrowed.

Lyra winced. "Yes, I'm aware of what happens to the messenger."

73

"Raina wasn't sure if you would show up today," Luther said. "I told her you would. I've had more experience figuring out what people are likely to do, you see. Raina is still new at the management end of things."

"What does that have to do with — Oh, never mind. I'm here." Lyra straightened her shoulders. "And, until Raina returns, I'm in charge."

Luther nodded once and ripped open the envelope. He pulled out the note and read it in a single glance. Then he read it again.

When he looked up there was ice in his eyes.

"Do you know what this says?" he asked.

"No," Lyra said. "But I gather it's a very short message."

"Here." Luther thrust the note into her hand. "Read it yourself."

The note was written in Raina's elegant secretarial school script. It was, as Lyra had suspected, quite short. She read it aloud.

Dearest Luther,
I have been called away on an urgent, personal matter. I do not expect to be gone more than a few days at most. I will telephone you at the earliest opportunity when I have a better understanding of the situation. In the mean-

74

time, please forgive me for my hasty departure.

Sincerely,
R.

P.S. Kindly do not interrogate my apprentice. She doesn't have any answers for you.

Lyra looked up and found Luther watching her with the cold, fierce intensity of a predator.

"She's in trouble," Luther said.

"I agree," Lyra said. She folded her arms. "And since you raised the subject, I may as well tell you that I have opened an investigation."

Luther looked stunned. "Into Raina's disappearance?"

"Yes." Lyra sighed. "I was worried, you see. She did not seem to be her normal self this morning. I'm well aware that there are some serious issues involving professional ethics here. Raina is my employer, after all, and she did make it clear that she was leaving town on a personal matter. I have a duty to uphold Kirk Investigations' reputation for honoring client confidentiality. However —"

"The hell with professional ethics and client confidentiality. Raina isn't a client anyway. She owns the firm."

"Yes." Lyra brightened. "There is a lot of gray area here."

"There's nothing gray about it. We're going to find her. Did you get anywhere in your *investigation*?"

Lyra went around behind Raina's desk and opened the large, leather-bound desk calendar. "Her appointments last week and yesterday were all routine, assuming you can call the Adlington case *routine.*"

"Except that she sent you to the Adlington interview."

"She thought it would be good experience for me. It seemed like a simple, straightforward client interview."

"Go on. What else did you check out besides her calendar?"

Lyra closed the calendar and opened the center drawer of the desk. She took out a notebook. "She uses this to record memos of telephone conversations with her business contacts and her clients. Unfortunately, she keeps the notes in shorthand, but the dates are plain to read, and so are the phone numbers and addresses. The last note is about the Adlington case. There's nothing after that. I was in the process of going through her files to see if there has been any recent activity. She keeps very good files."

"Raina used to work for a small law firm in New York that was in the trust and estate business for several generations," Luther said, his tone impatient.

"Yes, she mentioned that."

"Did she?" Luther's brows rose. "I'm impressed. Raina doesn't usually talk to people about her time in New York."

"Well, I tend to ask a lot of questions. Besides, one can hardly miss her classy East Coast accent."

Amusement gleamed briefly in Luther's dark eyes. "I can see why Raina says you have a talent for investigation work."

Lyra's spirits soared. "Did she tell you that?"

"Yes."

"That's . . . very nice to hear." Lyra cleared her throat. "As I was saying, there is nothing on her calendar that indicates today was going to be anything other than normal here at Kirk Investigations, and so far I have found no notes indicating recent phone calls to any of the businesses or people in her file of contacts."

Luther gave her a thoughtful look. "Kirk Investigations is a two-person agency, and of those two people, you are the only one who has had an unusual experience recently."

"Yes, and last night Raina did her best to take my mind off what happened at the Adlington residence, but aside from her concern for me — she was very understanding — I detected nothing unusual in her behavior."

"Neither did I."

And you know her ever so much better than I do, Lyra thought.

"I assume you took her home after you put me in a limo with one of your drivers?" she ventured.

"Yes, I took Raina home," Luther said.

"I don't mean to intrude on your privacy, but did anything take place that might have . . . upset her?"

"You mean, did we quarrel?" Luther's jaw tightened. He walked to the window and looked out at the street. "No."

"May I ask if you, uh, shared a nightcap?"

"I left her at three this morning," Luther said. He turned around. "That's what you want to know, isn't it?"

Lyra breathed a sigh of relief. "Yes, thank you. I don't mean to pry, but I'm trying to establish a timeline."

"A timeline?"

"Raina says that's the first thing to do in a

case. It makes sense. I grew up in the shipping and freight business. Timing is everything in that world, too."

Luther was clearly intrigued now. "Go on. Tell me about your timeline."

"Given our own personal recollections of the evening, I think we should assume that whatever disturbed Raina and sent her away from Burning Cove happened sometime between approximately six o'clock this morning and, at the latest, eight."

Luther studied her for a moment, curiosity replacing the cold steel in his eyes. "What makes you think you can narrow the time window to a couple of hours?"

"Raina stopped in here at nine. She was on her way out of town. That means her suitcases must have been in the trunk of her car. She wasn't sure exactly how long she would be gone, but she estimated three or four days. It takes time for a woman to pack for a trip of that duration. She was dressed for a long drive — trousers, comfortable shoes, a scarf for her hair. She seemed in a great hurry, but when I offered her coffee she said she had already had some with breakfast. Also, I know she took the time to read the morning paper."

"How did you figure that out?"

Lyra glanced at the copy of the *Burning*

Cove Herald on her desk. "She mentioned that the Adlington case was in the headlines and said something about how fortunate it was that the *Herald*'s crime reporter, Irene Ward, covered the story, because she got the details right and she even managed to insert Kirk Investigations into the piece. Good publicity for the firm."

"Your point is that Raina breakfasted, had coffee, and read at least the front page of the paper, but something happened soon after that which caused her to pack a bag, dress for a long drive, and rush here to leave a note for me."

"Yes," Lyra said. She tapped one polished fingernail on the desktop and focused very intently on Luther. "Raina mentioned that you operate a rather exclusive investigation business of your own and that you did intelligence work during the Great War and for a few years afterward. You've obviously had a lot more experience in this sort of thing than I have, but I can think of only a couple of things that could have turned Raina's world upside down between breakfast and approximately eight a.m."

"A telephone call or a telegram."

"Precisely."

"Damn. Raina's right. You do have the instincts for this work."

The remark, coming from a man who knew a lot about investigating, infused Lyra with a dose of self-confidence.

"Thank you," she said. "I think we should take a look around Raina's house. Perhaps we will find something that will reassure us or give us some idea of where she went. I don't suppose you have — ?"

"A key?" Luther said. "Yes, I do."

"Great."

"Not that we'd need one," Luther added. "Breaking into a house is child's play."

"I see."

Picking locks was apparently another job skill she needed to learn if she stayed in the private investigation business.

Luther moved to Raina's desk and picked up the phone.

"Who are you calling?" Lyra asked.

"I've got a very personal stake in this situation. That means I'm too close to it to be sure that I'm thinking logically, and you're good but you're an amateur."

"I prefer the term *apprentice.*"

Luther ignored that. "We need an expert, someone with a talent for picking up the feel of a scene."

"The feel? I'm not sure I understand."

"We also need someone who can look at things with an objective eye. Someone who won't get emotionally involved."

"Sounds like you're talking about a robot," Lyra said.

"Close enough." Luther spoke into the phone. "Burning Cove Hotel? Please ring Simon Cage's room."

CHAPTER 9

Luther Pell had been right about one thing, Lyra decided. The expert, clear-eyed investigator who never got emotionally involved was definitely not a robot, but there was a lot of steel under the quiet, self-contained surface of the man.

The gold-rimmed spectacles didn't fool her for a second. Everyone has a few secrets, but something about Simon Cage told her he either had a lot of them or else the ones he harbored were big. She was also very certain that he was quite capable of taking his to the grave. Those who tried to force those secrets from him might find themselves digging their own graves.

That, of course, made him fascinating. And unaccountably unnerving. She was still trying to decide how to interpret the unfamiliar chill of awareness that had jolted her senses when Luther had introduced him a few minutes ago. She had a feeling her intuition was sounding the alarm, but she wasn't sure why she should be worried. Cage was, after all, a friend of Luther Pell's.

Okay, maybe that was reason enough to be wary of the man.

Cage had the stoic, intriguing profile of a man who could deal with whatever life threw at him. She knew that, with his slightly rumpled linen jacket, spectacles, and briefcase, he was playing a part he had scripted for himself. He looked exactly as one would expect an antiquarian book dealer to look. His dark hair was cut short in the current style but there was no gleam of oil.

His green eyes were almost unreadable — almost but not entirely. Maybe his eyesight was poor. Maybe he really did need the gold-rimmed spectacles, but she doubted it. She suspected he wore them because he had convinced himself they made it difficult for people to see the man behind the glasses.

She glanced at the scars on his right hand. Yet another mystery.

He was watching her now with cool speculation. Suddenly she knew what he was thinking.

"No," she said. "I had nothing to do with Raina's disappearance."

Luther was about to insert his key into

the front door lock of Raina's pretty little Spanish Colonial–style villa. He paused and looked at her.

"What are you talking about?" he asked.

Lyra angled her chin at Simon, who was standing quietly to one side, the briefcase at his feet.

"Your so-called expert here is analyzing the situation, no doubt trying to figure out what might have changed recently in Raina's life," she said. "That's what real investigators do, right? Look for anomalies? Breaks in the pattern? It has dawned on Mr. Cage that I am the biggest anomaly around. Raina hired me four days ago, and yesterday a man involved in my very first case died — probably because of me. When it comes to ripples in the timeline, those two things do stand out."

Luther frowned. He looked as if he was about to argue with her observation. Instead he eyed Simon.

"Well?" he asked.

Simon pushed his spectacles higher on his nose. He did not appear embarrassed or chagrined.

"You know, I had intended to spend this afternoon by the pool at the Burning Cove Hotel, drinking iced tea and reading a good novel," he said. "Instead, I find myself standing here waiting to investigate the disappearance of a lady I have never met. So, yes, I am doing some analyzing, and it does, indeed, strike me that Miss Brazier is a very new employee at Kirk Investigations. Three days on the job and a man gets killed. The next day Miss Kirk goes missing. It adds up to a series of interesting —"

"*Coincidences,*" Lyra interrupted smoothly.

"I'm not a big believer in coincidences," Simon said.

The tone was polite but the message was unmistakable.

"Believe it or not, coincidences do happen," Lyra said. "It's obvious that you're the suspicious type, Mr. Cage. Let's see if you can put that unfortunate character trait to good use by finding a genuine clue inside Raina's villa. Because if you can't do that, your so-called expertise won't be of much use to us. You'll be free to return to the Burning Cove Hotel and sit by the pool."

She gave Simon a chilling smile, the one she reserved for powerful men who thought they were irresistible to women simply because they had a great deal of money or owned a large company. She had met a lot of that sort while working as her father's assistant at Brazier Shipping.

Simon blinked at the smile and regarded her as if she were a rare antiquarian book he might — just might — bid on at auction. "If you don't mind, I'm going to stay out of this discussion," Luther said. He pushed the key into the lock and opened the door. "We've got work to do and we're going to do it in a methodical manner. I will go first, because as far as we know I was the last one to leave the house before Raina took off. With luck I'll be able to notice if anything seems different or out of place. You two will follow me."

"Excellent plan," Simon said.

"Yes, it is," Lyra agreed.

She opened her handbag, took out a small notebook and a pencil, and snapped the bag shut. She could not fault Simon for playing a part, because she was doing the same thing today. Even though she was no longer sure she was cut out to be an investigator, Raina had entrusted her with the responsibility of running Kirk Investigations. She was going to do her job. Right now that job was finding out why Raina had disappeared.

She marched briskly past Simon and followed Luther into the tiled entryway of the small villa.

Simon picked up his suitcase, moved into

the shadowed space, and closed the front door.

For a moment the three of them stood quietly, absorbing the feel of the space. Lyra thought the interior décor was an excellent reflection of Raina — sophisticated and tasteful. There was, however, no hint of her East Coast origins. When Raina had arrived at the end of Route 66 in Santa Monica she had apparently embraced the California style.

The fashionable Spanish Colonial influence was everywhere in the villa, from the white stucco walls and the colorful tiles around the fireplace to the dark wooden beams in the high ceiling. The carpets, curtains, and furnishings were all done in rich Mediterranean golds, browns, and reds.

"There's no sign of any disturbance," Luther said. He walked slowly, deliberately, through the living room. "Everything looks the way it did last night."

"Were the curtains open when you left?" Simon asked.

Lyra and Luther both turned to look at him.

"No," Luther said.

Lyra surveyed the curtains. "Raina opened them the way she would on any normal morning. She was in no particular hurry at that point. But when she left she did not take the time to close them, even though she knew she would be gone for a few days."

"The kitchen," Simon said. "We need to look at that room first."

Luther led the way into the kitchen, a room done in yellow tiles trimmed in black and white.

"No dishes in the sink," Lyra announced.

"Raina's housekeeper comes in twice a week," Luther said. "This isn't one of her days."

"So we know that Miss Kirk took the time to clean up after breakfast," Simon said. He looked at Lyra. "Your theory is correct. Something happened after breakfast. A telephone call or a telegram most likely, although I suppose it's possible someone came to the door."

Lyra could not decide if she should be flattered by his acceptance of her logic or irritated because it had taken him so long to acknowledge that she was right. She decided to ignore the comment altogether. He was merely a consultant, after all. Her father had often complained that business consultants were a useless lot.

There was a notepad attached to the wall next to the phone. Lyra could see some marks on the top sheet of paper.

Simon spotted the notepad at the same time and crossed the room to take a closer look.

"A phone number, by any chance?" Luther asked. "That would be a stroke of luck."

Simon studied the squiggles and shook his head. "Unfortunately, no. Just some doodles, the kind you make when you're waiting for a long-distance phone call to go through. Let's try the bedroom."

Lyra sensed Luther hesitating, as if he did not want to have to walk into that room. She did not blame him. It was Raina's personal space, an intimate space he had shared with her. But he said nothing. Instead he led the way upstairs. Without a word, Lyra and Simon followed him.

The bedroom was an elegant boudoir done in shades of cream punctuated with splashes of red and gold. A pair of glass-paned doors opened onto a romantic little balcony trimmed with wrought iron. But unlike in the rest of the house, the signs of rushed activity were everywhere.

Shoe and hatboxes had been taken down from a shelf in the closet but not replaced. Drawers stood open. The items on the dressing table were in disarray.

Lyra glanced into some of the open drawers and then studied the closet.

"Looks like Raina took a few items of lingerie, a nightgown, and at least one change of clothes," she announced. She moved to the bed and raised the lids of some of the boxes. "But she didn't pack any high heels or evening shoes. She didn't take any hats, either."

Luther surveyed the boxes scattered across the bed. "She was in a hurry. Why did she waste time pulling most of the shoeboxes and hatboxes out of her closet?"

"Because she was looking for something," Simon said. "Whatever it was must have been hidden at the back of the closet."

He moved around to the far side of the bed and contemplated a closed shoebox. After a few seconds he reached out and touched it as if it were a live grenade. Lyra could have sworn she felt a shiver of energy in the atmosphere.

Intrigued, she moved closer to Simon to get a better view of the shoebox.

"Why that one?" she asked.

"I don't know." Simon looked at Luther. "I think it's important. Do you want to open it or shall I?"

Luther hesitated a beat.

"I'll do it," Lyra said. "That box belongs to Raina. I think another woman should open it."

91

Luther nodded. He looked relieved. "Go ahead."

She reached out to take the lid off the shoebox. The spectral fingers on the back of her neck made her hesitate. This time she had no difficulty interpreting the message from her intuition. There was something bad inside the box.

Aware that both men were watching, their eyes riveted on the box, she took a firm grip on her nerves and removed the lid.

For a few seconds she gazed down at the small pile of yellowed newspaper clippings. Then, very gently, she dumped them out onto the quilt.

Simon picked up one of the clippings. "The dateline is Bar Harbor. The date is 1925. Thirteen years ago."

He read the rest of the article aloud.

LOCAL WOMAN SWEPT OUT TO SEA. FEARED DEAD.

Jean Whitlock, the wife of Malcolm Whitlock, is believed to have vanished at sea during the recent storm. She is reported to have taken the couple's sailboat out by herself. Authorities fear she was caught by the sudden turn in the weather. Her hus-

92

band is said to be distraught. The Whitlocks were married for less than a year.

The way Simon handled the clipping gave
Lyra the impression he was doing more than
just reading the chilling report. It was
almost as if he were trying to learn something simply from touching the brittle
paper. She remembered what Luther had
said about Simon's ability to pick up the
feel of a scene.

Luther read another clipping. SEARCH
FOR MISSING WOMAN CALLED OFF.

Lyra picked up a clipping. "This one is
from a Boston paper. It's dated eighteen
months later."

She read it aloud.

GRIEF-STRICKEN HUSBAND OF WOMAN
LOST AT SEA DIES IN TRAGIC ACCIDENT

Malcolm Whitlock was found dead in his
Boston home early this morning. The family reports the cause was a fall down the
stairs.

After the loss of his wife in a boating accident off Bar Harbor, Mr. Whitlock moved
back to Boston and went into seclusion.
He never appeared in society. His family
said he was in deep mourning.

Luther looked at Lyra and Simon. "Raina brought almost nothing of her past with her when she moved to California. Clothes, some money, and the list of contacts she had worked with in the course of her secretarial job in New York. She has no family. No friends from back East, at least none that I know of, and no clients except the ones she has here in Burning Cove."

"There's always someone from the past," Simon said.

"Yes," Lyra said. She studied the newspaper clippings on the satin quilt. "Always."

"But in this case the two individuals from Raina's past — Mr. and Mrs. Whitlock — are both dead," Luther said.

"Lost at sea is not always the same as dead," Simon said.

Lyra looked at Luther. "I hate to admit it, but he's right."

"I am deeply humbled by your generous acknowledgment of the possibility that I might have a legitimate point to make," Simon said.

"Are you always this annoying, Mr. Cage?" Lyra asked.

"One does the best one can," Simon said.

"It's a wonder your best hasn't led people to suggest you take a long walk off a short pier."

94

Simon adjusted his glasses. "Actually, I frequently get that suggestion."

"No kidding," Lyra said.

Luther cleared his throat. "I suggest that we get back to the subject of Raina. Simon, what did you pick up from those clippings?"

Simon shot Lyra a quick, wary glance. She knew he did not want to say whatever he was about to say in front of her, but he had no choice. Luther was waiting.

"There's a lot of heat," Simon said. "Most of it is old, but there's a fresh layer. Very fresh. I think it's safe to say that Miss Kirk handled these clippings briefly this morning."

"What kind of emotion?" Luther asked.

Lyra could barely contain her curiosity. She suddenly had a million questions for Simon Cage, but it was clear this was not the time to ask them.

"Fear is the oldest emotion on these clippings," Simon said, speaking carefully. "The fresh stuff is mostly rage."

Lyra glanced at the clippings. "We need to know more about the Whitlocks."

"Irene Ward might be able to help," Luther said. "Several of her stories have gone national. She knows people, and she's got connections on the East Coast. I'll ask her to make some calls, talk to people who work in the morgues."

"Morgues?" Lyra asked.

"Newspaper morgues," Simon explained patiently. "It's where they store the papers and the notes the reporters made when they covered the stories."

"Yes," Lyra said, striving for patience. "I am aware of the purpose of newspaper morgues." She turned to Luther. "I will make those calls."

Simon shook his head. "Won't work. The clips and notes in a newspaper morgue are considered proprietary information. The person in charge of the files is unlikely to be helpful to an unknown private investigator who calls up out of the blue from the other side of the country. A professional journalist with good contacts stands a much better chance of getting useful information from a morgue clerk."

Lyra tried not to grit her teeth. "Oh."

Luther headed for the door. Lyra and Simon followed. At the bottom of the stairs Lyra remembered the notepad next to the phone on the kitchen wall.

"Hang on," she said. "I want to check one thing."

The men watched her walk quickly across the living room, through the dining room, and into the kitchen. After a moment they followed, stopping in the doorway.

"What are you looking for?" Simon asked.

"I don't think these are doodles," Lyra said. "Raina was a professionally trained secretary in New York. She knows shorthand. She uses it routinely to keep her investigative notes. We need to find someone who can translate these squiggles for us."

She started to tear off the top page of the notepad but changed her mind and took the whole pad instead. There might be earlier entries that could prove helpful.

"I know a professional secretary who is proficient in shorthand," Luther said. "Elena Torres manages the head office at the Burning Cove Hotel. Oliver Ward, the owner, says Mrs. Torres runs the entire hotel. Says he just tries to stay out of her way."

"He sounds like a very smart man," Lyra said. "A good secretary is the key to a successful business. My father often says he couldn't run Brazier Shipping without his secretary, Mrs. Lee. Unfortunately, Father never made the leap to the obvious conclusion."

Simon and Luther looked at her.

"What conclusion is that?" Simon asked.

He had the expression of a man who is unwillingly fascinated by the sight of a slow-moving train wreck, Lyra thought. Or maybe it was the look of a man who is standing on the tracks watching the train come toward him.

She smiled the smile she reserved for people who assumed she was not very bright. It was a smile that never failed to dazzle.

"What my father failed to realize is that a woman is fully capable of running Brazier Shipping," she said.

"You?" Simon asked.

"Me." She turned to Luther. "Let's ask Mrs. Torres to consult for us."

CHAPTER 10

Lyra Brazier was the woman he had hoped to find in Burning Cove. Damn near perfect, Simon decided. Sophisticated, modern — an interesting, spirited woman who was free to get involved in a short-term, no-strings-attached affair.

Perfect. Except she wasn't, and he could not figure out why.

In theory she was exactly what he was looking for, but the reality was that she was proving to be complicated and unpredictable. He did not need a complicated and unpredictable woman in his life. On top of that obvious fact, it was clear she had concluded he was going to be a problem she would just as soon have done without.

Okay, he wasn't the most diplomatic person in the world, but it wasn't his fault that she stood out as the glaring new element in Raina Kirk's life, the anomaly that disrupted the pattern. Facts were facts.

She was inexperienced in her new profession — she had been on the job at Kirk Investigations for a mere four days — but this afternoon she had displayed some insightful detective skills. She was the one who had picked up what might prove to be the first solid lead in the disappearance of Raina Kirk. It was the reason they were gathered in the inner office of Oliver Ward, the owner of the Burning Cove Hotel.

"Miss Kirk was obviously taught the Gregg method in secretarial school." Elena Torres examined the marks on the top sheet of the notepad Lyra had given her. "And I must say she has a very fine hand. But you need to understand that, over time, every professional develops a personal style of shorthand, one that incorporates her own shortcuts."

"I know," Lyra said. "My father's secretary explained that to me when she showed me how she transcribes dictation. It was like reading and writing another language. Amazing. It was thanks to her that I realized the marks on that paper might be shorthand. Do you think you can make anything of them?"

"Yes, I'm sure I can," Elena said. She picked up a secretarial pad and a pencil. "I'm a Gregg secretary, too."

Simon stood quietly in the back of the room, arms folded, his briefcase at his feet. Oliver had given his chair to his secretary to use while she studied the notepad. He now had one shoulder propped against the wall. He gripped the handle of a cane in his left hand. Simon recognized the stance of a man who has dealt with pain for a long time.

Oliver had once been a famous magician who had nearly been killed onstage. Simon had never seen his act but he was well aware of the man's legend. The dramatic end of Ward's career had made headlines across the nation and around the world.

Ward's wife, Irene, who had the crime beat for the local paper, had her own notebook at the ready. Luther had told her that they were going to need her help.

Luther himself was prowling the room. Simon had been doing odd jobs for him for a couple of years now, long enough to be aware that the restless pacing was out of character for him; evidence of a seething anxiety. Pell's impatience was laced with a barely concealed frustration. He was using anger to overcome his fear that something terrible had happened to his lover.

Simon passed the time trying to analyze exactly why he did not want to take his eyes off Lyra. It was alarming to know she had realized so quickly that he had been immediately suspicious of her. Most people either ignored him entirely or dismissed him as a stodgy antiquarian book dealer until it was too late; until he had discovered their secrets.

He had spent the past two years cultivating his unimpressive image. Lyra had taken one look at him and known exactly what he was thinking. *You don't fit the pattern, Lyra Brazier.*

That was true in too many ways.

She was striking, but not beautiful in the Hollywood mold. Her hazel gaze was intelligent and insightful, not soft, sultry, and seductive. He was no judge of women's fashions but even he could tell she possessed the hard-to-define qualities of grace and style. She was the kind of woman who could light up a room when she walked into it — not because she was glamorous but simply because she was interested in everyone in the room and people responded to that energy.

The magic was that there was no magic, he thought. Lyra's curiosity was genuine. He never ceased to be surprised by how rare that particular character trait was in both men and women. Most people were eager to talk about themselves, but their interest in others was too often limited to a consideration of how someone else might be of use or persuaded to climb into bed.

I may have gotten cynical.

Lyra should have been the cynical type. She was in a profession known for inspiring cynicism and a deep disappointment in human nature. Yet in spite of the serious circumstances they were investigating, she radiated a determined optimism that probably hinted at naïveté. He got the feeling she was one of those annoying individuals who always looked for the silver lining and refused to take a realistic view of people and situations.

Yet yesterday she had killed a man with a golf club and then danced the night away at a fashionable club.

"The Gregg method is completely phonetic," Elena explained. "It records the sound of the word, not the actual spelling." She finished transcribing, put the pencil down, and looked up. "Miss Kirk wrote *Labyrinth Springs Hotel and Spa.*"

Lyra's eyes widened. "You're sure?"

Elena glanced down at her notes. "As sure as I can be under the circumstances."

"Why would Raina meet an acquaintance at a spa?" Oliver said.

Luther went very still. "Maybe she isn't

meeting an acquaintance. Maybe that was an excuse. Maybe she checked in for personal reasons. What if she recently learned that she's ill, and she didn't want to tell me? She's undergoing one of those bizarre so-called cures they feature at health spas."

"Please don't panic, Mr. Pell," Lyra said. "That is not a useful emotion at the moment."

Everyone stared at her. Simon knew they were all thinking the same thing: No one told Luther Pell not to panic.

Luther shut up and started pacing again.

Simon looked at him. "Keep in mind that we don't know if Miss Kirk made that note on the pad this morning. She could have jotted it down yesterday or the day before."

Elena shook her head. "I think it's safe to say she wrote this today. There's an entry on the previous page that refers to her reservations for dinner for two here at the hotel last night."

"Raina took me out for dinner last night," Lyra said. "After that we went to the Paradise. You're right, Elena. The note about the Labyrinth Springs Hotel and Spa must have been written early this morning."

Oliver looked at Luther. "If Raina had a sudden, serious concern about her health, I doubt very much that she would have

104

chosen the Labyrinth Springs Hotel and Spa."

"Mr. Ward is right," Lyra said.

Irene looked thoughtful. "Yes, he is."

"I agree," Elena said.

"Why are you all so sure of that?" Simon asked.

"Because it's not a health spa." Lyra unfolded her arms and widened her hands. "It used to specialize in old-fashioned water cures, but a year ago Edith Guppy, the founder of Guppy's House of Beauty, closed her New York day spa and opened one in Labyrinth Springs."

"That's a resort town in the foothills several miles from Palm Springs," Irene said.

Simon nodded. "I've heard of it."

"That old hotel in Labyrinth Springs was on its last legs a few years ago," Oliver said. "I considered buying and renovating it myself, but I decided I liked Burning Cove a lot more than I liked the desert. Winters are all right, but in the summer you might as well shut your doors. About eighteen months ago a wealthy New York investor named Billingsley came along and picked up the place for a song. He poured a lot of cash into the hotel and completely renovated the old spa. Guppy moved in a year ago. Got to admit, affiliating with Guppy's

House of Beauty was a stroke of genius on Billingsley's part."

"The Labyrinth Springs Hotel and Spa has become popular with celebrities and socialites from Los Angeles in the past year," Elena said. "Men play golf and tennis. Women often go alone or with a female friend to take advantage of the special Day of Beauty at Guppy's spa. Clients can book as many days as they want, of course. Most select the three-day option, which includes the hotel room."

Lyra didn't say *I told you so,* but she shot Simon a smile that could only be labeled triumphant.

He sighed. "All right, I'll bite. How did you know about Guppy's House of Beauty?"

Lyra, Elena, and Irene stared at him as if he were from some other planet.

"Are you kidding?" Lyra said. "Every woman in the country who reads *Vogue* or *Harper's Bazaar* or any major newspaper knows the Guppy brand. Ads for Madam Guppy's signature perfume and her beauty products show up in all the best fashion magazines."

"I see," Simon said, feeling suddenly outgunned.

Oliver gave him a pitying glance. "Look on the bright side. Next time you have an occasion to purchase perfume for a lady, you'll know which brand to buy."

It occurred to Simon that he had never bought perfume for a woman. Flowers, yes. Drinks, yes. Dinner at fashionable restaurants, yes. But not perfume.

Lyra gave him a smile that was a little too sweet. "If you want to make an impression, be sure you buy Guppy's *signature* perfume."

He eyed her warily. "Which is?"

Irene looked up from her notebook. "Violet. I don't wear it, myself. It's a little too heavy for my taste."

"I don't care for it, either," Lyra said. "Irene is right. It's on the heavy side."

"I agree," Elena said. "It feels East Coast somehow. Not California."

Luther had been ignoring the byplay but he abruptly stopped pacing and turned around to look at the women.

"Why did Guppy leave New York?" he asked.

There was a short silence. Irene, Elena, and Lyra looked at each other. Irene shrugged.

"I'm sure the rent on Madison Avenue was sky-high," she said. "It was probably costing her a fortune to keep the spa open."

"I'll bet she wanted to go after the celebrity market," Lyra offered. "The Guppy image was starting to become a bit stodgy. Women of a certain age wear Violet. Younger women are turning to newer cosmetic lines. Guppy probably concluded that moving the spa to California and appealing to the Hollywood crowd would update the image of her brand. She's always been very shrewd when it comes to marketing."

Simon looked at Lyra. "You know a lot about marketing."

"I was raised in the business world," Lyra said.

And you took notes, Simon thought, *because you planned to take over your father's business empire.*

He wondered how much it had hurt when Lyra realized she was not going to inherit control of Brazier Shipping because she wasn't the son that her father had evidently wanted. *I know the feeling.*

Ruthlessly he shoved the past back into the shadows and focused on the present.

"Let's think about this," he said to Luther. "Miss Kirk told Lyra she was meeting an acquaintance, remember? The acquaintance probably chose the location. Given what we now know about the Labyrinth Springs Hotel and Spa, it's safe to assume that Miss

Kirk is not in the midst of a sudden health crisis."

Luther's jaw tightened. "None of this feels right."

"I agree," Lyra said. "And those clippings in the shoebox indicate that whoever called her is someone from her past."

Irene tapped her pencil against the notebook. "It's too late to telephone those East Coast newspapers. The offices will all be closed. But I'll start contacting the morgues first thing in the morning."

"The next step is to pay a visit to the Labyrinth Springs Hotel and Spa," Simon said.

"Yes," Luther said. "At the moment it's our only lead. I'm coming with you."

Oliver spoke up quietly. "Bad idea."

"He's right," Lyra said. "You should not go to Labyrinth Springs, Mr. Pell. Not yet."

Luther scowled. "Why the hell not?"

Lyra folded her arms and regarded him with a cool, commanding air. It was the look of a woman who was accustomed to giving orders and having them carried out.

"This is Raina Kirk we are dealing with here," she said. "We don't know for certain that she went to Labyrinth Springs, and if she did go, we don't know why. There are, however, some things we do know. First, she wanted to keep her actions a secret from all of us. Second, if she doesn't want us to know what she is doing, she will not welcome Mr. Cage and you barging into her personal business like a couple of maddened bulls entering a bullring."

Simon blinked. "Maddened bulls?"

"Figure of speech," Lyra said.

"My gut tells me Raina is in serious trouble," Luther said.

"My intuition tells me the same thing." Lyra inclined her head. "But if that's true, there is even more reason to approach this situation with caution."

Luther shot her a fierce look. "Got a better idea?"

As far as Simon could tell, Lyra was not intimidated.

"Yes, as a matter of fact, I do," she said. She turned to Elena Torres. "Would you please telephone the Labyrinth Springs Hotel and see if you can get a reservation for me for tomorrow night? It's about a four- or five-hour drive. I'll leave first thing in the morning. I should be there around noon at the latest. I'll put a sign in the window of Kirk Investigations today explaining that the office is closed for the rest of the week."

Elena gave her a knowing look and reached for the phone. "Will you be using

110

your real name?"

"Good question," Lyra said. "I need a cover name."

"Cage," Simon said. "Make the reservation in the name of Mr. and Mrs. Simon Cage. Newlyweds. We'll want the honeymoon suite if it's available."

"Don't be ridiculous," Lyra said, stunned.

"It's the perfect cover," Simon said.

What the hell am I doing? he thought.

CHAPTER 11

Raina surfaced from the hallucinations with the sense that she was alone. She knew the feeling well, because she had spent much of her adult life alone. She had not realized how empty her world had become until she moved to Burning Cove. There, in the warmth of the California sun, she had begun to discover the treasure of friendships with people she felt she could trust. In Burning Cove she had met Luther Pell.

Burning Cove and Luther and her new friends had given her the ultimate gift: the promise of belonging; the promise of home. But she was a woman with a carefully buried past. She had always feared that one day the specters of that past would rise up out of the grave. Now her nightmare had become real and she had to face it the same way she had everything else in her life — alone. She had to protect Luther and her new friends at all costs.

She suppressed the last fragments of a vision in which she was falling into a whirlpool of hot, violet-colored light and fought to take stock of her situation. A few vague memories flickered and sparked. The door of the hotel room opening. Terrifying monsters leaning over the bed — no, not monsters. Men with their faces covered in the rubber masks that were used in spas and salons to smooth wrinkles. She remembered her frantic struggle to get off the bed and escape. Broken glass. Darkness. Endless darkness. The rumble of a car engine. The strap of her handbag in her fingers. Fumbling with the clasp. More hallucinations.

Panic.

And then a vision of Luther reaching down into the violet whirlpool, trying to grasp her hand. But she kept falling . . .

She opened her eyes and discovered she was in a bedroom. Not the room she had been booked into at the hotel. She was lying on a large four-poster bed. The faint, lingering scent of a familiar perfume clung to the quilt and the pillowcases. It was the same fragrance that had wafted up from the bedding in room two twenty-one at the Labyrinth Springs Hotel — Madam Guppy's Violet.

I never did like that perfume. Too heavy.

113

At least she was no longer blindfolded. And her hands were free. The lamps in the room were on. That was a good thing, because the faded, floral drapes were pulled tightly shut across the window.

She sat up slowly. That was when she heard the clanking of metal links and became aware of an uncomfortable weight on her right foot. She looked down. The light from the wall sconce gleamed on the manacle around her ankle. One end of a metal chain was attached to the manacle. The other end was secured to an iron ring bolted to the wall.

She was wearing the trousers, shirt, and sport shoes she'd had on when she was in her hotel room. At least she was fully dressed. It was always easier to deal with disaster when one was wearing good clothes.

She got up slowly. The chain was just long enough to allow her to go into the adjoining bathroom. She could also get to the dressing table. It would not let her go as far as the door.

She went to the window and pulled the faded curtains aside. There was nothing to see except the solid wall of boards that had been nailed across the window.

Someone had gone to a lot of trouble to create a prison cell — far too much effort for just a single kidnapping. She knew then that she was not the first woman who had been chained in the very nice, somewhat old-fashioned bedroom.

She saw a plate of breakfast rolls, a large teapot, and a cup and saucer sitting on a small table. The design of the plate and the cup and saucer was familiar. The food she had ordered from room service had been served on dishes decorated with the same design. The rolls were not homemade. They looked as if they had come from a professional kitchen — a hotel kitchen.

It occurred to her that food might help settle her queasy stomach. She clanked her way across the room, picked up one of the rolls, and took a bite. It went down and felt like it would stay down.

She lifted the lid of the teapot and inhaled cautiously. The contents were only luke-warm, but that was not what made her decide to forgo a cup of tea. It was the faint trace of an all-too-familiar herbal scent that worried her. It triggered a memory. A pot of the same tea had been brought to her hotel room, courtesy of the hotel management. She'd poured herself a cup while she waited for her visitor. Not long after finishing the tea she had been plunged into the hallucinations. At some point she had collapsed on the bed.

She knew something about poisons. She would not drink the tea. She picked up the pot and went into the black-and-white-tiled bathroom. The towels were monogrammed with the logo of Guppy's House of Beauty: a violet orchid. She poured the tea down the sink and set the pot aside.

There was a glass on the white-tiled shelf above the sink. She used the soap to wash it out and then drank a full glass of water. When she was finished she clanked her way back into the bedroom, ate the rest of the breakfast rolls, and sank down on the edge of the bed. She examined the manacle around her ankle.

She was a captive locked in a deceptively pleasant prison. With the curtains pulled shut, one didn't even notice the boarded-up windows.

She knew a lot about outwardly attractive prisons, too. She had spent her short nightmare of a marriage locked in one in Bar Harbor.

She fought back a surging wave of panic and tried to think. She had been tricked. It wasn't the Ghost Lady who had made the telephone call that had brought her to Labyrinth Springs. Someone else — someone who knew the secrets of her marriage —

116

had made that call.

Her nightmares had come true. The violent psychopath she had married had not died in a fall down the stairs. He was alive and he had hunted her down. This time he would kill her.

But she was no longer the lonely, naïve young woman who had been easily deceived by a handsome, charming, wealthy older man.

The manacle. She had to do something about it before she could try to figure out a way to escape. She had faced a similar problem the last time she had been held prisoner. In Bar Harbor she had been able to save herself because someone had taught her how to sail. It had been weeks, however, before she had gathered the nerve to take the risk of sailing into the storm.

The good news this time was that she already knew how to pick a lock. A secretary learned a lot of skills when she realized she was working for a couple of ruthless killers. She had made it a point to discover her employers' darkest secrets, especially when she began to suspect that she was on their to-do list of future victims.

She tried to focus on the details of her surroundings, searching for something she could use to unlock the manacle. But the room was starting to twist and warp around her again, just as it had last night in room two twenty-one. The hallucinations slammed back, scenes from her nightmares.

A devastating lethargy settled on her. She fell back onto the bed.

Tears of rage and frustration leaked from her eyes. She knew then that she should never have eaten the breakfast rolls.

CHAPTER 12

Simon arrived at the beachfront cottage shortly before six the next morning. The first thing Lyra noticed was that he wasn't wearing his spectacles. The second thing that was immediately evident was that he was in a bad mood.

He looked at the three pink leather suitcases and the hatbox sitting in the small front hall.

"What the hell?" he said.

"We're supposed to be on our honeymoon, remember? A bride doesn't check into an expensive hotel with only one suitcase."

"Is that right? You've done this before?"

"I have attended a number of weddings as a bridesmaid. I spent a few months planning my own wedding until I discovered that my fiancé was sleeping with my former best friend. Trust me, I know how these things are done."

Simon surveyed her snug dark green skirt, yellow silk blouse, and dainty high-heeled sandals with a disapproving glare.

"You look like a fashion model," he said.

She gave him her most glowing smile. "Why, thank you."

He did not return the smile. "Does it occur to you that you might be going overboard with our cover story?"

"Would you prefer that I wear my trench coat and fedora? Somehow I don't think that would work with the image of Mr. and Mrs. Cage, newlyweds."

"We're wasting time." Simon picked up two of the pink leather suitcases and headed out the open door. "Let's get on the road."

She slung the strap of her handbag over her shoulder, gripped the handle of the remaining suitcase, picked up the hatbox, and hurried after him.

"Are you always this grouchy in the mornings?" she asked.

"I don't know. There's never been anyone around to complain."

"So you're not married, then?"

"No."

"Ever been married?"

"No."

He opened the trunk of the sleek maroon Cord parked in the drive and wedged two pink suitcases alongside his briefcase and a single, well-worn brown leather suitcase. When he was finished he eyed the hatbox and the remaining suitcase.

"Those will have to go in the backseat," he said.

She gave him her super-dazzling smile. "Why do I have the feeling you wish you could stuff me into the trunk and put the suitcases in the passenger seat?"

He ignored that. Instead he took the third suitcase and the hatbox around to the passenger's side of the convertible. The top was down. He leaned over and dropped the suitcase and box on the floor of the rear compartment.

He straightened and started around the front of the car. "Let's go. It's a solid four-and-a-half-hour drive to Labyrinth Springs, and that's assuming no car trouble."

She did not respond, nor did she make any move to get into the car. It was important to start as one meant to go on.

Simon got halfway around the front of the convertible before he stopped abruptly. Without a word he turned around and returned to the passenger's side of the vehicle. He opened the door for her.

She gave him a real smile and slipped into the butter-soft leather seat.

"Thank you," she said.

"That's right." He closed the door. "It's important to reward good behavior."

"This is going to be a very long drive, isn't it?"

"I have a radio. We won't have to amuse each other with scintillating conversation."

"Too bad. I'm quite good at conversation."

"Believe it or not, I already figured that out."

He rounded the long hood of the Cord, opened the door on the driver's side, and got behind the wheel. He took a pair of sunglasses out of his shirt pocket, put them on, and fired up the engine.

She pulled a green silk scarf out of her handbag, folded it into a triangle, and put it over her hair.

"Am I allowed to remind you that this honeymoon cover was your idea?" she asked, knotting the scarf under her chin.

"That would be rude," he said. He pulled away from the curb. "But I probably deserve it."

"I like a man who takes responsibility for his behavior." She opened her handbag again, took out a pair of sunglasses, and slipped them on. "If you regret suggesting I accompany you as your bride, why did you come up with the idea in the first place?"

"I couldn't think of any other way to keep an eye on you. And you were planning to continue the investigation on your own. Admit it."

"Of course I would have continued looking for Raina, with or without a fake husband."

"I knew it."

She settled back into the seat. "Besides, although you had no way of knowing it, this trip to Labyrinth Springs will allow me to cross off one of the items on my personal agenda."

He stopped the car at an intersection and glanced at her. "What's that?"

"Checking into a hotel with a man who isn't my husband."

"Is that your idea of a joke?"

"Nope. I'm serious."

"What else is on this agenda of yours?"

"Lots of things I haven't done because I wasted too much time trying to be the perfect daughter and prove to my father that I was mature enough and smart enough to take over his business. After I graduated from college I talked my father into hiring me. I started in the mail room of Brazier Shipping and worked my way up to the head office. I wanted to learn every aspect of the business. I was Father's assistant until a few weeks ago."

"What happened a few weeks ago?"

"I quit. It's complicated. I'm hoping my new career as a private investigator will make it possible for me to fill in my résumé."

"What résumé?"

"Just an expression. What I'm trying to explain is that when I get old I want to be able to look back on an interesting past."

"I saw the article in yesterday's edition of the *Herald.* Looks like you've already got an interesting past."

She shuddered. "What happened at the Adlingtons' residence doesn't count."

"Trust me, it counts."

"Why do you say that?"

"Because you're never going to be able to forget it."

She thought about that. "You're right. That is very insightful of you."

"Golly, thanks. Once in a while I impress myself. There's a map in the glove box. You're in charge of navigation."

"Lucky for you, I know how to read a map."

"Yeah, clearly my luck runneth over today."

She opened the glove box, pushed aside the flashlight and a few other items, and pulled out the map.

In spite of Simon's dour mood, she would have enjoyed the trip if their mission was not so serious. The road followed the coastline as far as Los Angeles. It was another picture-perfect Southern California day. The ocean sparked and dazzled with a diamond-sharp light. The breeze stimulated all her senses. And she was sitting very close to the most interesting man she had ever met. Simon drove the exciting car with cool, relaxed skill.

All in all it was a scene right out of a Hollywood movie. *This is where I was meant to be,* she thought. *Should have walked away from Brazier Shipping years ago and moved to Burning Cove.*

But as with so many things in this land of sunshine and glamour, appearances could be deceiving. That was certainly true of Simon Cage.

"Are you a real antiquarian book dealer?" she asked.

His hard profile got harder. For a moment she wasn't sure he was going to answer the question.

"Real enough," he said finally. "I've got a small shop on the first floor of my house in Santa Monica. But I make most of my money tracking down and authenticating antiquarian books for collectors."

"And working for Luther Pell?"

"I do occasional odd jobs for him, yes."

"Investigations."

"Yes."

"No offense, but you don't look like a professional investigator."

"You're not the first person to mention that," he said. "That's more or less the point when you're working undercover."

She flushed. "Right."

"Maybe I should get a trench coat. Can I ask where you bought yours?"

She shot him a scorching look. "That is not amusing."

"I'm not known for my humor."

"Understandable," she said. "I assume you have a gun."

"In my briefcase."

"Well, that's something, at least."

"The briefcase or the gun?"

"Ha. That was a desperate attempt at humor. Don't try to deny it. I know it when I see it."

"What about you? Got a pistol in one of those pink suitcases? The hatbox, maybe?"

This was embarrassing. A competent professional investigator ought to have a pistol and know how to use it. She was good with a bow and arrow because she had been on the women's archery team in college, but unfortunately firearms had not been included in the curriculum.

"I just started my job at the Kirk agency," she said. "Raina says I'm not ready to carry a gun. She says I need more experience."

"Don't be offended, but I have to tell you I find that reassuring."

She crossed her arms. "I am offended."

"Judging by what happened on your last case, it sounds like you can take care of yourself," Simon said. "In my experience, guns are overrated. They never seem to be available when you need one. You're usually stuck with whatever is handy. A golf club, for example."

She went cold and fixed her attention on the view through the windshield.

"What did I say?" Simon asked.

"Let's change the subject."

"You don't want to talk about your last case."

"It was also my first case," she said. "And no, I don't want to discuss it."

"I've had cases that ended badly, too."

"Is that right?" she said.

She glanced at the scars on his right hand but decided it was too soon to ask any questions about them. Scars, whether seen or unseen, were a very personal matter.

"Yes," he said.

"Who are you, Mr. Cage?"

"You know who I am."

His response was a fraction of a beat too slow, she decided. He had not been expecting that question. She smiled. It was good to know she could disturb the veneer of calm, cool control that Simon showed the world.

"What made you decide to pose as an antiquarian book dealer for your investigative work?" she said, feeling her way into the inquisition. "It seems an odd choice."

"It's not a role. I told you, I really am in the book business. I specialize in tracking down valuable antiquarian books, manuscripts, and maps for collectors. I have a reputation for being able to detect frauds and forgeries. You'd be astonished by how many people engage in deception in the antiquarian book trade."

"No, I wouldn't be surprised. There's a lot of money sloshing around in that world, just as there is in the art world. And a lot of obsessive collectors. That combination always makes for a lively business in frauds and forgeries."

"Yes, it does."

"How did you end up doing so-called odd jobs for Luther Pell?"

Again there was a slight hesitation before Simon answered. When he did, she got the impression he was choosing his words with great care.

"Luther came looking for me a couple of years ago," he said. "He'd heard I had a certain talent for locating rare books and that I could detect frauds and forgeries. He thought I might be useful to him on occasion."

"I can see where that sort of talent would be useful to a lot of people."

"It's a little more complicated than that," Simon said.

"I know."

Simon's hands tightened around the steering wheel. He kept his attention fixed on the two-lane highway.

"Is that right?" he said, his tone far too neutral. "What exactly do you think you know?"

"Yesterday when we were at Raina's house you sensed something important in that shoebox where we found the clippings. You detected it just by touching the box. Do you, by any chance, have some paranormal ability, Simon Cage?"

"Please don't tell me you're one of those people who is obsessed with psychic phenomena."

"I'm not obsessed with it but I do find the subject fascinating."

"Fascinating."

"It makes me curious," she said.

"Everything and everyone seems to make you curious."

"Well, yes, but the paranormal is particularly intriguing to me," she said, her enthusiasm sparking. "It apparently interests others, too. Are you aware that Duke University established the Parapsychology Laboratory several years ago?"

Once again Simon's hands tightened on the wheel.

"Yes," he said.

"And then there are Edgar Cayce's readings and his Association for Research and Enlightenment."

"Cayce is either delusional or a fraud. I'm betting on the latter."

"You can't possibly know that."

"Do you really take all that stuff about dream readings and astral projection seriously?"

"Well, no. But I think he and others are serious about the research, and I do believe the subject deserves to be studied. It's not as if a lot of well-respected people haven't tried to investigate the paranormal. Take Arthur Conan Doyle, for example."

"It does seem amazing that the man who created Sherlock Holmes could be so easily fooled, but here's what I know about mediums and fortune-tellers, Lyra. They are all frauds and con artists."

"I agree," she said. "I had some readings done by tearoom psychics, and I attended a séance. Houdini would have exposed all of them in a minute."

He shot her a searching glance. "I'm glad to hear you didn't fall for the con."

She wrinkled her nose. "You don't have to look so stunned and amazed that I was able to detect the fakery."

"Sorry. It's just that I know how easily even very smart people can be fooled, especially when it comes to the paranormal. People believe what they want to believe even when the evidence points in another direction."

"Just to be clear, while I don't believe one can talk to the spirit world or make predictions about the future, I do believe there are forms of energy in the world that we have not yet been able to detect with our modern instruments and gauges. I am convinced that the concept of paranormal energy deserves legitimate exploration."

"Figures."

Lyra smiled. "You know what?"

"What?"

"We should probably change the subject. A full-blown quarrel wouldn't fit our cover. We're on our honeymoon. At this point we should be utterly besotted with each other. The arguments come later."

Simon startled her with an unexpected crack of laughter.

"How would you know?" he said. "You told me you'd never been married."

"No, but I have been engaged. Once was enough. I don't ever plan to marry."

Simon thought about that. Then he smiled.

"You're a very modern-thinking woman," he said.

He sounded satisfied, she decided.

"Yes," she said. "And while we're on this particular subject, I realize it's a bit late to be asking the question, but I should probably know the answer before we check in to a hotel suite together."

"I told you I wasn't married."

"Yes, but is there, perhaps, a woman in your life who might not like the idea of the two of us registering as man and wife?"

"No."

"A man?"

"No."

"Aha. You're divorced."

"No."

She considered briefly.

"Engaged?" she ventured.

"Once upon a time. Like you, I've come to the conclusion that marriage isn't for me."

"Was she the one who ended your relationship?" Lyra asked.

"How did you guess?"

"Something about your very short, very brusque responses to my little attempt at interrogation. It was a messy ending, I assume?"

"Do relationships ever end in any non-messy ways?"

"Probably not. How bad was it?"

She could have sworn that this time Simon actually flinched in surprise. Then he shook his head, bemused.

"Do you really want to know?"

"I'm bored. Long drive. Can't get good radio reception this far away from a town. I would be okay if I was behind the wheel, but you're the one who gets to drive, because this is your car. So that means you are my only source of entertainment."

"I should tell you about my failed engagement so that you won't be bored?"

"Have you ever talked about it to anyone else?"

133

"Hell, no."

"Maybe you should," she said. "Might do you a world of good. It's clear you're a bit depressed."

"I'm not depressed," he said. "It so happens I'm not the chatty type. Unlike, say, you."

"Look at it this way. We're stuck with each other for now but after this case you and I will probably never see each other again. What have you got to lose by talking to me?"

"Has it occurred to you that I might find it awkward to discuss my private life with a complete stranger?"

"We're checking into a hotel as Mr. and Mrs. Simon Cage," she said. "Most people would consider that incredibly scandalous. I'd say that, under the circumstances, we are not complete strangers."

"What are we?"

"Professional colleagues. I told you why I broke off my engagement. I think I deserve to know your story."

"If you want to know about what happened to my engagement, you need to tell me more about why yours ended."

"I told you, I caught him in bed with a woman I considered a friend. She was going to be one of my bridesmaids."

"What made you fall in love with the guy

in the first place?"

"That's a bit more complicated. I was sure Hamilton was Prince Charming and Mr. Perfect all rolled into one. I've known him all my life. Had a secret crush on him for years. My parents loved him. They wanted him to marry my sister, Vivian. When she declined I was happy to take her place. Hamilton seemed fine with the idea. Mother and Father were thrilled. He's rich, so we knew he wasn't after my inheritance. He was going to take over my father's shipping company. I planned to help him run it. *What could possibly go wrong?* you may well ask."

A slow, knowing smile briefly transformed Simon's features. "You planned to *help* him run your father's company?"

She unfolded her arms and exhaled a long sigh. "Okay, you've got me. I had my heart set on taking over Brazier Shipping, but it had become clear that my father was never going to be convinced that a woman could run the firm. I also knew Hamilton well enough to realize he had no real interest in the business."

"So you figured you could get control of the company if you married Prince Charming?"

"It seemed the perfect solution. Hamilton is smart, funny, very handsome, and an

135

excellent kisser. We had a lot of fun together. So, yes, it would have been something of a marriage of convenience for both of us, but I convinced myself I loved him. I fully intended to honor my vows. I expected him to be sincere, too."

"You got conned."

She frowned. "No, I don't think so. Hamilton was fond of me. I think that, in his own way, he really did care for me."

"You got conned," Simon repeated, ruthless.

"In hindsight, I think I'm the one who conned Hamilton, and myself, as well."

"Huh. An interesting perspective. You may be right."

"Regardless, it all worked out for the best, because it forced me to face reality. I am now on a new and much more exciting path. There. I told you my story. Your turn. Did you find your fiancée in bed with someone else?"

"Maybe she found me in bed with someone else," Simon said.

"Not likely."

"Because I'm too dull and boring to get involved in an illicit affair?"

"I have no idea if you would allow yourself to be drawn into an affair. After the mistake I made with Hamilton, I do not consider

136

myself a great judge of men, not when it comes to their ethics and morals. But I am quite capable of judging their intelligence."

"What does my intelligence have to do with my morals?"

Simon sounded bemused, bewildered, and fascinated now.

"You wouldn't get caught in the act unless you wanted that to happen," she explained patiently. "You're too smart and too careful." She drummed her fingers on the windshield frame. "Still, that does bring up the question, doesn't it? Which was it? You caught her, or you made sure she caught you because you wanted her to end things?"

"Neither. Gloria decided I was either a professional con artist who was out to take advantage of her or simply delusional. She couldn't decide if I ought to be arrested or committed to an asylum for the insane."

CHAPTER 13

Lyra stared at him, wide-eyed, astonished, shocked.

Simon wasn't sure if he should be satisfied or alarmed. It was obvious that it took a lot to set her back on her heels. For the first time since they had left Burning Cove he felt at least somewhat back in control of the conversation. It was as if he had temporarily regained his balance, barely avoiding a hard fall, but was still on the tightrope.

Lyra, being Lyra, recovered fast. She gave him an accusing glare. "You said that to rattle my nerves. Admit it."

"Yes," he said. "But it also happens to be the truth."

In some perverse way he was enjoying the moment. He would no doubt regret it later, but, damn, at least he'd managed to pull her up short for a while. Not that she would learn her lesson. It wouldn't be long before he once again found himself struggling to keep up with her.

He had gone to Burning Cove hoping to find a fast woman, and he had found her. He just hadn't expected to end up with a lady who moved at lightning speed in unpredictable directions. This was probably one of those be-careful-what-you-wish-for situations, he decided.

Lyra settled back into her seat, the shock factor already giving way to curiosity. "Tell me about the delusions."

"It involves my ability to detect frauds and forgeries," he said. "I let people think I'm good at the work because of my extensive study and research and my vast experience."

"But you don't have any of those things?"

"Well, in my own defense I can say that I've spent enough time in academic and private libraries during the past few years to pick up a lot of the fancy language that goes with the antiquarian book business. I know how to sound like a pro. Want to hear me discuss the different editions of *Paradise Lost* and tell you why the one with engravings by Gustave Doré is worth so much?"

"No."

"I could also tell you why Milton is so important to the development of the English language and literature."

"Forget it."

"Care to discuss Christopher Marlowe's influence on Shakespeare, perhaps?"

"We're discussing you, not Marlowe, Shakespeare, or Milton. Do you have any formal academic degrees?"

"None. I lost my parents when I was eleven. Ended up in an orphanage. I started sensing things that no one else could detect when I turned twelve. At first I thought I was picking up the energy of ghosts or spirits. I woke up in the middle of screaming nightmares. Terrified the other boys, not to mention the staff and the director. Got a reputation for being mentally unstable. The director could have had me committed immediately, but she didn't. Instead, she called in three different doctors to examine me. The first two said I was a lost cause and that I should be sent to a state asylum."

"What happened?"

"A third doctor heard about my case and asked the director of the orphanage if he could examine me. She agreed immediately. I figured that would not go well, so I was making preparations to run away when Dr. Otto Tinsley showed up."

"That name sounds familiar."

Simon realized he was clenching his teeth. He forced himself to relax.

"Not surprising," he said. "He makes a

140

living giving lectures on the subject of paranormal research. The talks are accompanied by dramatic demonstrations of the Tinsley Paranormal Energy Detector. If you think Madam Guppy is good at marketing, you should meet Tinsley. He knows how to captivate an audience."

"I have never attended one of his lectures, but I've read about him in the press."

"Tinsley ran me through a lot of tests. When he was finished he assured me there was nothing wrong with me and promised to take me away with him. I was desperate to escape the orphanage. I would have gone with the devil himself. Tinsley conned the director. Told her he was sure he could cure me but that I would have to go with him. Marsden had him sign some papers, and the next thing I knew, Tinsley had adopted me."

"Did Tinsley treat you well?"

Simon hesitated. He had not seen that question coming.

"Almost like a real son," he said.

"If he adopted you, then you *were* a real son."

"It wasn't quite that simple."

"What happened?"

"For years, things went well. I grew up. We became business partners. Tinsley was

141

— is — obsessed with his paranormal research, but that kind of research requires money. He gets his funds by doing lectures and public demonstrations of his machine. He was barely getting by when we met. But after he put me in the act, the cash started flowing."

"The act? You mean you helped him give his psychic demonstrations? That must have been fun for a twelve-year-old kid. Just think, you were onstage doing genuine paranormal demonstrations."

Her enthusiasm threw him off balance again. It was not the reaction he had expected. Disapproval or laughter, maybe, but not this glowing excitement.

"Fun?" he repeated, trying to regain his balance.

"I've met a few Hollywood stars since I moved to Burning Cove, but I've never met a real psychic who gave demonstrations in front of audiences."

"I'm not a real psychic," he muttered. "Psychics pretend to read minds, talk to the dead, and predict the future. They're charlatans. I just . . . sense . . . certain kinds of emotions, that's all. I walked away from the Tinsley show about four years ago."

"How did it work?"

"The show?"

"Yes," Lyra said. "What was your job?"

He groaned. He should have known better than to go down this path, he thought.

"The act involved members of the audience asking for psychic readings on objects they had brought from home. Usually they wanted to know something about the history of the item. Tinsley would go into the crowd and select someone. He would escort the person onstage and then he would connect me to his damn machine with a metal band around my head and around one wrist. He gave me the object to hold and then he pulled a red curtain around me and the machine. After a few minutes he pulled the curtain aside with a flourish. I announced the results to the audience in a suitably dramatic voice. Satisfied?"

"No. Why the curtain?"

"It was an *act*, Lyra. A performance. You need to impress the audience with lots of stage props."

"Okay, I guess that makes sense. The machine was a prop, too, right? You didn't really need it to do your readings."

"As far as Tinsley is concerned, the machine is real. I told you, he's obsessed with it. But it doesn't actually work. The idea was to make it look like it could channel a person's latent talent. Tinsley wanted to create a lot of interest in the device so that people would buy tickets to the show and help fund his research. My job was to make the machine look as if it really worked."

"What kinds of things did people ask you to read?"

"Old jewelry. Family heirlooms. Sometimes they just wanted to know if an object was valuable. Occasionally they tried to do their own detective work. One woman brought a carving knife to the show. As soon as I touched it, I knew it had been used in a murder."

"You could tell just by handling it?" Lyra said, fascinated.

"Yes." Simon downshifted for a curve and thought about the sensations he had experienced when he touched the hilt of the blade. "It was the first time I had read an item that had been associated with extreme violence. I was so shocked I blurted out the word *murder*. The audience was stunned. The woman who had requested the reading yelled, *I knew it. I knew that bitch killed him.* Fortunately it was the last act of the evening. Tinsley and I packed up the show immediately and left town within the hour. The last thing we wanted to do was get caught up in the middle of a murder investigation."

Lyra said nothing. He glanced at her, trying to get a read on what she was thinking. She was smiling. Amusement sparkled in her eyes.

"What?" he said.

"The image of you and Dr. Tinsley scrambling to hightail it out of town before you had to explain things to the police is rather amusing, that's all."

"Trust me, it wasn't at the time."

"No, I imagine it wasn't. But I have to tell you it does sound a lot like a scene from a Laurel and Hardy movie."

Once again he was caught off balance. He shocked himself with a short, sharp crack of laughter.

"I guess you had to be there," he said.

"Did you leave the act because Tinsley was using you to make money to finance his research?"

The flash of reluctant amusement vanished in a heartbeat.

"There was no real research involved, Lyra. It was all a con. And I had a major role in it."

"How can you say that? Obviously you have some sort of paranormal talent."

"No, damn it." He paused. "What I have is a good sense of intuition. That's all."

"You've got a serious paranormal talent

and you're not about to admit it, not even to yourself. Why, exactly, did you leave the Tinsley show?"

"I got tired of being used."

"I don't think that's the whole story."

"That's all the story you're getting."

"Sooner or later you'll talk," Lyra growled in an exaggerated movie-villain voice. "Everybody does."

"To you?"

"Yep. The hard part is making them stop."

He had the horrifying feeling she was right.

CHAPTER 14

The phone rang just as Luther was trying to decide if he should take the risk of contacting one of his connections in the FBI. The problem with asking the Bureau for assistance in a missing persons case was that this particular missing person had a very murky past. He had no hesitation about calling in a favor, but the last thing he wanted to do was encourage the authorities to stir up the deep waters of that past.

He stopped prowling the room and seized the receiver. "Pell."

"It's Irene. I started making phone calls at five o'clock this morning. I have some information about the disappearance of Jean Whitlock and the death of her husband. Not sure how helpful it will be, though."

"Whatever you have is more than I've got now." Luther went back to the desk and grabbed a pencil and a sheet of paper. "Talk to me, Irene."

"There wasn't a lot of press coverage of Mrs. Whitlock's disappearance. Bar Harbor is a small place. The local paper stayed on the story for a while because the Whitlock name is an old one. The family has had what the wealthy like to call a summer cottage there since the late eighteen hundreds. There was nothing new in the clip files — Mrs. Whitlock took a sailboat out and ran straight into a storm. Body was never found. Husband distraught. However, being a small community means everybody knew everybody else's business. The clerk in the paper's morgue was kind enough to let me know that the Whitlock marriage was not a happy one."

"How bad was it?"

"Apparently Malcolm Whitlock was jealous and possessive. Jean was never seen in public without him. There was speculation that Malcolm was mentally unbalanced. Some people remembered certain incidents that occurred when he was a boy. Apparently he set some fires and a few pets went missing. The Whitlock family more or less gave Malcolm the house to get him out of Boston. He lived there year-round. His relatives never visited."

"Do the locals think he murdered his wife?"

"According to my source, everyone believes it's more likely that Jean Whitlock escaped the house and took the sailboat out in bad weather because she was trying to get away from her husband."

"What about his death?"

"Interesting, to put it mildly. The family maintains to this day that Malcolm was so distraught over the disappearance of his wife that he moved back to Boston, bought a house, and became a recluse. Never went out into society again. They claim he died in a fall down the stairs."

"I'm getting the feeling some people didn't buy that story," Luther said.

"No. The reporter's notes filed with the story in the morgue indicate that there were rumors Whitlock's family got him committed to a private asylum and that he died there. Suicide. I'm going to make a few more calls and see if I can dig up more details. I wanted to get this information to you first."

"Thanks, Irene."

"You're wondering if Jean Whitlock is now Raina Kirk, aren't you?"

"Yes, but there is another possibility. Maybe Jean Whitlock is the acquaintance who convinced Raina to meet her in Labyrinth Springs. You didn't find any photos, I take it?"

"No. The Whitlock wedding was a courthouse affair. No pictures. None in the Bar Harbor papers and nothing in the Boston press." Irene paused. "I wonder why Raina didn't confide in you. Why not ask for help?"

"I can think of one reason why she might be trying to handle this on her own," Luther said.

"She thinks she's protecting you from something in her past?"

"Yes."

He hung up the phone and went to the French doors that opened onto a balcony. He contemplated the lush gardens and the sun-splashed ocean beyond.

Did you go to Labyrinth Springs to meet Jean Whitlock, Raina? Or are you Jean Whitlock?

CHAPTER 15

That afternoon Lyra opened the French doors of the honeymoon suite and stepped out onto the wrought iron balcony. She gripped the railing and surveyed the elegantly manicured gardens in the courtyard of the Labyrinth Springs Hotel and Spa.

"Why wasn't Raina's car in the parking lot?" she said. "She left Burning Cove in her convertible. We should have seen it when we arrived. Maybe we're wrong. What if she isn't here?"

"Take it easy," Simon said. He crossed the sitting room and moved outside to join her at the railing. "We agreed that this is our starting point. It's the only solid lead we've got. There could be several reasons why we didn't see her car in the lot. She may have driven into town to do some shopping."

"I doubt it," Lyra said. "She was not in a shopping mood when she left Burning Cove yesterday."

"There's a shopping mood?"

"Of course," Lyra said. She studied the setting. "There isn't much around here, is there? Just a lot of desert. The town is barely a village. There's a sprinkling of nice houses and a few resorts, but it strikes me as a very odd location for a secret meeting with an acquaintance."

"Depends how you look at it. On the one hand, it's hard to be anonymous here. People staying at a resort like this notice the other guests on the golf course or at the pool. They see them in the bar and the dining room. That's one of the reasons they come to a fashionable hotel and spa in the first place."

"To see and be seen."

"Right. But there is one possible advantage to this particular location."

Lyra glanced at him. "What?"

"You could bury a body out there in the desert and no one would ever find it."

Lyra shuddered. "Thanks for that cheery thought."

She had to admit he was right. Beyond the hotel gardens and the oasis of green that was the golf course, the vast desert valley stretched for miles in every direction. It would be a simple matter to conceal a body in an unmarked grave.

She had taken a few minutes to read the pamphlet titled *History of Labyrinth Springs* that she had picked up at the front desk when she and Simon had checked in. The small, fashionable town had originally been a stagecoach stop. Later, the arrival of the railroad in nearby Palm Springs had transformed it into a destination for those who first came to take the water cures in the hot springs and then stayed to enjoy the sunshine in midwinter.

Over time, the water cures had lost their appeal. The smart set wanted swimming pools, tennis courts, and golf courses, all of which Palm Springs offered. For years the Labyrinth Springs Hotel had failed to keep up with the times and had been in danger of closing its doors. But the new owner had rescued it. Oliver Ward was right — persuading Madam Guppy to move her spa to California had been a stroke of marketing genius.

Unlike most of the buildings in town and the winter homes of the wealthy that were scattered around the valley and the foothills, the old hotel had been constructed in a style that was typical of late Victorian spa and beachfront resorts. It reminded Lyra of the Hotel del Coronado in San Diego — a sprawling, fanciful structure trimmed with

153

wide, shaded verandas. The lobby was a grand rotunda lit with a massive chandelier. Gazebos decorated the gardens. Guppy's spa occupied one entire wing.

The honeymoon suite was on the third floor. Evidently it had not always been intended for that purpose. Lyra had been relieved to discover that there were two bedrooms: a master suite and a much smaller suite on the opposite side of the spacious sitting room that had probably been intended for children or a lady's maid.

The bellhop had left all of the luggage in the master bedroom. Simon had waited until he was gone before moving his single suitcase and his briefcase into the small bedroom.

The sitting area was furnished with a sofa, two reading chairs, and a fully stocked liquor cabinet. A bouquet of flowers and a bottle of champagne were on the round table in the center of the room. The note on the table read Congratulations to Mr. and Mrs. Simon Cage. Compliments of the Management of the Labyrinth Springs Hotel & Spa.

"Too bad we can't simply telephone the front desk and ask to be connected to Raina Kirk's room," Lyra said. "If she really is in the middle of an investigation, that could destroy her cover. Besides, for all we know she's registered under another name."

"Don't worry, there are other ways to find out if she's here," Simon said.

"How? Plant ourselves in the lobby and see if she happens to walk past us? We can't sit down there for hours. People will notice. And what if she never even checked in? We can't waste time."

"You're not going to panic on me, are you?" Simon asked. He sounded only mildly concerned.

She narrowed her eyes. "I'm not panicking. I'm trying to come up with a plan."

"Save yourself the effort. I've already got one."

"Is that right? What is it?"

"Let's go downstairs, have tea on the veranda, and then take a stroll around the grounds. I'll tell you how we're going to find out if Miss Kirk is here and at the same time I'll get a feel for the layout of the resort."

Lyra gave him a determined smile. "*We* will get a feel for the layout of the resort. I realize you are under the impression that you had to bring me along because you didn't want me investigating on my own, but I've got news for you. We are professional colleagues."

"Luther told me you were hired on at the Kirk agency as an apprentice investigator."

"So?"

"So that makes you the *junior* colleague. I'm the one in charge."

"Sure," Lyra said.

She gave him a dazzling smile.

Simon got the man-watching-a-slow-moving-train-wreck look again.

CHAPTER 16

"Here's what you need to remember, Gerald," Lyra said. "You are an intelligent, good-looking man with a job. You have a lot to offer a woman. I understand what you're going through, because I went through a very similar experience, myself, with a man I planned to marry."

Gerald glanced at Simon. "Not Mr. Cage, I take it?"

Simon swallowed some of his cocktail and gave Gerald a warning look.

Gerald was a waiter. He had just delivered Lyra's pink lady and Simon's martini to the table. Simon was not certain how it had happened, but at some point Gerald and Lyra had fallen into an intimate discussion of Gerald's love life, which evidently had taken a downturn recently.

Simon was caught between amazement and exasperation.

Lyra gave Gerald a warm smile. "Mr.

Cage came along after my engagement ended. You could say he swept me off my feet. Ours was a whirlwind, runaway romance."

"Wow," Gerald said. "Just like in the movies, huh?"

"Yes," Lyra said. "And I'm sure there is a lovely young woman here in Labyrinth Springs just waiting for you to ask her out on a date. But you're going to have to forget what's-her-name and look to the future."

"Betty," Gerald said. "Her name is Betty."

"Not anymore," Lyra said. "From now on she is what's-her-name as far as you are concerned. It's all about focusing on the future, Gerald, not the past."

"Okay," Gerald said earnestly. "I'll try. Thanks for the advice."

"Anytime," Lyra said. "And thank you for the excellent service."

Gerald glowed. "You're welcome. Next time you come into the dining room, just ask for me."

"We'll do that."

Gerald hurried away. Simon looked at Lyra, who was seated on the opposite side of the table.

"Do you always end up becoming best friends with the waiters when you go out on a date?" Simon asked.

Lyra raised her brows and picked up her glass. "Gerald and I have a lot in common, and this is not a date. You and I are working a case, remember?"

"*I'm* working a case. You appear to be engaging in a very personal conversation with a man whose last name you don't know."

Lyra took a sip of her pink lady and lowered the glass. "Why are you annoyed?"

I have absolutely no idea, Simon thought. But that was not entirely true. It alarmed him that he had used the word *date.* It was Lyra's fault. She was wearing a slinky evening gown that framed her elegantly rounded shoulders and displayed a lot of skin in back. The gown was a mysterious cobalt blue and it gleamed in the candlelight. Long, lacy black gloves framed her hands and forearms. Her hair fell in deep, sultry waves. He did not want to take his eyes off her.

"I'm just trying to stay focused on our investigation," he said. "You're the one who pointed out that we don't have a lot of time to waste."

"Relax. I felt sorry for Gerald. It's obvious he's depressed, and when it came out that his girlfriend dumped him to go to Hollywood, I thought it would cheer him up to know that he isn't the only one in the world who's recently had a bad romantic experience." Lyra widened her eyes. "Say, maybe you should tell him about your fiancée ending your engagement. Sympathy from another man who has been through a similar experience would do him a world of good."

"Got news for you. Men don't talk about stuff like that."

"How can you say that? A few hours ago you told me all about how your fiancée ended your engagement."

"I meant men don't talk about stuff like that to other men. Gerald and I will not be having a conversation."

Lyra waved one gloved hand in graceful dismissal. "Suit yourself."

She took another sip of her pink lady.

Simon watched her for a moment. "People talk to you."

"Probably because I talk to them. If you want people to talk to you, I suggest you try learning how to make polite conversation."

"What I'm saying is you have a talent for getting people to open up to you. That's a useful skill in our profession."

Lyra's mouth tightened. "You make it sound like I manipulate people."

He shook his head. "No. You find people

genuinely interesting. That's why they talk to you."

"Here's a news flash for you, Simon. Most people are interesting for at least a few minutes. Everyone has a story. It does not follow that I want to listen to that story for hours and hours. But for a few minutes? Yes. I'm curious. People never fail to surprise me. You can learn something from everyone."

"Is that right? What did you learn from Gerald, aside from the fact that he's depressed because his girlfriend ditched him?"

Lyra raised her brows. "Weren't you paying attention? Among other things, I learned that we shouldn't order the fish tonight."

"Damn. You're right." Simon raised his martini glass in a small salute. "Like I said, you have a talent."

Her eyes suddenly filled with shadows. The breezy, sophisticated, glamorous veneer vanished in a heartbeat. For a brief moment he caught a glimpse of the hidden side of the woman.

"Got news for you," she said quietly. "My terrific talent for making conversation didn't do me any good at the Adlington residence."

He knew he needed to say something helpful, but he wasn't any good at this kind of conversation, either. "You wouldn't be a

161

decent person if killing a man didn't shock you to the core, even if that man was trying to murder you."

She watched him with her haunted eyes. "Have you ever killed anyone?"

I'm a lousy psychic. Should have seen this coming.

The most expedient thing to do was lie. He was pretty good at lying. The ability was an essential tool for someone in his business. They said that telling the truth was the easiest thing to do, because you didn't have to remember the details of a story and keep them straight. But in his experience, telling the truth about his past usually led to disaster. If he hadn't told his fiancée the truth he might have been a happily married man with two kids and a lawn to mow every Saturday by now.

Or maybe not.

On the other side of the table Lyra sat quietly. Waiting.

He got that small, nerve-jarring shock of awareness that crackled across his senses when he picked up an object that was saturated in hot energy. In that flash of dazzling clarity he realized he did not want to lie to Lyra Brazier. He was not sure why it was important to tell her the truth, but it was.

"Yes," he said. "I did kill a man."

"Does the memory still disturb you?"

"He still shows up in my nightmares, yes."

"Did it happen in the course of one of your investigations?"

"Yes."

"Do you want to talk about it?"

"No," Simon said. "Not tonight."

"Okay."

CHAPTER 17

What the hell had gotten into him? He had never meant to tell her about his time as a stage psychic, and he never brought up the subject of the McGruder case. True, she hadn't pried all the details of the latter out of him, but it was probably only a matter of time. He wondered if Lyra was a hypnotist. Maybe that was how she got people to talk to her.

Simon pondered that possibility as he stood in the shadows of the hotel hallway and watched Lyra lure the night clerk out from behind the front desk.

"It's a lovely evening for a swim, isn't it?" she said, breezing through the lobby. She was dressed in a fluffy terry cloth robe and slippers. Her words were slightly slurred. She sounded and acted happily intoxicated. "I can't wait to enjoy a dip in one of the hot pools."

It was three o'clock in the morning. The

last of the guests had gone to their rooms nearly an hour earlier. The night clerk had been dozing in the inner office. When he heard Lyra announce her intended swim he woke up and shot out the doorway. His name tag read HIRAM.

"Madam, please, you can't go swimming," he yelped. "Not at this time of night. The bathhouse is closed."

Lyra waggled her fingers at him and winked. "Don't worry, Hiram, I'm sure I'll find a way in. I'll bet you have a key."

She opened the lobby doors and went outside into the moonlit gardens.

Hiram rushed around the end of the desk and charged after her. "Madam, you must not go into the bathhouse unless there are attendants available. Madam Guppy and the hotel management have very strict rules. Swimming alone in the mineral pools is not allowed. It's dangerous."

"You are welcome to come with me," Lyra sang out.

She disappeared into the gardens. The horrified clerk followed.

Simon waited until they were both out of sight before he emerged from the hallway.

He went to the front desk and opened the guest register. He flipped back to the previous day and went quickly through the list of people who had checked in.

Raina Kirk was not on the register, but he hadn't expected things to be that simple. Only three single travelers had arrived on that date, however. Two of them were women — Miss J. Granville and Miss E. Coulson. He made a note of the names and the rooms they had been assigned.

He closed the register and checked the wooden board behind the desk. The keys for the rooms that had been assigned to Miss Granville and Miss Coulson were gone, indicating they were in their rooms. He had not noticed any single women in the bar or the dining room, but that was not unusual. Women traveling alone often ordered room service.

Lyra's lilting laughter drifted in from the gardens. It sounded like she was on the far side of the courtyard. That meant the clerk was still safely out of the way.

In addition to the night clerk's office, there was another office door marked PRIVATE. He took out the lockpick he had slipped into the pocket of his evening jacket and started around the end of the front desk.

Lyra's voice was louder now. She was singing "Too Marvelous for Words." He got the message. He changed his mind and went back around the front desk.

He was lounging against the desk, banging the service bell, when Hiram escorted Lyra back into the lobby. She gave him a sparkling smile.

"Oh, hello, darling," she said. "I am trying to convince this nice man to let me take a swim in one of the bathhouse pools. He says I can't swim alone, and he refuses to join me. Would you like to take a swim?"

"Not tonight, dear," Simon said. "I've got a headache. Let's go upstairs. I think we both need some sleep."

He crossed the room to take her arm. Hiram was visibly relieved.

"Good night, sir," he said. "Madam."

"Good night, Hiram," Lyra said. "Thank you for showing me around the gardens."

"Anytime, Mrs. Cage," Hiram said.

He hastened into the inner office.

Simon kept his grip on Lyra's arm and steered her toward the stairs. When they reached the landing on the next floor she made to pull away from him. He realized he did not want to let go, but he could not think of a good excuse to hang on to her. Reluctantly he released her.

"Next time you can play the role of the ditzy dame who's had too many cocktails," she said.

"I doubt if I could top your performance," he said. "You were magnificent in the part."

"I was, wasn't I? Those drama classes I took in college finally paid off. Well? Were you successful?"

He smiled. She was a little giddy, and it wasn't from the pink ladies. He recognized the sensation because he was experiencing a similar rush of exhilaration. It was the energy of action; of moving forward on a case. Maybe the new lead would go nowhere, but at least there was a path.

"We're about to find out," he said. "Raina Kirk's name was not on the register, but two single women checked into the hotel yesterday in the afternoon."

"Do you think one of them was Raina?"

"It's possible. There's only one way to be sure. I've got the room numbers. We knock on doors and see who answers."

"This could and probably will get very awkward," Lyra warned. "Unless we get lucky with the first door, we're going to wake up a stranger who will no doubt be extremely annoyed."

"In that case we go into our act."

"Which is?"

"Intoxicated honeymooners who got lost on the way back to their suite."

"Embarrassing, but I suppose it's all we've

168

got to work with."

Simon glanced at his notes. "We'll start with room three twelve."

"What is the name of the guest in three twelve?"

Simon consulted his notes. "Coulson."

They climbed to the third floor and walked down the hall to three twelve.

"I'll knock," Lyra said. "Why don't you stay out of sight? We know the occupant is a woman. If it's Raina, she'll recognize me. If it isn't Raina, whoever is inside will be alarmed at the sight of a man."

"You're right. Go ahead."

Lyra rapped lightly on the door. There was no response.

"It's three in the morning," Simon said. "Whoever is inside is probably sound asleep. You'll have to knock louder."

Lyra shot him a quelling look but she did not argue. She raised her hand, made a little fist, and knocked again. Sharply.

There was a moment of silence inside and then a woman spoke. Her voice was thick with sleep.

"Who's there?" she called.

Lyra took a quick breath and stepped back. She glanced at Simon, shook her head, and mouthed the words, *Not Raina.*

"Sorry," she said, raising her voice.

"Wrong room."

She turned quickly, motioning to Simon.

"Let's get out of here," she whispered.

But it was too late. The door opened abruptly. An attractive woman in her late twenties or early thirties peered out. She was dressed in an expensive silk robe. Her hair was pinned up in curls. She studied Lyra with sleepy blue eyes.

"Who are you?" she demanded. Then she noticed Simon and frowned. "What's going on here?"

"I'm so sorry we awakened you," Lyra said. "We are looking for our friends. They invited us up to their room for a nightcap after the bar closed but we must have got the number wrong."

"House phone's on the table down the hall," the woman said, clearly irritated. "Call the front desk and get the right room number."

"Excellent idea," Lyra said, edging away. "We'll do that. Again, we do apologize."

The woman muttered something in response and closed the door. Simon heard the key turn very firmly in the lock.

Without a word, he and Lyra went several steps down the hall.

"Good story," he said softly when he was sure they were out of earshot of the woman in three twelve. "Better than mine."

"Thanks."

"Also, you managed to avoid giving her our names. Very professional."

"Do you think so?"

"As a rule, it's always better not to give out any more information than absolutely necessary. Less stuff to remember that way."

"I'll keep that in mind."

They went down to the second floor and began what turned out to be a very long hike through the quiet east wing of the hotel.

"If Raina is in two twenty-one she's going to be furious when she finds out we followed her," Lyra warned.

"Don't start having second thoughts now. We're here because you and Luther Pell are convinced Miss Kirk is in trouble, remember?"

Lyra straightened her shoulders. "Right. You agreed with us, as I recall."

"I did. Relax. If Miss Kirk is angry about our presence here at the hotel, we will tell her Luther Pell sent us to make sure she's all right. She won't blame us. I understand she's been seeing Pell exclusively for a while now. If that's true then she must know that very few people say no to Pell."

Lyra looked more cheerful. "True."

Room two twenty-one proved to be the very last one in the hallway. It was a short distance from the service stairs and the fire escape.

"The name of the guest who checked into this room is Miss Granville," Simon said.

"If this is Raina's room, she certainly took the least convenient suite in the hotel," Lyra said. "I'm sure she travels first-class. A room next to the service stairs is hardly her style."

"It was a good choice if she wanted privacy," Simon pointed out. He glanced back down the hallway. "The neighboring rooms are empty."

"How do you know that?"

"I checked the keys hanging behind the desk. The one to this room was gone but the keys for the neighboring rooms were still on the hooks."

"You're right," Lyra said. "She must have wanted privacy. Otherwise I'm sure she would have objected to being stuck at the end of the hall."

"Maybe the person she came here to meet is the one who doesn't want to be seen coming and going from Miss Kirk's room," Simon said. "They could both be using the service stairs to meet privately."

"You know, I'm learning a lot from you. I should probably start taking notes."

He told himself it was a good thing she considered him useful — it was a step up from his previous status as an object of her insatiable curiosity. Nevertheless, he was irritated.

"Instructors get paid," he said. "Remind me to bill you when we're finished."

"I'll do that."

They stopped in front of two twenty-one. Lyra rapped sharply.

There was no response.

She knocked again. Louder this time.

When no one came to the door she looked at Simon.

"Now what?" she asked.

He heightened his senses and raised his hand to knock.

The scars burned.

Slowly he lowered his hand and gingerly touched the doorknob. The jolt of hot energy made him grimace.

Lyra had gone still beside him. "What's wrong?"

"I don't know," he said, keeping his voice low. "But something violent happened in this room."

She did not question the observation or accuse him of imagining things. She took his words as a statement of fact.

"We've got to get inside," she whispered.

He tried the doorknob. It was locked. He reached into his pocket, took out the small lockpick, and went to work.

"You may want to look the other way," he said. "Because this is illegal as hell."

"Where can I buy one of those things?"

"Any hardware store or locksmith will sell you one. The trick is learning how to use it without getting arrested."

"How did you learn?"

"Practice, practice, practice."

The lock gave way. He pushed the door inward. The lamps were off inside the room but the drapes were open. A wide shaft of moonlight angled across the floor. The bed was empty, still made up.

Simon moved into the room, crossed to the window, and pulled the drapes tightly shut. He switched on a floor lamp. Lyra followed him and closed the door.

Together they surveyed the empty room.

"Housekeeping turns down the beds every night," Lyra said. "But no one has been in here to prepare the room this evening."

Simon walked slowly through the space, opening drawers and the closet door. All empty. He got down on one knee and looked under the bed.

"Nothing," he said. "No clothes. No suitcase. No makeup on the dressing table.

But something happened in here."

"The bed," Lyra said. "It's wrong."

He came to stand beside her. "Why do you say that?"

"It was not made up by a professional."

"Professional?"

"A trained, experienced housekeeper did not make up this bed," Lyra declared. "The bedspread is wrinkled and not draped evenly. The pillow shams are very sloppy." She pulled back the bedspread. "And just look at the way the sheets have been folded at the corners. Not the work of a professional. This bed was made in a hurry by someone who doesn't know how to do a proper job of it."

"You can tell all that just by looking at it?" Simon asked, impressed.

"I've stayed in a lot of expensive hotels, and I grew up in a family that has always employed a professional housekeeper. A well-made bed is a work of art. Take a look at your bed when we get back to our room. You'll see what I mean."

"I believe you." Simon leaned down and touched the bed. Once again the scars burned. He raised his hand and took a step back. "The last person in this bed was badly frightened."

"By an intruder?"

"Under the circumstances I think that's a reasonable assumption. Let's check the bathroom."

"We have to remember that there's no way to know if this is Raina's room," Lyra said. "It could belong to the woman whose name is in the hotel register, Miss Granville. Maybe she checked out early."

"The key is gone from the board behind the front desk, remember?"

"Oh." Lyra cleared her throat. "Right."

Simon glanced at her, not certain how to respond. The rising tide of her fear was a disturbing force in the atmosphere. She was scared and trying not to show it. He wanted to reassure her but he had nothing to offer except false hope. He knew her well enough now to know she would not want that.

He continued into the bathroom and paused to flip the light switch. The space gleamed with green and pink tiles. The porcelain fixtures matched the pink tile work.

"What happened to the towels?" Lyra said.

Simon glanced at her. "What do you mean?"

"There aren't any. The bed was made by someone who doesn't know how to make up an elegant bed. The towels are missing from the bathroom. You're right — things are very wrong in this room."

Simon looked at the drinking glass holder on the wall above the pedestal sink. It was empty. "Whoever tried to clean up in here was in a hurry."

He crouched and looked under the big sink. A shard of glass sparked in the shadows. He picked it up.

And sucked in a sharp, hissing breath when the flash of raw emotion arced through him. He shut down his senses and got to his feet.

Lyra studied the sliver of glass. "Do you think it's a piece of the missing water glass?"

"Yes. It was shattered. I think whoever was surprised by the intruder tried to use it as a weapon. If the person was successful, there may be blood."

"Not if someone cleaned up afterward, and that's what appears to have happened. Whoever it was used the towels."

"Probably." Simon looked around. "But in my experience, killers rarely manage to get rid of all of the blood, especially if they're working in a hurry."

Lyra froze. "Killers?"

He grimaced. "Sorry. I was speaking of some past investigations I've handled."

He found the small brownish splatters underneath the claw-footed bathtub.

"She drew some blood, all right," he said. "Raina?"

"Whoever was in this room was fighting for her life," Simon said evenly. "But I don't think anyone was murdered in here."

"Then what happened?"

"Given what little information we've got, I think there's a possibility that the guest who was booked into this room was kidnapped."

Lyra's eyes widened in shock. "That makes no sense, not if Raina was the person in this room. She has some money of her own, but there's no wealthy family to pay ransom. No family at all —" She broke off on a soft gasp. "Luther Pell. He's not family, but it's no secret he and Raina are a couple. Pell has a lot of money."

"A kidnapper would have to be a complete fool to send a ransom note to Pell. Talk about dining with the devil."

"You're right," Lyra said. "Mr. Pell is a very dangerous man. They say he has mob connections."

"He does."

"But it's possible whoever took her doesn't know that."

"It's also possible ransom is not the goal here," Simon said. He tossed the shard of glass into the trash basket. "This could be about something else besides money. Let's get out of here."

He turned off the lights and went through the doorway into the main room. Lyra followed.

He walked around the bed and cracked open the door. There was no one in the hallway.

"All clear," he said quietly.

He heard the dressing table drawer open. He quickly closed the door and turned around in time to see Lyra reach into the drawer and remove a piece of paper.

"What did you find?" he asked.

"It's a list of spa appointments for yesterday afternoon, the day that Miss Granville checked in to the resort. A massage, a facial, and the steam room."

"Assuming Raina was using the name Granville, why would she waste time in the spa? She came here to meet someone."

"She may have decided she had to book a few appointments in order to keep her cover story intact," Lyra said. "A woman who checked into an expensive resort that specializes in exotic beauty therapies and didn't take advantage of the facilities would cause people to ask questions."

"Maybe."

Lyra glanced at the schedule. "This is

interesting. Next to the words *Violet Herbal Facial* there's a note: *Request Miss Frampton.*"

"Does it look like Raina's handwriting?"

"No. It's in the same hand as the list of treatments. Whoever prepared this schedule wrote the note. It's obviously the name of a specific treatment lady."

Simon considered that for about half a second. "I wonder if Frampton was the person Raina came here to meet."

Lyra looked skeptical. "I doubt it. I think it's more likely she's a spa employee. We're jumping to a lot of conclusions here, aren't we? We still don't know if Raina was the guest in this room."

"There is another possibility," Simon said. "Maybe Raina's acquaintance was the single woman who was booked into this room."

"We need more information. I think I should book a spa day tomorrow and try to get some answers about Frampton."

Simon hesitated. "I'm not sure that's a good idea."

"Don't be ridiculous. It fits perfectly with our cover. I'll be fine. The spa is bound to be a busy place. There will be lots of people around. What could possibly go wrong?"

"Well —"

"We both know we've got to figure out

fast if someone named Frampton is involved in this thing. Gossip flows like a river in a spa or a salon. I'm in the best position to see if I can figure out who Frampton is."

"Because everyone talks to you?"

"Sooner or later. Usually sooner."

CHAPTER 18

"Welcome to Guppy's House of Beauty, Mrs. Cage. I'm Madam Guppy. I will be doing the initial evaluation of your beauty needs and recommending the treatments and therapies that will be most beneficial for you. Here at Guppy's House of Beauty we take a scientific approach to matters of skin care, diet, and exercise."

"I'm aware of your reputation, Madam Guppy," Lyra said. "You are a legend in the beauty business, as I'm sure you're well aware. When my husband asked where I wanted to go on our honeymoon I thought of the Labyrinth Springs Hotel and Spa immediately. He would have preferred Hawaii, but I was quite firm. Besides, I went to Hawaii last year on holiday."

"I see," Madam Guppy said. "May I ask what sort of work your husband does?"

Her full name was Edith Guppy. She was in her very late thirties or early forties, a sophisticated woman who had been blessed with a classic profile, an elegant figure, and a French accent. The owner of Guppy's House of Beauty must have been truly stunning in her younger days, Lyra thought, and she was certainly aging well. Guppy was a walking testimonial to the treatments, therapies, and products she sold.

She was dressed in a stylish, crisply tailored suit the exact shade of deep violet that was the signature of her famous brand. The snug-fitting jacket had wide, sharply defined lapels, and the narrow skirt fell to precisely the right place on her calf. Her stacked-heel shoes were the same color as her suit.

There was a great deal of violet everywhere in the salon and spa. The front desk staff and the treatment ladies wore violet-colored uniforms. The walls and the upholstery of the furniture were the same shade.

The dramatic color was everywhere in Guppy's office, as well, Lyra noted. That was where she was now. The front desk staff had explained that Madam Guppy personally interviewed and assessed the needs of every client who booked a treatment at the spa.

The receptionist had also confirmed that Frampton was the name of one of the treatment ladies who did facials. Lyra was pleased with herself. She had been in the spa for less than half an hour and she had already identified Frampton. The investigation was starting off well. She could hardly wait to tell Simon.

"My husband is in the antiquarian book business," Lyra said. She waved a hand in a vague gesture. "He advises collectors and archivists. I find it all quite boring, but he is passionately devoted to his work. One might say he is obsessed with it. It is very difficult to convince him to take any time off, but a man can hardly avoid his own honeymoon."

Edith cleared her throat. "I couldn't help but notice that you are very fashionably dressed, Mrs. Cage. And I understand you and your husband booked the honeymoon suite, one of the most expensive in the hotel. A full day here at the House of Beauty is a rather pricey luxury. I didn't realize there was a lot of money to be made in the book business."

Lyra raised her brows ever so slightly. "My husband is descended from an established New York family. They're in banking. Old money. My family has done quite well in shipping here on the West Coast. New money, but I find it spends just as easily. Not that it's any of your business."

Edith reddened beneath her masklike

veneer of makeup. The high color was not a sign of embarrassment, Lyra decided. Guppy was annoyed. Evidently she was not accustomed to being treated in such a high-handed manner.

Lyra smiled, a deliberately cool smile. She could play the frivolous, shallow, arrogant society lady role as well as anyone. She had been raised in the exclusive social world of San Francisco. People had no trouble buying the image she projected when she went into the act. She was not sure how she felt about that. On the one hand, it made a great cover here at the Labyrinth Springs resort. But knowing that others were so quick to conclude she actually was shallow, self-centered, and probably not very bright was irritating.

"Speaking of your overpriced spa," she said, "I booked the full-day package, which includes a facial."

"All of our packages include a facial," Edith said. "My spa is well-known for them. We offer several different versions. Each is scientifically designed for specific skin needs. Good skin is one of a woman's most important assets."

"I agree, and I am very particular about my facials," Lyra continued. "In fact, I would like to request a certain treatment lady for that service today."

Edith frowned. "Which one?"

"I believe her name is Miss Frampton. She was highly recommended to me by a friend in San Francisco who spent a few days here at the resort some months back. She assured me that Miss Frampton gave her the best facial she has ever had. Said her skin positively glowed afterward."

"Miss Frampton is highly qualified," Edith said. "But according to your chart, another equally skilled treatment lady, Miss Drake, has been assigned to you today."

"I would prefer Miss Frampton."

"I'm afraid she's fully booked."

"In that case," Lyra said, "I'll reschedule my spa day. Perhaps Miss Frampton will be free tomorrow."

She rose and collected her handbag.

Edith practically leaped up out of her chair and came around the end of the desk. "That's quite all right, Mrs. Cage. I'll see about rearranging Miss Frampton's schedule today. I'm sure it won't be a problem."

"Thank you."

"We do try to accommodate our clients," Edith said. Her vivid blue eyes sparked with barely concealed irritation. "Follow me, please."

Not waiting for a response, she opened

186

the door of the office and stepped out into a hallway carpeted in violet. The corridor was a long one. It was lined with treatment rooms on both sides.

Some of the doors were open. Lyra glanced into the rooms as she went past. She saw massage tables covered in violet sheets. In other rooms there were bizarre metal and electrical devices that she knew were designed to stimulate and tighten various portions of the female body. One door was marked PARAFFIN BATH. It was closed. The little sign out front announced that a treatment was in progress.

Midway down the hall a door opened and a treatment lady stepped out. Lyra caught a glimpse of a woman lying on a table. The client was tightly swaddled in wet sheets that appeared to have been soaked in an herbal bath of some sort. Her face was coated with a green paste and her eyes were covered with slices of cucumbers.

Lyra shuddered. Disturbing images from the nightmares she had experienced after she had seen Boris Karloff in *The Mummy* flashed through her head. She made a note to refuse any treatments that involved being wrapped in sheets.

Edith stopped in front of a violet door. "This is the evaluation chamber. My assistant will provide you with exercise clothes as well as a robe and slippers. When you are ready I will perform the examination and prescribe the specific therapies, products, and exercises that you require."

Lyra walked into another violet-hued room scented with Guppy's signature fragrance. A three-sided mirror stood in one corner. A large metal cone-shaped device sat on a table in the middle of the space. There was a chair positioned at each end of the table.

The windows were set high up close to the ceiling. Light filtered in, but the room felt claustrophobic. *Get a hold of yourself, woman. You're here to find Raina. You have a job to do. Stick to the plan.*

The plan, such as it was, had seemed like a good one when she came up with it last night in room two twenty-one. It had still appeared sound when she and Simon sat down to a breakfast of eggs, toast, and grapefruit that morning. But now, for the first time, an uncomfortable frisson of ghostly energy was sparking across her nerves.

A stern, middle-aged woman dressed in a spa uniform appeared from behind a curtain.

"You may undress in here, Mrs. Cage.

188

Please remove all of your outer garments. You will find your exercise shorts and top on the bench. There is also a robe hanging on the hook. The slippers are under the chair. Your spa experience ends in the steam chamber. After you are finished with that treatment you will find your clothes waiting for you in the adjacent dressing room."

A short time later, dressed in a fluffy violet-colored terry cloth robe and slippers, Lyra sat in front of the wide end of the metal cone. She inserted her face a short distance into the front of the cone.

A light came on inside the cone, partially blinding her.

Edith Guppy sat on the opposite side of the table and peered through the magnifying lens positioned at the narrow end of the device.

"My dear Mrs. Cage, you have been neglecting your complexion," Edith announced. "Proper hydration and stimulation of the skin are absolutely essential to maintaining a youthful appearance. Never fear, by the time you leave today, you will be a new woman."

"That will certainly be an interesting experience," Lyra said.

Edith sat back and got to her feet. "If you will step in front of the mirrors and remove your robe we will assess your measurements and weight. I believe you are rather too full-figured for the modern style."

"Do you think so?" Lyra got up, blinked several times to un-dazzle her eyes, and undid the sash of her robe. "Mr. Cage has not complained about my figure."

"Well, he is unlikely to do so, isn't he? A gentleman would hardly wish to be rude to his wife."

Lyra smiled. "Obviously you don't have a problem being rude."

Edith squared her already sharply squared shoulders. "As your beauty consultant, it is my duty to point out your flaws so that they may be corrected. A wife who hopes to keep the attention of her husband must strive to perfect and maintain a fashionable figure. You would not want Mr. Cage's eyes to wander, now, would you?"

"If I catch Mr. Cage's eyes wandering I will put a strong purgative in his soup."

Edith looked pained. "You have an odd sense of humor, Mrs. Cage. But never fear. I will see to it that you receive the appropriate physical exercises to tone your entire body. Your first treatment will be the herbal wrap."

"Is that the therapy the woman who was wrapped up like a mummy was receiving in one of the rooms we passed on the way here?"

Edith was in the process of using a measuring tape on Lyra's waist. She looked up, scandalized.

"You make the procedure sound unpleasant," she snapped. "Rest assured that by the time it is finished you will feel relaxed and refreshed and your muscle tone will be vastly improved."

"I'm going to skip the mummy wrap procedure."

"I insist. The herbal body wrap and the paraffin bath are the foundation of all the other procedures."

"What is involved in the paraffin bath?"

"The client reclines in a bathtub. Warm paraffin is poured over the body and smoothed onto the face. The paraffin hardens, forming a protective shell. After about twenty minutes the paraffin is peeled off. The skin is left smooth, supple, and hydrated. It is a very popular treatment, I assure you."

Lyra had a sudden vision of herself as a wax statue.

"I'm going to pass on the paraffin bath, too," she said. "I am somewhat claustrophobic. The thought of being encased in wax gives me the chills."

Edith Guppy's jaw clenched. Her eyes got steely. "Very well, Mrs. Cage. If you insist on declining the herbal wrap and the paraffin bath, I will remove both treatments from your schedule. But I must warn you that you will not get the full effects of your day here at the spa without those two essential procedures."

"I'm sure the facial will make up for it."

Edith snapped the measuring tape off Lyra's waist and stood back. "You may put on your robe now. An attendant will conduct you to the massage chamber."

It was going to be a very long day, Lyra thought.

CHAPTER 19

They used the service stairs to smuggle her out of the hotel.

Simon stood at the far end of the long, empty hallway and studied the door that opened onto the service stairs. It was the only explanation that made sense. The kidnappers could not have taken their captive down the main stairs and out through the lobby. They would have had to go past the front desk and any guests who happened to be in the vicinity.

The only other alternative was the fire escape ladder on the side of the building, but it was visible from the parking lot and the service buildings below. The risk of being seen would have been too great.

He wrapped his hand around the knob of the stairwell door, gritted his teeth, and heightened his senses. The shock of the emotions that had been laid down on the metal hit like a small flash of lightning.

Violence with a sharp twist of anxiety whispered through him. The kidnappers had been determined but nervous. As long as they were in the hallway they were in danger of being seen.

He opened the door. The shadowed stairwell was illuminated by a low-watt bulb on each landing. He was on the second floor, so he did not have far to descend. He started down the steps, trying not to make any noise.

Although he doubted Lyra would learn anything useful in the spa, he was very glad now that she was spending most of the day there. She would be safe, surrounded by other hotel guests and the staff. He was free to concentrate on his investigation. That was a very good thing at the moment, because if he got caught on the service stairs it would be relatively easy to explain his presence. Absentminded antiquarian book dealers were expected to get lost. Trying to come up with a good reason why the absentminded book dealer's wife had also gone down the back stairs of the hotel would be a lot more difficult.

His *wife*.

He realized he was adapting too easily to the role he was playing. He wondered how Lyra felt about having a fake husband. As far as he could tell, she found the experience an adventure.

When he reached the ground floor he heard muffled voices and caught the odor of roasting meat. He was near the hotel kitchen. The stairs continued down another level. At the bottom he opened the door.

He emerged into a large, poorly lit space that served as both pantry and storage room for the kitchen. Canned goods, large serving dishes, cutlery, and neatly folded table linens filled the shelves.

On the far side of the space was a door. He opened it — got another hot jolt of anxiety-tinged energy — and stepped outside. He found himself in a narrow lane that was obviously used for deliveries.

It could just as easily have been employed to remove a captive from the hotel.

He thought about that for a moment. The timing would have been critically important. The kidnappers must have been certain that a vehicle was waiting in the delivery lane. Certain that the likelihood of being seen was very slight.

Inside job. That was the only explanation that fit with the facts.

He made his way along the lane, just another hotel guest out for a walk; one who had taken a wrong turn and found himself in the back of the establishment.

He rounded a corner and saw a handful of small trucks and several aging, battered cars. The employees' parking lot. One vehicle stood out: a flashy new Buick Roadmaster convertible. It was an expensive car for a waitress or a bellhop. Maybe it belonged to someone in management.

He walked past the parked vehicles, his senses elevated, and touched the doors of each car.

He got a hot blast of energy from the driver's-side door handle of the new Buick. It felt different from what he had picked up in room two twenty-one and on the service stairs door.

Fear. Desperation. A terrible need to escape.

He yanked his fingers off the handle. He had been right. The kidnapping of the woman in room two twenty-one had been an inside job. There was no way to know for certain that Raina Kirk had been the target, but given his strict "no coincidences" rule, he had to assume she was the one who had been taken.

He thought briefly of calling Luther but decided to hold off until he had talked to Lyra. She might have an idea of how to handle him. Pell was in an unpredictable mood, a grenade just waiting for someone to pull the pin. If he rushed to the scene and tore the Labyrinth Springs resort to pieces, they might never find Kirk — at least not alive.

In the meantime, they now had another very strong lead.

The next step was to identify the owner of the Buick, because the sense of surging panic and desperation had come from the last person who had opened the driver's-side door.

CHAPTER 20

"You said one of your acquaintances recommended me, Mrs. Cage?" Janet Frampton leaned over the treatment table and began painting Lyra's face with a green paste. "I'm very happy to hear that. I'm glad she was satisfied with my services. I pride myself on delivering a superior facial."

Lyra looked up at her. Janet was young, attractive, and enthusiastic. Her hair was pinned up beneath a violet cap. Her smartly tailored uniform was enhanced with a handsome Bakelite necklace composed of graduated violet beads.

"Lovely necklace," Lyra said.

"Thank you. It was a gift from Madam Guppy. I was the top-performing treatment lady last month. I sold more products than any of the others."

"How long have you worked here at the House of Beauty?" Lyra asked.

"About a year. I was employed at a spa in

Los Angeles, but when the opportunity to work at Guppy's House of Beauty came up, I grabbed it, even though it meant moving away from L.A."

"I assume that's because the money is better here?"

"Most of the guests from the hotel do tip generously," Janet conceded. "But the main reason I accepted this position is because it offers the chance to learn the most advanced scientific beauty techniques. Madam Guppy trained in Europe, you know. Paris."

"Yes, I believe her experience in Europe was mentioned in the brochure."

"She creates all of her own formulas and she designs most of the exercise equipment. My goal is to open my own spa someday. That's why I want to learn from the best."

"That's an exciting plan," Lyra said. "Very wise of you to train with such a famous expert in the field. Where would you like to establish your spa?"

"I've been giving that a lot of thought," Janet said. She dabbed green paste on Lyra's nose. "It will have to be in a location that is easily accessible for ladies of means, of course. It will also have to be a fashionable destination. New York is out of the question. I could never afford to move there, and besides, one can hardly compete with the Red Door. Pasadena is a possibility, but it would be difficult for a small spa to stand out there."

"Perhaps a vacation setting? Burning Cove, for example?"

"A place like Burning Cove would be perfect, but I imagine it would take a great deal of money to establish a spa there. I would have to affiliate with a big resort or hotel, I think. It would be hard to convince one to finance a newcomer like me."

"What about the San Diego area? If you set up a location near the Hotel del Coronado you might be able to attract a few movie star clients. According to the press, stars love the Del. All you would need is one or two big names to use your services and you'd be golden."

"That would be a dream come true." Janet sighed. "But I really have to be practical. I'm going to need a financial backer. Someone like Mr. Billingsley."

"The owner of this resort?"

"Right. He invited Madam Guppy to move her business here. Paid for everything — the new spa wing, the fancy treatment rooms, all the exercise equipment that Madam Guppy designed."

"You should think about establishing an image, the way Madam Guppy has done. It sounds like you've already identified your market — socialites and women with money. Now you need to design an eye-catching logo and concoct a signature product like Violet perfume."

Janet paused the brush in midair. "Wow. You really know a lot about business, Mrs. Cage."

"I was raised in a business-minded family." Lyra reminded herself that she was not there to listen to a young woman dream big dreams. Time to change the course of the conversation. "I think you will be very successful when you do go out on your own. You obviously have a talent for the skin care business. You understand the importance of hydration."

"Proper hydration is absolutely critical."

"My San Francisco acquaintance was not the only person who recommended you," Lyra continued.

"Really?" Janet glowed. "A guest here at the resort, perhaps?"

"Yes, as a matter of fact. I didn't get her name. We met in the dining room last night. I complimented her on how good her complexion looked. She said she'd had it done by you."

"I had several clients yesterday. I wonder which one said such nice things about my services."

"I don't know her name, either, but she told me she had asked for you because another lady had mentioned you, a very fashionable woman who had lived in New York and was an excellent judge of quality when it came to spa services."

"New York," Janet said, her tone reverent. "I remember a client with a posh New York accent. She was very elegant. Tipped quite generously."

"I wonder if she is still here at the resort."

"Oh, no. I heard she checked out in the middle of the night."

Lyra shivered.

"Are you cold, Mrs. Cage?" Janet said.

"I'm fine," Lyra said quickly. "Just felt a bit of a draft, that's all. Pity your New York client was unable to book a second facial. You missed out on another generous tip."

"Yes."

This time Janet's response was crisp and final. It was clear she did not wish to continue the conversation.

"I wonder why she cut short her vacation," Lyra mused.

"A family emergency, I believe." Janet put the brush aside. "Now, then, we will let that set for fifteen minutes. The herbal therapy is designed to condition the skin for the next step in the facial."

"There's another step?"

Janet brightened again. "Oh, yes, the most important part of the procedure. You will slip on one of Madam Guppy's specially designed face masks. It will smooth out all those little lines and wrinkles."

Lyra felt the icy touch of spectral fingers. "What does this mask look like?"

"I have one right here."

Janet opened a drawer and took out a violet rubber mask that had been fashioned to fit over the head and face. There were holes cut into it for the eyes, nose, and mouth. It looked like something out of a horror movie.

"I'm going to skip the mask," Lyra said.

"There's nothing to worry about," Janet assured her. "It fits quite tightly and is somewhat uncomfortable, but one wears it for only thirty minutes. The results are worth it, believe me."

"No rubber mask," Lyra said.

The only thing she could imagine that would be worse was being locked in a coffin.

"Very well." Janet exhaled a long sigh. "The masseuse warned me that you had strong opinions about certain procedures."

"That would be the masseuse who tried

to beat me to a pulp," Lyra said. "What's next on my schedule?"

Janet frowned and picked up a sheet of paper. "I see you're booked for the Guppy Body Sculptor."

"How does that work?"

"You will be positioned between two sets of electrically driven metal rollers that will glide up and down your body from your calves to your waist. The rollers stimulate and tone the thighs and hips."

"It sounds like a mangle, one of those machines people use to iron sheets and tablecloths. I could get crushed between the rollers."

Janet chuckled. "Nonsense. Madam Guppy designed the Body Sculptor to ensure that it conforms to the shape of the female body."

"I'll warn you right now that if I get flattened, Mr. Cage will be very annoyed."

An hour later, feeling like a freshly ironed bedsheet, Lyra was ushered into the exercise room. Strange, fearsome machines gleamed malevolently in the glare of the overhead fixtures.

"It looks like a medieval torture chamber," she said.

Miss Sylvan, the treatment lady in charge

of the exercise room, glared.

"Each of the Guppy Toning Machines is designed with one purpose in mind," she declared. "To make you a new woman."

Lyra spotted a large gyroscope that was big enough to accommodate a person. She could see how it worked. The user climbed inside, secured her wrists and ankles, and then set the gyroscope into motion. For the first time that day her spirits rose.

"I'll start with that machine," she said. "It looks like a carnival ride. I think it would be fun."

"I'm afraid the Guppy Exercise Gyroscope is out of order," Miss Sylvan said.

Lyra groaned. "Of course it is. This is my lucky day."

"We will start with the Guppy Electric Thigh Shaper."

CHAPTER 21

At four o'clock, wrapped in a large towel, her hair in a terry cloth turban, Lyra was ushered into the steam chamber by a uniformed attendant.

"You will find it a very relaxing experience," the woman said. "There's a pitcher of Madam Guppy's special iced herbal tea on the table. It will keep you properly hydrated. I will come and fetch you in fifteen minutes."

Lyra moved into the tiled room. The humid atmosphere hit her with the force of an ocean wave.

She peered through the billowing steam. "Am I the only one in here?"

"Yes," the attendant said. "There are no other clients scheduled for this time today."

She closed the door.

Lyra paused to give herself a moment to adjust to the temperature and the thick air and then staggered to the nearest bench and collapsed.

Relief swept over her. For the first time since she had entered the spa, no one was pummeling her muscles, painting her with strange herbal concoctions, or standing over her while she performed dreadful exercises on weird machines that had clearly been designed by a sadist. Her thighs were still quivering from the electric vibrating belts on the thigh-toning machine, and her pectoral muscles would never be the same, thanks to the Guppy Bust Improver.

She needed a drink — a real drink, not the dreadful iced herbal tea in the pitcher on the table. She had been served a glass of the stuff a short time ago when she had been in the so-called refreshment room. She had taken a few sips and then, when the attendant wasn't looking, she had poured the rest into the nearest potted plant.

What she craved now was something stronger than the tea. An ice-cold cocktail would be perfect. For a few seconds she fantasized about a pink lady, or maybe a sidecar or a martini.

Not much longer. She just had to get through the steam room treatment, and then she would be able to escape the spa.

She settled back and thought about what she had learned. The treatment women had all been eager to chat with a client who found them and their work interesting. Most of the conversations had concerned the methods and techniques they employed. Their job also involved selling Guppy House of Beauty products, so Lyra had received a lot of earnest sales pitches.

Nevertheless, sprinkled into the chatter had been some gossip about other guests. The most fascinating bit of information was that the woman in room two twenty-one was not the first guest who had checked out in the middle of the night in the past year.

She could not wait to inform Simon that her day at the spa had not been a waste of time. She had done some genuine investigative work today. Okay, maybe she didn't have the icy nerves it took to make a career out of the business, but she would damn well do whatever had to be done to help find Raina.

She lounged against the back of the bench, letting the moist heat do its work. She just hoped she wasn't going to be sore for a week.

The steam grew heavier, forming a fog-like mist. She could barely see across the room to the opposite wall. The temperature in the chamber was rising rapidly. Her whole body was damp, and a strange kind of lethargy was sinking into her bones. This wasn't her first experience in a steam room. Something was wrong. It was time to leave, but for some reason she could not muster the energy to get up off the bench and go back into the dressing room.

The humid atmosphere was supposed to relax her, but it was proving to be too much after the long day of exercise, massage, and skin treatments. The memory of a conversation she'd had with a therapist who worked at an elite spa in San Francisco flickered somewhere at the edge of her thoughts. *You want to be careful with heat. Dehydration can set in very quickly, and it can be lethal.*

A shadowy form materialized in the mist. It sent a fortifying jolt of panic through her. Lyra managed to push herself to her feet.

"Who's there?" she called out, trying to sound firm and in control.

There was no answer. Lyra listened closely but she did not hear any footsteps. She collapsed back onto the bench. The steam chamber *felt* empty, she concluded. But more shadowy figures were appearing and disappearing in the fog. Ghosts?

She didn't believe in ghosts.

The steam took on strange colors. The walls began to warp and bend.

Fear shivered through her. *Dehydration can*

set in very quickly, and it can be lethal.

She had to get out. Now.

It took three tries to get up off the bench again and a surprising amount of effort to trudge back to the door. Every step drained her strength. The tiled walls spun faster. A heavy darkness tugged at her senses.

She could not afford to faint. She had heard stories of people dying in steam rooms.

She finally reached the door. She gripped the knob and twisted.

Nothing happened. The doorknob did not turn. She really was getting weak.

She tried again, using both hands this time. The door did not budge. It dawned on her that it was locked.

Fear spiked again, giving her a rush of panicky energy. She used a corner of the towel to wipe the steam off the window set into the upper portion of the door and peered into the dressing room. There was no one in sight. The attendant who had shown her into the steam chamber was gone. There were no other clients; no one to unlock the door.

Someone had made a terrible mistake. The attendant had closed the steam chamber for the day without bothering to make sure the last client was out.

Lyra raised a hand and pounded on the door.

"Help. I'm in here. Open the door."

There was no response.

She turned slowly, trying to focus on her surroundings. There was no other door. The only way out of the chamber was through the dressing room.

She yanked off the terry cloth turban and pulled it on over one hand. She summoned everything she had and smashed her covered fist into the glass pane in the door.

The glass cracked. Several shards fell out. Cool air wafted through the opening. She took a couple of deep breaths and struck another blow. She was still feeling light-headed, but the panic eased. She had a way out.

She used her turban-covered fist to knock the remaining bits of jagged glass out of the frame. When it was empty she leaned through the opening and groped for the doorknob. The key was not in the lock.

There was no help for it; she was going to have to wriggle through the door's now-empty window frame. It was large enough, but it was at least four feet from the floor. She needed to elevate herself so that she would have the leverage required to scramble through the frame.

She took another deep breath of the unsaturated air on the other side of the door and staggered back across the steam chamber. She grabbed the arm of one of the wooden benches and hauled it across the floor. The damn thing was heavier than she had expected. It didn't help that she was still feeling the weight of the strange exhaustion that had settled into her bones.

When the bench was finally in position she unwrapped the large towel she was wearing and flung it over the bottom of the door frame.

Stark naked now, she stepped up onto the bench and half dove, half fell into the dressing room.

She landed awkwardly and lay quietly for a moment, waiting for her pulse to slow down. It didn't.

Dehydration can be lethal.

She had to move. She had to get some water. There were several stall showers at the far end of the room.

Slowly she staggered past the rows of lockers to the front door. It was locked, too. There was no window in it. *Well, of course there isn't,* she thought. It was the door to a dressing room, after all.

Great. Another problem. But at least she could breathe now. Most of the heavy air in the steam room was still trapped in the chamber. She would figure out how to get out of the dressing room right after she got some water.

She crossed to the sink, grabbed a paper cup from the dispenser, and started drinking water.

When she'd had her fill, she pulled aside the curtain of the nearest shower, turned on the faucet marked cold, and stepped under the spray. She was so tired she had to plant one hand against the tiled wall to keep herself from crumpling. She tried to focus on how to escape from the dressing room. The steam from the main chamber was starting to pour through the shattered window in the door. It wouldn't be long before it filled the dressing room.

Maybe she could keep some of the mist out if she could figure out how to hang towels over the opening. She had to buy some time while she came up with a way to escape the dressing room.

Footsteps pounded out in the hall.

"Lyra. Lyra, are you in here? Answer me, damn it."

Simon.

The tide of relief threatened to overwhelm her.

He pounded on the door. "Lyra? I'm coming in."

She wanted to throw herself into his arms. And then she remembered that she was naked and standing in a shower. She was starting to feel better, but she did not have the energy required to dry off and get into a robe.

"Simon." She tried to shout but her voice sounded weak. *"Simon."*

She heard the door of the dressing room slam open. Instinctively she closed the shower curtain.

"In here," she said.

A strong, masculine hand gripped the edge of the shower curtain and whipped it aside. Simon examined her from head to toe in one swift, assessing glance.

"Lyra." His voice was raw. "What the hell happened?"

There was a lot of heat in his eyes, but she didn't think it was lust or even mild sexual interest. For some reason she found that depressing. It was a silly reaction on her part. Probably caused by the effects of the shock and dehydration. Still, she was standing nude in front of him. In a shower, no less. That ought to have had some effect on his passions.

Maybe he didn't have any passions.

No, she knew better. The man had passions, but he was very, very good at concealing them beneath his antiquarian book dealer façade.

"Accident," she managed. "Got locked in the steam chamber. The heat. It was turned up too high. Had to break the window to get out. Front door was locked, too." She frowned. "How did you get in?"

Without a word he held up the lockpick he had gripped in one hand.

"Oh," she said. "I really need one of those." She remembered she was still nude. Belatedly, embarrassment struck. "Would you mind handing me a towel?"

Her request shattered the strange mood that had come over him. He turned away to grab one of the oversized towels. The shower curtain fell back into place. She turned off the water.

"Here," Simon said.

He reached around the edge of the curtain to hand her the towel. She sighed. He was probably more embarrassed than she was.

She wrapped the towel around herself and pulled the curtain aside. Simon took a couple of steps back.

"Are you all right?" he asked.

"Yes." She ran her fingers through her wet hair, pushing it back behind her ears. "I think I got dehydrated from the heat and the steam. But the shower and a few glasses of water helped. I'm feeling better now. Thank goodness you came along when you did. I don't know how to pick locks. I doubt if I could have escaped from this room. How did you know to come looking for me?"

"I . . . had a feeling something was wrong. Let's get you out of here."

"My clothes. They're in locker number ten." She went down the aisle formed by the lockers and opened number ten. Her things were neatly stored inside. She collected them and moved to one of the curtained dressing rooms. "I'll just be a few minutes."

She whisked the curtain closed, unwrapped the towel, and dressed with fingers that shook. When she was ready, she pulled the curtain aside and saw Simon. He was at the door of the steam chamber, studying the broken glass. As she watched, he gripped the doorknob. She was standing several feet away from him but she could have sworn she sensed a flash of ominous energy.

He released the doorknob and turned to face her. His eyes were fierce.

Her mouth went dry — not from dehydration.

"You're going to tell me it wasn't an accident that I got locked in the steam chamber, aren't you?" she said.

"Did you really believe it was an accident?"

"Let's just say I was trying to remain optimistic."

"That attitude is not particularly helpful in our business."

CHAPTER 22

"Believe me, I am as distressed about this unfortunate incident as you are, Mr. Cage," Ridley Billingsley said.

Simon fought back the rage that threatened to override common sense.

"That's not even remotely possible," he said. "My wife could have died in that damn steam room."

They were gathered in the office of the owner of the resort. Billingsley was East Coast, from his patrician airs and his elite private school accent to his bespoke suit and striped tie. There was no doubt he was genuinely alarmed by the incident in the steam room, but Simon was sure that Ridley's real source of distress was the possibility of bad press for his hotel.

Simon could have told him that the last thing he and Lyra planned to do was go to the local paper — the unfortunate accident story worked well for them — but he wanted

Billingsley to sweat. The owner of the resort made a good target, and right now Simon needed a target for his fury.

At the moment he was playing the outraged husband, which, he reflected, was not a hard role to get into. Not at all. He was seething. Whoever had tried to murder Lyra was most likely connected to the spa, but Billingsley was ultimately the man in charge of the resort, including Guppy's operation. Simon knew it would look odd if he didn't start at the top. He would deal with Guppy later.

For her part, Lyra was playing the badly shaken lady who was on the verge of collapsing. She sat in a chair, looking stricken, and sipped a glass of water.

"It was an accident, I assure you." Billingsley gave Lyra a beseeching look. "On behalf of Madam Guppy and the entire staff of Guppy's House of Beauty, I offer you our most sincere apologies, Mrs. Cage."

Lyra dabbed at her eyes with a hankie. "I just don't understand how it could have happened. Where was everyone?"

"The spa was forced to close unexpectedly early due to electrical issues," Billingsley explained. "In the confusion the attendant in charge of the steam chamber forgot there was one client in that room.

Maintenance is working in the spa now, trying to locate and repair the faulty wiring, but I'm told that the problem is most likely what caused the chamber to overheat."

"I see," Lyra said. She put down the glass and appeared to collect her shattered nerves. "I had planned to book another Day of Beauty, but I've changed my mind."

"I understand," Billingsley said. "You will, of course, receive a refund on the appointments you booked today."

"I should think so." Lyra rose to her feet. "Let's go, Simon. I need a drink."

Simon hesitated. He wasn't through with Billingsley, but Lyra's instincts were right. He got to his feet.

"Yes, dear," he said.

CHAPTER 23

"I really do need a drink," Lyra said. "A *real* drink. In the steam chamber I fantasized about an ice-cold martini or a sidecar. For some reason a pink lady didn't sound like the right cocktail for the moment. There was some herbal tea provided, but the stuff was dreadful. I didn't bother with it because I'd tasted it earlier and had to pour most of it into a plant."

Simon stopped pacing the suite and turned to face her. "How about another glass of water?"

Lyra made a face. "I've had so much water in the past hour I'm in danger of floating out the door and down the hall. I'm fine, Simon. Really. Why don't you fix both of us a cocktail? And then I'll tell you what I found out today while I was being mangled and maimed and nearly murdered at Guppy's House of Beauty."

He eyed her. "Are you telling me you

found out something in addition to the fact that someone tried to kill you?"

"Yes. And don't look at me like that. I'm not keeping anything from you. We haven't had a chance to talk until now. I'm finally feeling somewhat normal."

She did appear fully recovered, he decided. She was dressed in a floral-patterned dressing gown and curled up in a large reading chair, one leg tucked under the other. Her still-damp hair was parted in the center. She had left it loose around her shoulders to dry.

She had not bothered to apply any fresh makeup after they had returned to the room. All of the outward elements of glamour had been scrubbed or showered away, and yet she was more compelling, more intriguing than ever.

He had almost lost her today.

That thought was going to keep him awake tonight.

"All right," he said. He crossed to the liquor cart and took the lid off the silver-plated ice bucket that room service had filled a short time ago. "After you tell me what you discovered, I'll tell you what I found in the employee parking lot. But first I'll fix both of us a drink. I think I need one, too."

He tried to focus his thoughts while he mixed the cocktails. He was finally getting himself under control, but the what-ifs kept screaming silently in his head.

What if Lyra hadn't realized what was happening in time to save herself? What if she hadn't been thinking clearly enough to realize she had to smash the glass window in the door? What if she hadn't had enough strength to haul the bench over to the door so that she could use it as a platform? *What if he had lost her?*

At that last thought he had to suppress another storm of emotion. He usually declined jobs that involved working with a partner, and this was the reason why. The sense of responsibility was distracting. This case was getting dangerous. He did not want to have to worry about protecting someone else, especially a complete amateur, now that it was clear they were hunting a killer.

"Don't even think about it," Lyra said. "You can't ditch me or send me back to Burning Cove. Besides, I would like to remind you that posing as a couple was your idea."

Simon stifled a groan and finished pouring the martinis into the glasses. He carried the cocktails across the room and handed one to Lyra.

"How did you know?" he asked.

"What you were thinking?" Lyra took a sip of her drink and lowered the glass. "You're getting easier to read."

"Easier?"

"I can get a fix on most people within a few minutes, but with you it's much more difficult. This martini is excellent, by the way. Exactly what the doctor ordered."

"Do you ever make mistakes when you try to read people?"

"Sure. The biggest mistake I ever made was thinking that my fiancé was the right man for me."

"You've had an interesting life, Lyra."

"It's a lot more interesting now. Ready to hear what I learned in the spa?"

Simon swallowed some of his martini and sat down. He leaned forward, resting his elbows on his thighs, and cradled the glass in both hands.

"Yes, but first, we need to be realistic," he said. "Someone tried to murder you today. That means our cover is no longer working. Whoever made Raina disappear —"

"It was Raina who vanished from room two twenty-one, by the way. I confirmed it today."

He stilled. "Are you certain?"

"Yep."

He sighed. "That explains why someone tried to murder you."

"I don't think so. I was very subtle."

He winced. "Right. Subtle. Do you realize what this means?"

"Sure," Lyra said. "It means we need a new strategy."

"What it *means* is that I should put you on the train to Burning Cove. You'll be safe there. Luther Pell will make certain of it. I'll continue the investigation on my own."

Lyra took another sip of the martini and lowered the glass. Her eyes glittered with determination.

"No," she said. "I can't walk away now. You need me."

"Do I?"

"I'm a good investigator, Simon. I'll prove it. One of the things I learned today is that Raina is not the only woman who has disappeared from this hotel in the past year or so."

He went very still. "Are you positive of that?"

"Yes." Lyra set her glass aside. "I talked to several of the treatment ladies in the spa. In addition to Raina, at least three other women who were booked into that room checked out in the middle of the night."

"Lyra, people check out of hotels early all the time. Why would the staff of the spa pay any attention?"

Lyra gave him a triumphant smile. "Because the women all had appointments at the spa that were canceled. Trust me, the treatment ladies remember who cancels at the last minute, just as they remember who tips and how well. But the main reason they recalled the room number is because two twenty-one has a reputation for being haunted."

Simon got the edgy sensation he always got when another piece of a pattern fell into place. "You're sure?"

"Yes."

"How did you discover that?"

"The thing about spas and salons is that gossip is part of the experience. The missing women all had a few things in common. In addition to the fact that they were all wealthy, they all checked in alone. No husbands or companions or personal maids. They were all booked into the haunted room. Every hotel has one, you know."

"A haunted room?"

"Right," Lyra said. "It's practically a requirement for an older hotel."

"What's the story behind the haunting of

two twenty-one? I assume you got that, too?"

"The rumor began to circulate several months ago because a woman was found dead in that room."

"A hotel guest?"

"No. The dead woman was a treatment lady who worked in the spa." Lyra paused. "She supposedly died from an overdose of heroin. Now you can understand why the treatment ladies made a special note of that particular room."

Simon gave himself a few seconds to process the information. "You are nothing short of amazing, Lyra. People really do talk to you."

"You see? I told you that you need me."

"All that spa conversation nearly got you killed."

"Maybe," Lyra said. "We should keep in mind that the incident in the steam room could have been an accident."

"No. It wasn't an accident."

"All right, I admit that under the circumstances it seems unlikely. But if you're right, it only goes to show we're getting closer to finding Raina."

"What it goes to show is that you don't know what you're doing. You're an amateur." Simon got to his feet and began to pace the room. "The fact that someone tried to murder you means you blew your cover, and mine, too. Whoever is behind this is onto us now. They'll try to hide all of the evidence."

Lyra's eyes glittered in an ominous fashion. "Stop lecturing me. I contributed vital information to the investigation. Admit it."

He came to a halt in front of her. "You kicked over a hornet's nest, that's what you did."

She jumped to her feet. "At least we've got a lead. Do you know what I had to go through to get that information?"

"You think I'm ever going to forget that you almost got steamed to death?"

"Forget the steam bath experience. I'm talking about a painful massage, weird stuff painted on my face, hot and cold baths in water that stank of sulfur and who knows what other minerals. Not to mention the dreadful instruments of torture in the exercise room. I didn't even get to try out the one machine that looked like it might be an interesting experience."

He stared at her, riveted. "What?"

"The big gyroscope. You get inside and roll around like a ball. It was out of order."

"You thought that would be an interesting experience?"

"What can I tell you? It looked like a carnival ride. Everything else looked painful and scary. Never mind, my point is that I did my job today and now we have information we can take to the police."

"You really think that will help Raina? In case you haven't noticed, we're in a hurry here. Bringing in the police will not only cost us time, it will cost us whatever edge we still have."

Lyra folded her arms very tightly and glared. "I picked up some clues and another lead. What did you accomplish today?"

"I found the damn car."

Her hands dropped to her sides. Her eyes widened. "Raina's car?"

"No. The one they used to take her away."

"It's here? At the hotel?"

"It's in the employees' parking lot. A nice new Buick convertible. It belongs to a bartender named Kevin Draper. He told his pals here at the hotel that he came into a small inheritance from an uncle."

Excitement lit Lyra's eyes. "How do you know it's the right car?"

He paused a beat and then shrugged. She didn't seem to have a problem with his psychic side.

"The heat on the driver's-side door handle," he said. "Whoever drove that car last

229

was scared. Frantic. Close to panic. He was probably afraid of being caught."

"Psychic heat."

He nodded. "It sounds crazy when you say it out loud, doesn't it?"

"No, it sounds like a reasonable explanation for what you sensed."

"Whatever is going on here is an inside job, Lyra."

She nodded. "I agree. If a gang is kidnapping women from this hotel on a regular basis, they would need a vehicle that wouldn't arouse suspicion or curiosity. A car that is seen regularly in the parking lot. That means they have to have at least one person inside."

"At least two or three, I think. In addition to the actual kidnapping, someone has to change the hotel records and explain the late-night checkouts."

Lyra began to walk in a circle around the table in the middle of the sitting room. "How do they identify their victims? And why did they take Raina? As you said, it would be extremely risky to try to force Luther Pell to come up with ransom money. I have no doubt that he'd pay whatever it cost to get Raina back, but after she was safe he would spend the rest of his life hunting the kidnappers."

"And given his connections both in the criminal world and the government, sooner or later he would find the people who took Miss Kirk. When he did, he would be . . . ruthless. You'd think the kidnappers would know that, but bad guys make mistakes in judgment all the time. Look, I don't have all the answers. That's why it would have been in our best interest to keep from drawing attention to ourselves. Now that you've effectively destroyed our cover, we're going to have to change course."

"If you would stop yelling at me we could get to work on a new strategy."

"I am not yelling."

"Technically, no, but you are definitely reading me the riot act," Lyra said. "Okay. You've made your point. I don't need to hear any more lectures. I would like to remind you again that I went through a rather stressful experience today. I know I didn't handle things the way you think I should have, but I got solid information, damn it."

He couldn't tell if she was angry or crushed. He wasn't sure what to do next.

"Are you going to cry?" he asked.

She glared. "No, I am not going to cry. That would be extremely unprofessional."

"Yes, it would."

A sharp rap on the door made them both flinch in surprise.

"Bellhop. I have a delivery for Mrs. Cage."

Simon looked at Lyra. She shook her head.

"I didn't order anything," she whispered.

"Just a minute," Simon called.

He crossed the room, opened his briefcase, and slipped the gun out of the holster. He motioned to Lyra to step out of the line of sight and then went to the door. Leaving the chain on the lock, the gun concealed against his thigh, he opened the door.

A young man dressed in the livery of the hotel stood in the hall. He had a stack of violet-colored boxes wrapped in elegantly tied violet ribbons.

"Mrs. Cage's spa purchases," the bellhop said.

"Oh, I forgot about those," Lyra said.

Simon stared at the stack of violet boxes. "You bought all that stuff today?"

"No more lectures, please," Lyra said. "Let the man in."

Simon grunted, unhooked the chain on the door, and stepped back, careful to keep the gun out of sight.

The bellhop hustled through the door. "Where would you like these, Mrs. Cage?"

"Set them on the table, please," Lyra said.

She found her purse, unsnapped it, and took out some money. "Here you go. Thank you so much."

The bellhop looked thrilled with the tip. "Anytime, ma'am."

He went out the door and sauntered down the hall, whistling.

Simon closed and locked the door. He put the chain back on and turned to watch Lyra untie a ribbon on one of the boxes.

"I can't believe you were shopping while you were in the middle of conducting an investigation," he said.

"When you spend a day at a spa you're expected to make a few purchases. The treatment ladies work on commissions as well as tips. It would be rude not to buy some of the products."

She lifted the lid off one of the boxes and took out a violet jar.

"What is it?" Simon said.

"Guppy's House of Beauty night cream. It's guaranteed to restore the radiant glow of youth."

"You're not old," he blurted, unthinking. "Your radiance is just fine."

She wrinkled her nose. Her eyes sparkled with amusement. "Thank you. But it was made clear to me today that a wife must devote herself to a rigorous program of regular skin care and exercise in order to hold her husband's attention. After all, to quote Madam Guppy, we would not want Mr. Cage's eyes to wander."

"Mr. Cage has not been able to take his eyes off you since the moment he first saw you."

There was a fraught silence. It reminded Simon of the tense pause that occurred between a lightning strike and the sound of thunder. You knew there was power and energy and danger in the atmosphere. You just didn't know exactly when and where the explosion would take place.

Lyra watched him with a steady, unflinching gaze. He got the feeling that she was once again trying to get a fix on him; trying to read his mind.

"Is Mr. Cage unable to take his gaze off me because he's afraid that when I am out of his sight I will jeopardize his investigation?" she asked, her tone suspiciously polite.

"That, too," he admitted. He walked slowly toward her and stopped a foot away. "But mostly he can't take his eyes off you because you are . . . unpredictable. Complicated."

She nodded very somberly. "Unpredictable is good. So is complicated."

"A mystery," he said.

"Oh, yes, I like being a mystery. I like it very much."

She set the jar of night cream aside and turned away from the stack of violet boxes to face him. She lounged back against the table and, stretching her arms out to either side, gripped the edge with both hands.

"I could say the same about you," she said. "You're complicated. Mysterious. You are, however, becoming a little more predictable."

"Help me out here — are we still quarreling, or have we started flirting?"

"You're not sure?"

"Unlike you, I have a hard time with the nuances of social interactions of this nature."

She gave him a slow, sultry smile. "Give it some thought. With your keen investigative skills I'll bet you can figure out what's going on here."

"You," he said, "are also dangerous."

"That is the most romantic thing anyone has ever said to me."

"For some reason I doubt that."

"It's the truth. People who meet me always think they know exactly who and what I am — the frivolous, spoiled daughter of a wealthy shipping tycoon. A woman whose only job in life is to marry well, provide a couple of heirs to the family fortune, and host charity galas. But I don't plan to do any of those things. Would you like to kiss me?"

"Yes," he said. "But under the circumstances that probably would not be smart."

"Maybe not, but it would be unpredictable and complicated and mysterious."

"And dangerous."

"Definitely," she said. "At the very least we might be able to resolve the biggest question that currently confronts us."

"What question is that?"

"A kiss might help us decide if we want to have a full-blown affair when this case is over."

Everything inside him was tight and hard. The atmosphere was charged and intense. He was standing on the edge of a cliff looking down at the crashing waves of a storm-tossed sea. There was no way to know what dangerous currents were waiting for him beneath the surface. He realized he didn't give a damn. He was going to dive in and take the risk.

He clamped his hands over hers, trapping her against the table. He leaned in very close.

"I already know my answer," he said. "But

if you're not sure —"

"Not yet."

He covered her mouth with his own, intending a slow, exploratory kiss; a kiss that would allow him to maintain control. He had to move cautiously, because it was clear now that she was not the woman he had hoped to find in Burning Cove. Yes, she was fast, single, and reckless, but she was so much more — wildly unpredictable and dangerous. A thrilling mystery. And she didn't give a damn about his past or his weird talent.

He managed to keep a tight rein on the kiss right up until she yanked her hands out from under his, gripped his shoulders, and gave a soft, urgent cry against his mouth.

"Simon."

And just like that the kiss spun out of control. His senses — all of them — were caught up in the whirlwind. He gripped her waist, lifted her off her feet, and crushed her against his chest. He wanted to feel every inch of her.

"Touching you is like touching lightning," he said against her mouth.

"I'm not sure that's a compliment," she gasped. "But I know what you mean. I'm getting the same sensation. I've had a lot of experience with this sort of thing, but I have never felt anything quite like this. It's very exciting."

"That's one word for it."

He deepened the kiss, silencing her. She moved her fingers up to the back of his neck. She was pressed so tightly against him now he knew she had to be aware of his fierce erection. He moved his lips to her throat and inhaled the intoxicating scent.

"Simon," she whispered.

He groaned and reluctantly raised his head. "I know. We've got more important things to do tonight."

She took a deep breath. "Right." She pulled herself together and stepped back. Her eyes brightened with anticipation. "You have a new plan?"

"No, it's the same old plan I came up with this afternoon." He ran his fingers through his hair and turned away, giving himself a moment to regain control. "The owner of the Buick gets off duty in the bar at two in the morning. We're going to have a chat with him."

"Excellent plan."

"Gosh, thanks. I have been doing this kind of thing for a while now."

"No need for sarcasm," Lyra said. "I really am impressed. So we're going to confront Kevin Draper and get some answers."

"We're not going to talk to him here at the hotel. We need privacy for this conversation. We're going to follow him after his shift ends tonight. With luck he'll go to a bar for a late-night drink or drive straight home. Either location will work."

"What if he goes to a girlfriend's house?"

"I'm told he doesn't have a girlfriend." Simon paused. "Which strikes me as odd."

"Boyfriend?"

Simon shook his head. "The housekeeper I talked to said Draper isn't seeing anyone. She told me he was delighted to show off his new Buick when he first got it. Everyone wanted a ride in it. But after a few days he stopped inviting people to take a drive with him. She described him as being in a low mood lately. Withdrawn and depressed."

Lyra smiled. "Your informant was a maid? Well, well, well. Sounds like people talk to you, too."

"Sure, but only if I pay for the information or scare the living daylights out of them."

"I'm assuming that in this case you paid for the details about Draper's private life?"

"She's got a sick husband who can't work. They need the money."

"Sounds like the money went to a good cause," Lyra said. "Which approach do you intend to take with Draper?"

"Judging by the car he's driving, cash probably won't get his attention, at least not the amount I have in my wallet. I'll probably go with fear. It's cheaper."

Lyra gave him a disapproving look. "Do you think that's wise?"

"I have no idea. But it usually works."

CHAPTER 24

Ridley Billingsley let himself into his private quarters on the third floor of the hotel and headed straight for the liquor cabinet. He grabbed a bottle of whiskey and poured himself a stiff drink. He needed something to settle his nerves.

It was all coming apart. His beautiful game was in danger and it was his own fault. He should never have agreed to arrange the kidnapping of Raina Kirk. He had known from the outset that it was a risky thing to do. Yes, the client had offered a small fortune for the job, but he didn't need the money. He had inherited all he would ever need. His game had never been about making money. It was about a much more gratifying reward — the thrill of power and the satisfaction of listening to the women plead with him. Nothing excited him more than savoring the helpless terror in their eyes when they realized they were his to do with as he pleased.

But Guppy had insisted on taking the Kirk commission. She said the client knew everything about their operation and had threatened to go to the press if they didn't grab Raina Kirk. Guppy said that when they delivered Kirk to the client it would all be over. Finished. They would be out of it.

He knew better. After all, he was in the extortion business himself. Once you had leverage over someone, you never gave it up. Leverage was raw power, and he now held that power over some very important people, including a couple of tycoons and a potential congressman who might become president.

Knowing that someone was not only aware of the game he and Guppy had been running for the past year but had forced them to carry out a special, commissioned kidnapping was infuriating. There would be more requests for "favors" in the future. That's how it worked. No one knew that better than him.

Glass in hand, he started to prowl the suite, pausing every few steps to swallow some of the whiskey. It was the interview with Cage and his wife that had forced him to admit to himself the situation was deteriorating rapidly. In spite of Guppy's assur-

242

ance that the disaster in the steam chamber could be handled with the claim that it had been a terrible accident, he sensed in his bones that it had put his precious game at risk.

It was Guppy's fault. He never should have gone into partnership with her. She had been incredibly convincing, however, and back at the start of their association in New York he had believed she was the key to fulfilling his vision.

The threat of an impending disaster had forced them to close down the spa and move west. Initially he had taken great satisfaction in redesigning the game and luring fresh players. But now, once again, disaster threatened, and all because of Guppy.

He made another circuit around the room and stopped to refill his glass. He needed to calm down and think. He and Guppy had not realized the danger when Cage and his wife had checked in, but when Mrs. Cage had insisted that Frampton provide her facial, they had known something was wrong. Guppy had panicked. The result was the botched attempt to get rid of Lyra Cage in the steam chamber.

The arrangements for the routine kidnappings were carefully planned. In the end, no one talked. No one went to the police. But Cage and the woman were a different kind of problem. They had to disappear permanently, and it had to look like an accident.

He picked up the house phone. "Get me Madam Guppy."

"Yes, Mr. Billingsley," the hotel operator said. "I'll ring her suite."

Guppy answered after only one ring. "Yes?"

"It's Billingsley. We need to talk. Tonight. The usual place. Usual time."

He did not wait for her to acknowledge his orders. She would show up. She had as much to lose as he did.

He glanced at his watch. He had a few hours to kill before he met with the bitch. He went into the bedroom, pushed the bookcase out of the way, and spun the combination lock on the hidden wall safe. He opened the door. There was a pile of cash inside that he kept on hand in the event he needed emergency bribe money. There was also a bottle filled with the drug. He took the stuff with him when he traveled to Los Angeles. It made it easy to handle the streetwalkers. They weren't as satisfying as the socialites but sometimes he needed additional stimulation.

He took out one of the two envelopes inside.

He crossed to the bed, unzipped his trousers, and pulled himself free of the briefs. He dumped the photos onto the bed and shuffled through them, looking for the ones that aroused him the most. He tossed the Merryweather images aside. She had been scared but not scared enough. He had seen the rage behind the fear. It ruined the experience for him. Made him nervous.

He picked up another photograph and studied the image of himself kneeling between the legs of the helpless woman. She was the socially prominent fiancée of a banker. The chain around her ankle was clearly visible. He liked that. The photograph made him look powerful. Potent. The woman was properly terrified.

He started to stroke himself, straining for an erection.

Thirty minutes later, he gave up. He could never come when he was actually with a woman, but afterward the photos allowed him to fantasize his way to a climax. At least that was how it had worked in the past. Lately, however, the pictures no longer stimulated him as much as they once had. He needed something more invigorating, the kind of stimulation he got with the prostitutes. When he was with them he could do as he pleased.

But Guppy would not allow him to do any physical damage to the women who were chosen for the game. She insisted it was too risky. He was forced to limit himself to the photographs.

He had figured out in his teens that his impotence was caused by women. All his life they had laughed at him. It was only when he had them chained to a bed that they finally realized he was the one in control. That was when they cowered and pleaded. That was when he saw fear in their eyes.

He collected the photos, got to his feet, and went to the nightstand. He took the pocketknife out of his trousers and carved a neat slash across the throat of Angela Merryweather.

He felt the stirring in his loins. Excitement rushed through him. One by one he went through the pictures, using the knife to cut the throat of each woman. Within minutes he was in the rush of an explosive climax.

When it was over he sank down onto the bed to savor the aftermath. For a long time he gazed at the photos. After a while he gathered them up and stuffed them back into the envelope.

He knew now what he had been missing. The only thing that stood in his way was Guppy. For her, the kidnappings were simply a business that brought in a great deal of cash and made it possible to secure extortion materials over some important, influential people. She would never allow him to kill the women. There was no profit in that.

He would have to get rid of Guppy before he could do what he had to do to reclaim his manhood.

The phone rang, jarring him out of the hot new vision of his future. He went into the sitting room of the suite and picked up the receiver.

The voice on the other end was familiar. He could not believe the bitch had the nerve to try to blackmail him. The rage boiled up inside him again, ruining the euphoric aftermath of the orgasm.

"Yes, I'll meet you, but we must be careful," he said. "We must not be seen together, not at this time of night. The paraffin chamber in the spa. Thirty minutes."

CHAPTER 25

Kevin Draper finished polishing the last cocktail glass and slipped it into the overhead rack. He tossed the white cloth into the basket and headed for the door. He was beat. He used to look forward to meeting the late-night crowd at the illegal casino in town, but lately all he wanted to do after closing was go home and pour himself another whiskey, a big one.

Throughout his shift he had been sneaking sips from the glass he kept under the bar — just enough to keep him going but not enough to get in the way of his work. He could not afford to lose the job. His sideline as an occasional chauffeur depended on maintaining his position as a bartender. It had been made clear to him that he wouldn't be of any use if he started getting drunk on the job. A driver had to be reliable.

It had seemed so easy back at the start. A

lot of money in exchange for some driving. *Nobody gets hurt,* the voice on the phone had assured him. He just had to keep his mouth shut and be available when he was needed.

He opened the door marked EMPLOYEES' ENTRANCE, let himself out into the desert night, and walked down the lane that ran behind the hotel. The handsome Buick was one of three vehicles left in the parking lot. At this hour the only other staff on duty were the night clerk, Hiram, at the front desk and Pete, a bellhop who covered room service if someone ordered a late-night snack. The guests all had liquor cabinets in their rooms, so there was no call for drinks from the bar.

Nobody gets hurt.

He repeated those words to himself several times a day now.

He got behind the wheel of the Buick and cranked up the powerful engine. It really was a beautiful car. Men admired it. Women loved it. At first he'd given his coworkers free rides. A couple of the maids and some of the treatment ladies who worked in the spa had made it obvious they were available for dinner and a movie in town. Back at the start he had dated nonstop for a while. But somewhere along the line he had lost interest in that kind of thing.

He no longer looked forward to meeting his buddies at the casino, either. He just wanted out of the gang, but he was afraid that leaving would cost him his life. He didn't know much — had made it a point to know as little as possible — but if he tried to quit he was pretty sure the voice on the phone would conclude he was a threat.

Nobody gets hurt.

He drove away from the resort and turned onto the main road that would take him through the small town. The house he was renting was about a mile past the shopping district.

The sky glittered with stars and the moon was almost full, but the desert was a vast, dark world at night. There were no street-lamps between the hotel and the town. After he passed through the short shopping district with its galleries and boutiques, there was another eerie stretch of darkness before he got to his house.

When the headlights first appeared in the rearview mirror he noticed them because there was never any other traffic on that stretch of pavement at that hour. His first thought, as it usually was lately, was that it might be a patrol car. But the headlights were too fancy. They were the lights of an expensive speedster.

Panic twisted his insides and made him go stone-cold. Maybe the voice on the phone had concluded that his services were no longer needed.

Or maybe he was imagining things. Lately he jumped at shadows.

He held his breath when he turned into the dirt lane that led to his house. The speedster did not follow him. Instead it continued on down the road.

A dizzying wave of relief swept over him and left him shivering in reaction. He parked in front of the small house and went up the front porch steps, fumbling with his keys. He let himself into the living room, headed straight for the kitchen, and grabbed the whiskey bottle.

He was halfway through his first drink when he heard the knock on the door. Jolted, he nearly dropped the glass. Whiskey splashed on the floor. For a brief moment he considered running out the back door. But without the car, he wouldn't get far.

Nobody gets hurt.

He put the glass down and went into the living room. Twitching the faded curtain aside, he peered out the window. The weak bulb above the door revealed two people standing on the porch — a man and a woman. The man was carrying a briefcase. He recognized them from the hotel. Mr. and Mrs. Cage. The honeymooners.

He thought about the gossip that had been circulating around the hotel all evening. Something about Mrs. Cage having been accidentally locked in the steam chamber.

He'd had nothing to do with that. He was a bartender. He didn't work in the spa. What could they want from him at this time of night?

Dread mingled with bewilderment. He gave up trying to make sense of the situation and opened the door.

"What are you two doing here?" he asked. "Are you lost?"

"Kevin Draper?" Cage said.

"That's right."

"In that case we have the right house. I'm Simon Cage, and this is my wife, Lyra. We'd like to talk to you."

"I recognize you from the bar. Look, I heard about what happened to Mrs. Cage today, but I had nothing to do with it, I swear."

"We want to discuss another matter," Cage said. "The woman you kidnapped from room two twenty-one earlier this week."

"What the hell are you talking about?"

Kevin yelped. "No one was kidnapped."

He tried to slam the door shut, but somehow Cage's briefcase was in the way, wedging it open. And now there was a gun in Cage's hand.

Mrs. Cage smiled a reassuring smile. "We're private investigators. We just want to ask a few questions, that's all."

"But I don't know anything," Kevin said. His throat tightened. "You've got the wrong person."

"Please let us in," Mrs. Cage said. "We might be able to help you."

Kevin looked at her, desperate to believe she was telling him the truth. Then he switched his attention to the gun in Simon Cage's hand. Someone had said that Cage was a book dealer who specialized in really old volumes. A man in that line of work should have appeared awkward or even downright ridiculous with a pistol in his hand. But Cage looked dangerous.

"Private investigators?" Kevin said, stalling for time.

Mrs. Cage offered him a reassuring smile and a card.

He glanced at the business card. "Kirk Investigations?"

"Don't worry," Mrs. Cage said. "We are not criminals. We're professionals, and we're here to help."

She sounded sincere.

Kevin realized he really did believe her. He backed away from the door. "Okay, but I'm telling you, I don't know anything."

CHAPTER 26

One look at Kevin Draper was all Lyra had needed to know that the gun was not going to be necessary. Draper wanted to talk. He needed to talk. He was out of options and desperate to share the weight of whatever burden he carried.

"You won't need your pistol, Simon," she said. She did not take her attention off Draper. "Mr. Draper wants to help us."

Simon hesitated and then lowered the gun. He did not, however, stash it in the briefcase. He kept it in his hand, pointing at the floor.

Lyra gave the living room a quick glance, taking in the sagging sofa and the threadbare upholstery on the two chairs. The coffee table consisted of a couple of wooden boards perched on four concrete bricks. Evidently Kevin had spent all of his newfound money on the Buick. He certainly hadn't used it to redecorate.

"Why don't we all go into the kitchen," she said. "You two sit down and talk. I'll make us some tea."

Simon and Kevin stared at her as if she had spoken in some unknown language.

"I don't have any tea," Kevin blurted.

Simon's lips thinned. "This isn't a social visit."

Lyra ignored him. She smiled at Kevin. "Coffee?"

"I ran out a couple of days ago," he mumbled.

"Cola?"

Kevin flushed, evidently relieved to be able to give a positive answer. "In the refrigerator."

"That will be perfect," Lyra said. "Let's all go into the kitchen and have a cola."

She did not wait for an answer. She walked decisively across the room. The men followed her and took seats on opposite sides of the battered kitchen table. Simon set his briefcase on the floor beside his chair. He put the gun within easy reach.

Lyra opened the refrigerator, wincing when she saw the mold growing on several items. She took out three of the elegantly shaped cola bottles and opened a drawer to look for something she could use to pry off the tops.

"We're here because we are looking for a woman who called herself Miss Granville," she said.

Kevin froze.

Lyra pretended not to notice. She found the bottle opener and went to work. "Granville disappeared from room two twenty-one at the hotel. We know she was taken against her will. We know your car was used to abduct her. We are also aware that other women have vanished from that room. We assume you were involved in those kidnappings, as well."

"I didn't kidnap them," Kevin said, his voice trembling. "I was just the driver. None of them were hurt. How do you know so much?"

"Mrs. Cage explained that we are private investigators," Simon reminded him. "This is what we do. We find answers."

"None of them got hurt," Kevin said again. He sounded frantic. "I swear it. I saw them afterward. They were all okay."

Lyra looked at him. "Is Miss Granville all right? Is she safe?"

Kevin hesitated. Then he seemed to collapse in on himself. "I don't know. Granville was different."

"How?" Simon asked.

"I was told there wouldn't be a pickup

with her." Kevin stared down at the scarred wood table. "With the others I was told to expect a phone call that would tell me when to pick up the women."

"What did you do after you picked them up?" Simon asked.

"I took them to a spot that was within walking distance of the train station. Told them to buy a ticket to L.A."

Lyra felt the ghostly fingers on the back of her neck. "Were any of the women hurt?"

"No," Kevin said quickly. "That's what I've been trying to tell you. No one got hurt."

"Did any of the women talk to you about what had happened to them?" Simon asked.

Kevin hesitated. "Most of them never said a word. Some cried. They were blindfolded, so they couldn't see my face. When I let them out of the car they were relieved. Couldn't wait to get on the train. But there was one — the last one. Classy. Blond."

Lyra carried the cola bottles to the table and set them down. "She talked to you?"

"Yeah," Kevin said. "A little. The others were sort of numb, but the blond one was angry. I was afraid she might call the police when I let her out of the car. But she didn't. I watched to make sure she got on board. She bought a ticket for Pasadena."

"What was her name?" Simon asked.

"Merryweather. Mrs. Angela Merry-weather. Room two twenty-one." Kevin sighed. "It's always room two twenty-one."

He grabbed his bottle and gulped down the contents.

A man clinging to a small piece of something resembling normalcy amid the debris of a life that has spun out of control, Lyra thought.

"What did Mrs. Merryweather say to you?" she asked.

Kevin looked more bleak than ever. "She was blindfolded like the others, but I could tell she figured me for a loser. She asked me how much I got paid for doing such a dirty job. Said she hoped I enjoyed spending the money, because it was going to cost me my soul."

"Do you enjoy spending the money?" Lyra asked gently.

Kevin closed his eyes briefly. When he opened them Lyra knew he had given up all hope. He believed himself to be doomed, and like others facing the end, he had things he wanted to confide. He yearned for peace of mind.

"At first, sure, I had fun with the money," he said. "I thought the car would make it all worthwhile. But it didn't. After the second job I wanted out, but it was too late. I can't quit. They'll kill me. I'll be a dead man when they find out I talked to you. They've got spies everywhere in that damn hotel."

"We may be able to protect you," Simon said. "No guarantees, but if you do exactly as we tell you, there's a reasonable chance you'll survive."

"No," Kevin said. "You don't know these guys. Hell, I don't know them, either. All my instructions come by phone. But I can tell that the women I take to the train station are terrified."

"Who tried to murder Mrs. Cage in the steam bath chamber at the spa this afternoon?" Simon asked.

"I heard it was an accident," Kevin said. He looked at Lyra and grimaced. "I hoped it was, because if it wasn't —"

"If it wasn't an accident it means you can no longer tell yourself that nobody gets hurt," Lyra concluded.

Kevin nodded. "Deep down I knew it was just a matter of time before someone got killed. I was afraid it would be one of the women. Looks like it will be me instead."

"I want a name," Simon said. "Who locked Mrs. Cage in the steam room and turned up the heat?"

"I don't know," Kevin said. "And that's the truth. It's not like they tell me anything.

I'm just the damned driver. I get a phone call an hour before I get off my shift. I make sure the car is parked right outside the service lane door. Two guys whose faces I never see because they wear rubber masks bring the woman down the service stairs in a big laundry basket. She's always unconscious, like she passed out, y'know? They put her in the trunk of my car and disappear. I drive her to the pickup point, get her out of the car, and carry her inside the cabin."

"Where is the cabin?" Simon asked.

"About half an hour from the resort," Kevin said. "In the foothills. The place has been abandoned for years. I leave the woman there and go home. That's it until I get another call a few days later telling me to collect the guest — that's what the bastard on the phone always calls the woman, a *guest*. She's awake this time, but blindfolded, and her wrists are bound. I drive her back to Labyrinth Springs and drop her off outside of town. I untie her hands and make sure she has her purse. I tell her that when she can no longer hear my car engine she can take off the blindfold. She's supposed to walk into town and get on the train. I let her know I'll be watching to make sure she follows orders."

"What about the luggage?" Simon asked. "You said the women have their handbags when they get on the train, but what about their suitcases?"

"Once they are on board I make sure the luggage is loaded onto the baggage car. No one takes any notice. The porters know the hotel always handles the luggage for the guests who arrive and leave by train."

"You said you were told not to expect a call to take Miss Granville to the train station," Simon asked. "Any idea why she was treated differently?"

"No."

"Tell me exactly how Granville was handled," Simon said. "What was the first thing that made you think the pattern had changed?"

Kevin frowned. "Pattern?"

"Just answer the question," Simon said.

"Yeah, sure," Kevin said. "Well, to begin with, I got the call too soon."

"What do you mean?" Lyra asked.

"Until now there has always been at least two months, sometimes three, between the jobs," Kevin said. "But I got the call to pick up Granville about ten days after I took Merryweather to the station. I got the feeling right then that there was something different going on."

262

"Who was responsible for tidying up room two twenty-one?" Lyra asked.

"I dunno. One of the housekeepers, I guess. I never asked."

"Because you didn't want to know?" Lyra suggested.

Kevin nodded glumly.

Simon sat quietly for a moment. Lyra knew he was sorting through options and coming up with a strategy. She almost smiled when she sensed the instant it all came together in his head. He really was getting easier to read.

He looked at Kevin. "Here's what's going to happen next. You will pack a bag now. Take only what you absolutely need. Then you will get in your car and lead us to the cabin where you take the women. After that you will keep driving."

"Where?"

"Burning Cove."

"Are you out of your mind?" Kevin slammed his bottle down with so much force the entire table trembled. "I can't afford a hotel there. Movie stars and rich people vacation in Burning Cove. Everyone knows that. Besides, it would be easy for the gang to find me there. It's a small town."

"Allow me to finish," Simon said. "When you arrive in Burning Cove you will go directly to the Paradise Club. Any gas station attendant can tell you how to get there. You will ask for Luther Pell. He or a member of his staff will be expecting you. He will see to it that you are protected, unless —"

"Unless what?" Kevin asked, alarmed.

"Unless something bad happens to the last woman you transported to the cabin. Miss Granville from room two twenty-one."

"Nobody gets hurt," Kevin said quickly.

"You'd better hope that's the case with Miss Granville, because she's very important to Mr. Pell," Simon said. "He's the one who sent us to find her."

"Shit," Kevin whispered. "He'll probably kill me."

"Only if Miss Granville does not survive the kidnapping."

"How can you be sure of that?" Kevin demanded.

"I can't," Simon admitted. Absently he massaged the scars on the back of his hand. "But in this case I think I can talk him into doing me a favor. He owes me. As I said, all bets are off if the woman who called herself Miss Granville is injured or killed."

Kevin stared, panic-stricken. "But there's nothing I can do about that. All I can tell you is that she was fine when I left her at the cabin."

"You do have one other option, Kevin," Lyra said. "You could head for Mexico."

"Don't you think I already considered that?" Kevin shook his head. "It takes money to live there, just like anywhere else. I don't have any cash left. Spent it all on the car. I guess I'll take my chances in Burning Cove."

"I'll call Luther Pell and tell him you're on the way," Simon said.

"I knew it was going to end like this." Kevin dropped his head into his hands. "I wish I'd never gotten involved. I was just the driver."

"I've got a few more questions," Simon said.

CHAPTER 27

Edith Guppy unlocked the service entrance door at the back of the spa and let herself into the dark interior of the storage room. She switched on her flashlight and went quickly toward the central hallway, heading for the paraffin bath room where her *business partner* was waiting.

When the current situation had been resolved, it would be time to get rid of Ridley Billingsley. He and his money had certainly been useful but there was no question that his mental state was deteriorating rapidly. She sensed the photographs of him humiliating the women were no longer enough for him.

She had encountered others like Billingsley in the old days during the war. They got excited when they hurt people but sooner or later they needed more intense stimulation. They needed to kill. That sort had their uses, but eventually they became unreliable and had to be terminated.

She detested having to call Billingsley her *business partner.* She had built Guppy's House of Beauty from scratch. Every dime of the money she had smuggled out of Europe toward the end of the war had gone into the New York spa. The operation had been a smash hit from the day it opened, thanks to her talent for marketing.

She had run into financial difficulties during the worst of the Depression. She had been facing bankruptcy when she met Ridley Billingsley. She had known immediately that she could use him to keep Guppy's House of Beauty in business, but the price had been high. To gain his interest and his money, as well as access to his social connections, she had been forced to agree to let him play what he called his "game."

She hadn't minded the game. It had proven useful for obtaining the extortion photos. The fact that the women were clearly being assaulted in the pictures was not a problem. The images were just as potentially damaging as scenes of consensual sex would have been. When it came to sexual assault people always blamed the woman. She was viewed as having put herself into a reckless situation. Even if the police could be persuaded to act, the potential humiliation of having her naked body displayed in the scandal sheets or before a jury was more than enough to keep the victim quiet.

The new business plan had gone well in New York, right up until the disaster. Not even Billingsley's money could save the spa.

Facing the threat of ruin yet again, she had closed her doors before the rumors hit the front pages of the New York papers. She had conceived a new plan, but once again the Billingsley fortune was required to implement it.

He was a New Yorker born and bred. She had not expected him to agree to finance her venture out west. To her surprise, he had been enthusiastic about the idea of buying the old resort in Labyrinth Springs and transforming it into a destination spa for the Los Angeles crowd.

Things had started off brilliantly, thanks to her sharp advertising skills. Her name was once again golden in the world of beauty. The rumors in New York had been squelched with the aid of the Billingsley money and a convenient heart attack that had killed the powerful man who had threatened to destroy her. She had never told Billingsley that she was the one who had caused the tycoon's heart to stop in the middle of a lavish dinner.

Shortly after opening, the new California location of Guppy's House of Beauty had established itself as an exclusive destination for the Hollywood set. That was more than enough to guarantee success in California. The wealthy socialites on the West Coast had soon followed, and now the resort was starting to attract guests from the other side of the country.

The state had lived up to its reputation as a land where reinvention was not only possible but was expected. It was a world where a woman could bury her past and build a new future.

There had been a few problems from time to time, but nothing she couldn't handle. She had to keep control of Billingsley during the photography sessions. There was no question that he was unstable and getting worse. And one of the treatment ladies had tried to steal the drugs. That issue had been taken care of with an overdose in room two twenty-one.

Nothing had proven to be nearly as complicated or as dangerous as the problems she had taken care of during the war.

She went down the main hallway, past the treatment rooms and the exercise chamber. She stopped at the entrance to the paraffin bath and braced herself for the confrontation with Billingsley. He always acted as if he was the one in charge, but she knew his weakness. She had learned long ago that a woman who knew a man's cravings always had the edge. She really was going to have to get rid of Billingsley. As soon as the current situation was resolved she would arrange for him to have a heart attack.

The lights were off inside the room. That was not unusual. Billingsley insisted they hold their meetings in the darkened room to minimize the possibility of someone noticing the unusual activity after hours in the spa. She had a hunch the truth was that he liked issuing his orders from the shadows. He had a taste for high drama.

She did not need to turn on the lights. She had designed the treatment room and knew every inch of it by heart. There was a deep porcelain bathtub, a large tank for the paraffin, and a pitcher that was used to pour the heated wax over the client.

She smelled warm wax and realized the paraffin tank had been left on. That was a violation of the rules. Not only was it dangerous, it was a waste of electricity. In the morning she would speak to the treatment lady responsible.

Annoyed, she switched on the lights and

went across the space to turn off the heater. She stopped, stunned, when she saw what was in the bathtub.

The door opened. She spun around.

"You fool," she said. "What have you done?"

CHAPTER 28

Lyra watched the headlights of Kevin Draper's Buick grow faint and finally disappear into the night.

"Think he'll choose Mexico instead of Burning Cove?" she asked.

"I don't give a damn," Simon said. "We got a solid lead from him. Right now that's all that matters."

"Yes, and you will note that we did so without resorting to violence."

"Sure. Take all the fun out of it."

"We got more information out of him doing things my way. Admit it."

"He was a broken man," Simon said. "Falling apart."

"Yes."

"One thing that is clear now is that this is not a normal kidnapping. We need to know why the gang changed the pattern when they grabbed Raina."

Lyra shivered. "It feels like time is running out."

They were standing on the front porch of the long-abandoned cabin in the desert foothills. In the distance small splashes of light marked the town and the Labyrinth Springs resort.

Lyra heard Simon move. She turned around in time to see him aim his flashlight at what appeared to be the only new element of the cabin — the lock on the front door.

He took out his lockpick and went to work. A moment later she followed him into the cabin. There was only one room. The floorboards were bare and scarred. There was no paint left on the walls. The curtains on the single window hung in shreds. A broken wooden chair and a filthy mattress were the only items of furniture.

"It was probably built by a prospector," Simon said. "No electricity. No running water. No bathroom."

"Not the sort of place that would draw attention from passersby," Lyra said.

Simon walked slowly through the space, examining every inch of it in the beam of his light. "Invisible from the nearest road. You'd have to know it was here to find it. All in all, a strategic location for a gang of kidnappers."

He sounded cool and emotionless, as if he were a disinterested observer, but Lyra could feel the energy in the atmosphere. She knew he was using his other senses to explore the scene of the crime.

"Yes, but why aren't they using it to hold the captives?" she said. "According to Draper this was just a pickup and drop-off point."

"Obviously they didn't want Draper to know where the women are held while they make the ransom arrangements. He wasn't a real member of the gang."

"Just the driver," Lyra said. She watched Simon crouch beside the stained mattress. "Find something?"

"Raina was here, all right. The mattress has a lot of old energy infused in it, but the freshest layer feels like the same heat I picked up on the bed in room two twenty-one. I don't think she was unconscious, at least not the whole time she was here."

"If Raina awakened, she would have tried to escape or fight."

Simon moved his hand on the mattress. "There's something else going on. She's struggling, but it's not in panic. There's anger and desperation, but she's more cool-headed this time."

"What does that tell us?"

"She had a goal. An objective."

"Obviously she didn't escape. What else would she have been desperate to do?"

Simon lifted the edge of the mattress and aimed his flashlight at the floorboards underneath. "Leave a message for whoever came looking for her."

Lyra saw the object in the circle of light. She took a sharp breath.

"That's Raina's notebook," she said. "She managed to hide it under the mattress."

Simon picked up the notebook and got to his feet. "Let's get out of here. We need to call Luther Pell and tell him what we learned tonight."

"Right," Lyra said. "He deserves to know we've made real progress. The poor man must be half out of his mind with worry."

"Speaking of which, got any idea how I should handle him when I call him? I want to tell him that we're making progress, but I don't want him sending in the FBI or some of his mob pals. Got a feeling that would get Raina killed. Whoever is behind this can't afford to leave her alive."

Neither of them added the qualifier — if she was still alive. *We both need to think positive,* Lyra thought. She focused on the question.

"Pell needs to feel like he's taking action,"

she said. "He needs a job. Give him one."

"Good idea. I think I know exactly how he can make himself useful."

Lyra led the way out to the car and got into the passenger's seat. Simon climbed behind the wheel. He handed her the notebook and then turned the key in the ignition. He drove cautiously down the old rutted road, headlights switched off.

Lyra waited until they reached the narrow strip of pavement that would take them back to Labyrinth Springs. When Simon turned on the headlights she switched on her flashlight and flipped open the notebook.

Her first reaction was acute despair. "We've got a problem. I forgot that she keeps her notes in her secretarial code. If she did leave a clue we'll have to find a professional who can transcribe it for us."

"She might not have had time to write down any useful information," Simon said. He changed gears and drove faster. "She may have simply left that notebook behind because she hoped that it would eventually be found and recognized."

Lyra flipped through the pages, frantically trying to make sense of the cryptic circles and swirls. When she got to the last entry she gave a small yelp.

"Simon."

"You found something you can read?"

Lyra looked up, excitement spiraling through her. "She did have time to write a name. What's more, she wrote it out so that anyone can read it. *Guppy.*"

CHAPTER 29

"I've got a name for you, Luther." The familiar static of a long-distance call crackled on the line. Simon clamped the pay phone more tightly to his ear. "Mrs. Angela Merryweather. My informant says she lives in Pasadena. She's in her late twenties. Rich. Blond. Movie-star pretty."

He glanced out the open door of the phone booth. Lyra was leaning against the fender of the Cord, her arms crossed. There was no one else around. The gas station was closed for the night. Luther had answered his phone halfway through the first ring. He had listened, tense and silent, while Simon gave him a quick summary of events.

"Why do I care about Angela Merryweather from Pasadena?" Luther growled.

"She was kidnapped from the resort shortly before Raina disappeared. There's a gang operating out of the hotel and spa. According to my source, Merryweather wasn't as terrified as the others. She was angry."

"So she might be more inclined to talk — is that what you're saying?"

"Maybe. We need information. Details. A description of the place where the victims are held would be extremely useful. Given the logistical problems and the timing involved, I'm sure the location has to be fairly close to Labyrinth Springs."

"Pasadena is about a hundred miles from Burning Cove," Luther said. "If I leave now I can be there before dawn. Any idea what we're dealing with here?"

"Draper, the guy who drove the women to and from the pickup location, explained some of it when he showed us the cabin where the women are held at one point. The ring targets wealthy women who are connected to influential men — industrialists, politicians, bankers. Draper didn't know anything about how the ransom arrangements work, but after the money is paid the women are released. Draper says they're usually so frightened they don't talk. The families have obviously kept things hushed up, which means the gang is holding some form of leverage over their heads."

"There have been no attempts at extortion. I haven't heard anything from the kidnappers," Luther said.

"This is not a standard kidnapping. Whoever grabbed Raina must be aware of the risk of trying to extort money from you. Draper confirmed that the gang is handling things differently this time."

"How?"

Simon exhaled slowly. "I was hoping you wouldn't ask that question. All I can tell you is that Draper made it clear this kidnapping doesn't fit the pattern. He was told he would not be contacted to pick up Raina and transport her to the train station."

"That was the way the other kidnappings worked?"

"Yes."

"The bastards are going to murder Raina," Luther said in a voice that came from the coldest circle of hell.

"They won't do that until they get whatever it is they want," Simon said. "Listen to me, Luther — Angela Merryweather is our best option at the moment. She may have been blindfolded, but she might remember something we can use. Traffic. Music. Voices. Smells. Anything will help. It's a big desert. We've got to get a starting point."

"I'll get on the road as soon as we hang up," Luther vowed.

"Thanks. There's something else we should probably consider."

"What's that?" Luther asked.

"It's also possible the kidnappers made a mistake. Maybe they took the wrong woman."

"They grabbed the wrong woman, all right," Luther said.

The promise of a brutal vengeance was carved into every word. Simon glanced at Lyra again. He understood exactly how Luther felt. He forced himself to focus on the conversation.

"One more thing," Luther said. "Did this Kevin Draper know when the kidnapping ring set up shop in the hotel and spa?"

"He said he got the first phone call about a year ago," Simon said. "He seems sure that's when the kidnappers went into business."

"That's when the hotel reopened under new management, according to Oliver."

"And when the spa was opened. Guppy is the only name on the last page of the notebook. It wasn't written in shorthand. I'm sure Miss Kirk was trying to tell us that Edith Guppy is very much involved in this."

"I don't see how the kidnapping ring could operate without the cooperation of someone high up in the hotel," Luther said.

"I agree. We also think that at least one of the treatment ladies, Miss Frampton, is working with the kidnappers. Someone locked Lyra in the steam room this afternoon and turned up the heat. Lyra would have died if she hadn't managed to break the glass in the door."

"What the hell?" Luther's voice sharpened. "Someone tried to murder Lyra?"

"Yes. The hotel is insisting it was a terrible accident, and we're pretending to go along with that story, but there's no doubt it was a deliberate attempt to kill Lyra."

"She's in over her head. Get her out of there. Send her back to Burning Cove on the train."

"I strongly suggested she leave Labyrinth Springs. She, uh, declined."

"Declined?"

"She won't go, Luther. Says she's got a job to do. Short of handcuffing her and driving her back to Burning Cove myself, there's not much I can do except keep an eye on her. Besides, she's got all the right instincts. People talk to her. She's the one who convinced Draper to tell us everything tonight."

Luther was silent for a moment. Then he exhaled heavily.

"Take care of her," he said. "Raina will never forgive me if something happens to Lyra."

Simon watched Lyra through the phone booth door. "Don't worry, I won't let her out of my sight. Can I count on you not to do anything drastic to Kevin Draper, assuming he decides to head for Burning Cove? At the moment he's our only solid link to the gang. We need him alive, at least for now."

"I'll keep him alive as long as he's useful. But if anything happens to Raina —"

"Understood. I explained that very carefully to Draper. There's a good chance he won't show up in Burning Cove anyway. He may decide to head for the border."

"I'll have my people watch for him. If he shows up they'll make sure he doesn't disappear. How can I reach you after I talk to Angela Merryweather?"

"Call the front desk. Ask them to give me a message about a sick relative. I'll find a pay phone and call you back."

"You don't trust the hotel phones."

"No. Draper says the gang has spies everywhere."

"Maybe you should check out. Find a safer place to stay."

"The answers are at the resort, Luther."

"I understand. I don't like it, but I understand. Just promise me you'll take very good care of Lyra."

Simon did not take his eyes off her. Determination and courage radiated from her in invisible waves of energy that he could sense even from several feet away. She was risking her life for a woman she barely knew, a woman with a murky past, and there was no way to stop her.

Lyra was reckless, impulsive, and complicated, but in that moment he knew that she would never betray those who trusted her. Somewhere inside him a fierce beast stirred and stretched out long talons.

"I'll take care of her," he vowed.

CHAPTER 30

"*Shit,*" Simon hissed very softly. He yanked his gloved fingers off the doorknob. "That hurt."

"Are you okay?" Lyra asked.

They were standing at the back door of the spa. Simon had insisted they both wear gloves to avoid leaving fingerprints. His were sleek driving gloves. She had been forced to use a pair of fashionable gauntlet-length gloves that she had brought for evening wear. Next time she would be sure to pack driving gloves.

"I'm fine." Simon gingerly wrapped his fingers around the knob again. "I wasn't expecting it to be so hot, that's all."

"I assume you're talking about the special kind of heat that you can sense?" Lyra said.

"Leather gloves mute that sort of energy but they don't block it entirely. Whoever went through this door last was worked up. Excited. Nervous. Enraged." Simon paused.

"The sensations came from at least two different people. Maybe three. Hard to tell."

"Are they still inside?"

"I don't think so. The heat isn't red-hot. It's a couple of hours old, but it's muddy."

"Muddy?"

"Some of it feels really twisted." He reached down, opened the briefcase, and took out his gun and a lockpick. "Wait out here while I take a look around."

Lyra's first instinct was to argue, but common sense told her he was better equipped to go in first. He was the one with the gun. She added a pistol to the list of items she needed to purchase if she was going to stay in the investigation business.

Simon got the service door open. He moved into the heavily shadowed space and stood quietly for a moment. She felt energy shift in the atmosphere.

"This room is empty," he said. He walked across the space to the interior door and opened it. He aimed his flashlight down the central hallway. "No one in the hall, either. You can come in. Bring the briefcase."

She gripped the handle of the briefcase and tried to hoist it. The case didn't move. "This weighs a ton."

"The case is lined with a steel plate," Simon said. "Can you manage it?"

She leaned down and used both hands to lift the briefcase.

"No problem," she gasped.

She staggered into the room and kicked the door shut behind her. "What are we looking for?"

"Anything that might tell us where they are holding Raina. The only other alternative we've got is to visit every building, house, shed, or barn within a two-hour radius of the pickup location. It's not as if we've got a handy road map of all the abandoned cabins scattered around this desert. We need a starting point." Simon paused. "What is that smell?"

"It's Violet perfume," Lyra said. "Guppy's signature scent. I told you it was a bit heavy."

"Heavy is right. A man could choke on it."

"Brace yourself. The entire spa smells like this."

There was enough moonlight seeping through the half-closed blinds to reveal shelves filled with Guppy's House of Beauty products. Stacks of neatly folded sheets and towels were piled high in one corner. Robes hung from hooks on the wall.

"Don't switch on your flashlight," Simon said. "There are windows in here. I doubt if there is anyone around outside at this hour of the night, but you never know."

"There aren't any windows in the central hallway," Lyra said. "Guppy's office is at the far end, just off the lobby. There is a window in that room, but there are also blinds and drapes."

"That should work."

Simon started down the hall.

Lyra hurried after him, lugging the briefcase.

The doors of all of the treatment rooms were closed.

"I hope Luther Pell gets some useful information out of Angela Merryweather," she said.

"Luther is very good at interrogation. He takes a different approach than you do but he knows how to get people to talk."

"In other words, he'll scare the daylights out of poor Mrs. Merryweather?"

"Only if it's absolutely necessary."

"She was kidnapped. She is probably still traumatized."

"Luther will understand that."

They reached the end of the hall and stopped in front of the door marked OF-FICE. It was locked.

Simon made short work of the lock, switched off his flashlight, and opened the

288

door, gun in hand.

There was no one inside. The curtains were tightly pulled across the single window.

"You take the file cabinet," Simon said. He switched on his flashlight. "I'll check the desk and the safe."

"You can crack a safe?" Lyra asked, impressed.

He glanced at the imposing steel safe in the corner and shrugged. "It looks like a standard combination lock. Shouldn't be a problem."

Lyra set the briefcase down with a small sigh of relief. "So many things for me to learn."

"I wouldn't put safecracking at the top of your list of priorities."

"Why not?"

"It's illegal, for one thing."

"Details."

She opened the first drawer of the cabinet and started flipping quickly through the file folders. Most were clearly labeled with names.

"Client files," she announced. "Names. Dates. Services purchased and how much was spent on products."

Simon looked up from a desk drawer. "Is there a file for Granville or Angela Merryweather?"

"Good question." Lyra swept the flashlight beam across the neatly labeled tabs. "No."

"Is there a file on you?"

"That," she said, "is also an interesting question. Yes, here I am." She plucked the folder out of the drawer and flipped it open. "Looks like the others. My name, the services I received, and the products I bought. There is also a note that I requested Miss Frampton for my facial. It's underlined."

"Anything else?"

"Such as the fact that I was scheduled to be steamed to death? Nope."

"Locking you in the steam chamber was a last-minute impulse on someone's part. There wasn't time to come up with a smart plan." Simon paused. "Huh."

Lyra glanced at him and saw that he was using his flashlight to study the desk calendar. "Find something interesting?"

"Maybe. There's a note here about ordering supplies for tea."

"Madam Guppy brews her own special teas for clients. I was given some to drink shortly before I went into the steam chamber. I didn't like it, so I tossed most of it into a potted plant. There was another pitcher of the stuff in the chamber, but I didn't drink any."

"Who gave you the tea?"

There was a sharp edge to the question.

"Miss Frampton, the facial treatment lady. Why?"

"A few months back I had a case involving a chemist who was obsessed with ancient herbals. He was dealing his own homemade tonics to a select clientele. They all died what appeared to be natural deaths."

Shock lanced through Lyra. "Good grief, are you talking about the murderer the press called the Mad Chemist? The fake doctor who claimed to have found a cure for diseases of the lungs? McSomething?"

"McGruder. I was able to convince him to hire me to find a particularly rare edition of *Culpeper's Complete Herbal.* I learned a lot when I did the research for that case."

"The press said the FBI cracked that case."

"The Bureau asked Luther to handle it. He always gives the credit to the local police or the FBI. The last thing he wants is publicity for Failure Analysis."

"He gave the McGruder case to you?"

"We worked it together." Simon tapped the desk calendar. "Like I said, I learned a lot. At least two of the ingredients on this list are strong enough to knock you out. There are also some very interesting plants and mushrooms, the kind that can produce visions, if you know how to use them."

"The tea," Lyra whispered. "I was drugged before I went into the steam chamber."

"Did you hallucinate?"

"Yes. I thought I saw figures moving in the steam, and I felt very disoriented and unbalanced. I assumed I was just exhausted from the exercises and dehydrated by the heat. Thank goodness I didn't drink too much of the tea."

"We need to talk to Frampton. See if there's a file on the employees in that cabinet."

Lyra opened another drawer and saw a row of folders. "Yes. Here's one for Frampton."

"Address?"

"Yes."

"Take it. We don't have time to read it here."

"We're going to confront her tonight, too?"

"We can't afford to wait until tomorrow."

"You're right." Lyra tucked the file under her arm and closed the drawer.

Simon opened the briefcase and took out a stethoscope. He inserted the earpieces into his ears and placed the bell of the stethoscope near the lock. Gently he turned the dial.

"What are you doing?" Lyra asked.

"Listening for the lock to click. Hush."

Yet another job skill she needed to learn. Lyra made a note to add it to her growing list.

Simon worked the combination for a minute or two. There was a click and the door swung open.

He aimed the flashlight inside. "Some cash. All neatly stacked and bundled. Receipts."

"Probably the money and associated records from this week's sales," Lyra said.

"Nothing else in here." Simon closed the safe and got to his feet. He took the file from Lyra, dropped it into the briefcase, and headed for the door. "Let's go."

He led the way with his pistol and flashlight. Lyra took a fortifying breath, hoisted the suitcase in both arms, and trudged down the hall behind him. There were, she concluded, a few drawbacks to being an apprentice investigator and junior professional colleague.

Ahead of her Simon methodically brushed the back of one hand against each doorknob.

"Hey, Simon?" she said.

"What?"

"The papers said that McGruder was

found stabbed to death in his laboratory. A steel letter opener was used to kill him, as I recall. The police had a lot of theories, but I don't think they ever found out who did it."

"They didn't look very hard."

"Was it you or Luther? You said the two of you worked the case together."

"Do you ever stop asking questions?"

"No."

Simon grunted. "It was me. I told you, guns never seem to be available when you need one."

"It must have been a horrible experience, stabbing a man."

"Yes, it was. Probably a lot like striking someone in the head with a golf club."

She shivered. "Probably."

He stopped abruptly in front of the room marked PARAFFIN BATH. "Put the briefcase down."

"Gladly. But what's wrong?"

"A lot of energy. Different people, I think. But it's a few hours old."

Simon twisted the knob and pushed the door inward. He swung the beam around the room. Apparently satisfied that it was empty, he moved inside.

"There's a bathtub in here," he said.

Lyra came to stand in the doorway. "There's a reason they call it a paraffin bath, you know."

Simon aimed the flashlight into the tub. "Looks like someone decided to take a late-night bath."

"What?" Lyra took a few steps into the room. She stared down into the tub. "Dear heaven."

A full-sized wax figure of a woman reclined in the tub. *No, not a wax statue,* she thought. *A woman shrouded* head to toe *in hardened paraffin.*

Comprehension iced her nerves.

"Murder," she whispered.

Simon studied the paraffin-shrouded body. "I can't make out her face."

"Paraffin baths are one of the treatments offered here," Lyra said. She gazed at the body in the tub, shaken. "They're supposed to soften the skin. Earlier today I declined that particular therapy, along with the mummy wrap."

"Any idea who she is?"

"I'd have to peel the paraffin off her face in order to try to identify her. I really don't want to do that."

"Don't worry, we're not going to touch the body. She'll be discovered in the morning by someone on the spa staff. If we report this tonight, there's a high degree of probability we'll land at the top of a list of suspects. We can't afford to get tangled up in a murder investigation. We'll lose too much time trying to talk our way out of it."

"Agreed," Lyra said. "Finding Raina is our first priority. Wait. Point your flashlight at her again."

Simon did so without comment. Lyra took a cautious step toward the tub and forced herself to take a closer look at the victim. The hardened paraffin had formed a thick white shell over the entire body, including the head. The woman appeared to be nearly nude, but there was a chunky beaded necklace around her throat.

Lyra got a queasy feeling in the pit of her stomach.

"Miss Frampton, the woman who gave me the facial treatment today — the one who did Raina's facial — wore a necklace of violet Bakelite beads that was the same shape and size as that necklace. She said it was a gift from Madam Guppy, a reward for selling the most products last month."

CHAPTER 31

"What are we going to do now?" Lyra stalked across the front room of the suite, arms tightly folded. "We can't just sit around and wait for something else to happen."

"We could do that," Simon said. "But it would be smarter to get some sleep."

Lyra stopped in the middle of the room and glared at him. They had made it back to their suite by way of the service stairs. As far as they could tell, no one had seen them. Simon had poured each of them a glass of whiskey. Then he had settled into a reading chair to drink his nightcap. He looked far too calm, she decided. Controlled. In charge of the situation.

It was annoying.

She, on the other hand, could not sit still. She had swallowed some whiskey and begun pacing the room. She could not get the picture of the woman encased in paraffin out of her head.

"I couldn't possibly sleep," she announced.

"There's nothing else we can do until we hear from Luther." Simon glanced at his watch. "It's nearly dawn. He should be in Pasadena soon, if he isn't there already. Even if he's successful in locating Angela Merryweather and persuading her to talk, it's going to be a while before we hear from him."

"We should confront Guppy."

Simon leaned his head against the back of the chair and appeared to give that idea some serious thought. After a moment he straightened and shook his head.

"Not yet," he said.

"Why not?"

"It will be interesting to see how things play out after the body is discovered later this morning."

Lyra circled the table in the center of the suite. "Do you think Guppy is the killer? She would certainly know how to operate the paraffin equipment. But so would any of the treatment ladies."

"Why would Guppy take the risk of staging such an elaborate scene in her own spa? Encasing the body in wax is more than a bit extreme. A murder staged as an accident

298

would have made more sense. Whoever tried to kill you certainly wanted your death to appear accidental."

"Good point," Lyra said. "Maybe the killer is simply insane. Frampton's death might have nothing to do with the gang of kidnappers."

"Trust me, it's connected. There are no coincidences in a murder investigation."

"But the paraffin bath is so bizarre. Not to mention time-consuming. The killer had to go to a lot of work to heat the paraffin and pour it over the body. Kevin Draper emphasized that the gang is running a business. The last thing they would want to do is draw the attention of the police with a killing that looks like the act of a madman."

Simon set his empty glass aside. "I'm not so sure about that. When you think about it, there is a certain logic to making Frampton's death appear to be the work of a crazed fiend. It will point the authorities in the wrong direction. They certainly won't be looking for an organized ring of kidnappers."

Lyra sighed. "I see what you mean."

"It's also possible someone is sending a message."

Lyra glanced at him. "To other members of the ring?"

"Maybe. There are too many questions, Lyra. We need more information. We can't just flail around. Not now. We have to assume we are being watched. I doubt we are in danger here in the hotel, because two more deaths would be very difficult to explain to the police. In addition, if Guppy and her gang are onto us, it's almost certain they know that our client is Luther Pell."

"And no criminal in his right mind wants to draw the attention of Luther Pell."

"Right. The kidnappers must know that we are closing in on them. They'll panic. If I were in their shoes I would be looking for a way out. That starts with getting rid of Raina, but it will have to be done in a manner that won't point to Guppy and her spa."

Lyra looked at him, curiosity overriding her worries. "If you were the leader of the kidnapping ring, what would you do?"

Simon hesitated. "Do you really want to know?"

"Yes. Don't worry, I do realize we are speaking hypothetically."

Simon propped his elbows on the padded arms of the chair and put his fingertips together. "Hypothetically speaking, if I thought Pell was closing in, I would shut down the business and disappear."

"You're talking about the kidnapping business?"

"Right. I would eliminate all of the other members of the ring — I'm sure it's a small group — and then I'd frame one person to make certain Pell was satisfied, because I'd know he wouldn't stop looking until he was certain the ringleader was dead."

Lyra caught her breath, stopped for a couple of seconds, and then continued pacing. "And Raina?"

"The safest option is to make certain that Miss Kirk does not survive. She's a huge risk. Even if she has been blindfolded or drugged this whole time, there's no getting around the fact that she knows too much. She's a professional investigator, after all. She will have paid attention to even the smallest clue."

Lyra came to a halt and shuddered. "That sounds so . . . so —"

"Ruthless?"

"Yes."

"We're dealing with a ring of kidnappers that is willing to commit murder," Simon reminded her. "Given the identity of the victim and the fact that there has not been a ransom demand, we have to assume that whoever did this never intended for Miss Kirk to survive."

"Yes, I know," Lyra said. "But we were also speaking hypothetically. Your theory assumes that the killers are functioning like a small but well-organized mob. For them the kidnappings are business as usual. If things go bad in business, you do, indeed, close down the shop and let the employees go. But there are some unusual factors in this situation."

"Believe me, I'm aware of that. The biggest question is, why did they take the risk of grabbing Luther Pell's lover in the first place? The answers may be in Miss Kirk's past, but we don't have time to search for them."

"We must find Raina first." Lyra came to a halt again. "We made so much progress tonight. We know we're dealing with a ring of kidnappers who have been getting away with their crimes for at least a year. We know they've broken their pattern. But now we've come to a full stop."

"Every case is like this," Simon said. "There are times when things move so quickly you can barely keep up and times when you have to wait for more information. You get used to the ebb and flow."

"I'm not sure I will ever get used to the ebb part."

"Having second thoughts about becoming

302

a private investigator?" Simon asked.

"I was already reconsidering it after what happened at the Adlington house the other morning."

"Understandable."

"When this is over I may decide to pursue another career path. But first we have to find Raina."

Simon did not respond. Lyra turned her head and saw that he was watching her with his hard-to-read eyes. She studied him intently for a few seconds and then abandoned the effort. She was getting better at reading him, but this time she had no clue to his thoughts.

After a moment he got to his feet and walked deliberately toward her. He stopped directly behind her but he did not touch her.

"For what it's worth," he said, "I think you would make an excellent investigator. Raina Kirk told Pell that you've got a talent for the work. I agree."

"Do you really think so?"

"Yes," he said. "It's not just that you're curious by nature. And it's not that you have an amazing ability to get people to talk to you. There's something else that makes me think you were doomed to be an investigator."

"What?"

"You want to help people find answers to the questions that keep them awake at night. I should warn you that this kind of work can be extremely frustrating, because a lot of people won't thank you for the answers you give them."

"Because they won't like those answers?" Lyra asked.

"More often than not, that's the result. A wife who hires you to find out if her husband is cheating on her won't like it when you confirm her suspicions. Families who ask you to find a missing relative will be devastated if it turns out the relative is dead or, worse yet, vanished for a very good reason."

"But they still want answers."

"Yes. And so do you."

"Is that what it's like for you?"

"In a way. I need to use my talent. If I don't —"

She touched the side of his jaw. "If you don't use it you'll feel like you don't have a purpose. You'll drift through life."

"Something like that."

"Do you want to kiss me again?"

Simon's eyes heated. "Yes."

She smiled. "It's okay by me."

"Just okay?"

"Better than okay. I'd like you to kiss me."

He put a warm, strong hand on either side of her waist and drew her closer. "When I drove to Burning Cove to report to Luther Pell, I told myself that I would check in to a nice resort, spend some time by the pool during the day, and drink cocktails at the Paradise at night. I wanted to find a free-spirited, single woman, preferably a divor-cée, who was not looking to get married."

"You wanted a short affair. A vacation fling to take your mind off your last case. No strings attached."

"That was the plan," Simon said. "I told myself I would look for a reckless, indepen-dent lady who held modern, sophisticated views when it came to relationships."

"You found her."

Lyra stood on tiptoe, wrapped her arms around his neck, and brushed her mouth across his. Testing her powers of seduction. Hoping she had not misread the heat in his eyes.

"Lyra."

Her name was a husky whisper on his lips.

He tightened his grip on her waist, pulled her close, and took control of the kiss. The fierceness of his response thrilled her and briefly overwhelmed her senses. The atmo-sphere in the room was suddenly charged with a hot, sensual energy. She would have collapsed if he had not held her so tightly.

She had run a number of experiments with kissing over the years and had become adept at the art. But no man had ever kissed her like this. She knew that for the first time in her life she was experiencing something beyond casual sexual attraction, an emotion that was more intense, more compelling. Passion. The kind that left a woman breathless, the kind that could change her life. And this was it. Regardless of the outcome, this was a kiss she would never forget.

She launched herself into the storm.

CHAPTER 32

Angela Merryweather studied the stranger standing in the middle of the living room and told herself she had been a fool to let Luther Pell into the house. What smart woman opened a door to a man at four thirty in the morning?

Everything about him set off warning bells. Her intuition told her he was ruthless and driven. She suspected that he carried a gun under his elegantly tailored jacket.

When he had arrived a short time ago and told her why he wanted to talk to her, she had known the smart thing to do would be to send him away and lock the door. But instinct had warned her it would not be that easy to get rid of him. And deep down she desperately wanted to talk to someone about the terrible thing that had happened to her. She wanted someone to believe her and tell her it was not her fault that she had been kidnapped and violated. She yearned for an avenging angel or the devil — she no longer cared which one showed up so long as he promised to destroy those who had hurt her.

The rage seethed inside her night and day. It kept her awake and stole the light from every aspect of her life. Her marriage was falling apart because of what had happened. She knew the only reason Bradley had not filed for a quiet Reno divorce was because it would ruin his plans for a political career. He felt trapped in the marriage, not only because he needed her money but because the damned photos could destroy him. He blamed her for the disaster. That was what hurt the most. They had been friends and lovers at one time. Now he despised her and she yearned to be free of him. But she could not shake the heavy burden of guilt she carried. She felt responsible for the threat that was hanging over his head. She could not bring herself to walk out because the kidnappers would still have leverage over him. The photos could do enormous damage regardless of whether or not she and Bradley got a quiet divorce. The press would make him look like a cuckold.

Bradley would be furious if he knew that she was about to confide her secret to a stranger. But Bradley was not home this morning. He was gone a lot these days, preferring to spend his time at the office and the beach house.

"I'm sorry your friend is missing, Mr. Pell, but I don't see how I can help you," she said.

"I want you to tell me everything you can about the kidnappers and the place where you were held," Luther said.

"I was warned that not only would I pay a heavy price if I did not keep quiet, my husband and my family would also be badly hurt."

"Blackmail?"

"Yes."

"They've got something on you? Secrets?"

"They didn't know anything about me or my family, really. Just that we have money and that my husband is preparing to go into politics. So no, they didn't dig up any deep, dark secrets. They created new ones."

"Why you?"

She sighed. "I don't think I was targeted directly. I suspect I was the victim of some very clever advertising aimed at women in my position. Women of means."

"Wealthy women who move in certain social circles?"

"Yes. Every two months since the spa opened last year I received a handwritten invitation from Madam Guppy offering me a week of tranquility and three full days of exclusive, personally designed spa treatments. It's billed as a vacation for the fashionable woman who needs time away from the demands of family and society, time to fortify the mind and rejuvenate the body. I ignored the invitations until I finally decided to accept one."

"Sounds like the kidnappers put a lot of hooks in the water, see who takes the bait, and then select one."

She winced. "Talk about fishing in a barrel. Only wealthy women can afford Guppy's spa. I'm sure those are the only ones who receive the invitations. The vast majority of the ladies who move in my social circle would be lured by the promise of a few days of peace and privacy during which they can indulge themselves at an exclusive hotel and spa. The rich suffer from strained nerves and stress, too, just like everyone else, Mr. Pell."

"I know." He paused a beat. "Photographs?"

She raised her brows. "You're very insightful. Yes, they took photographs of me with a man. I was chained to a bed. I was nude. They threatened to mail them to all of our friends, the people at my husband's club,

310

his business acquaintances, and the press. Bradley would be ruined before he even got his campaign off the ground."

"The photos would destroy him and humiliate you."

"Technically, I wasn't raped, Mr. Pell, but only because the bastard who assaulted me could not get an erection. The photographs don't show that, however. They were taken from angles that make it appear he forced himself inside me. Going to the police wouldn't do any good, because I never saw his face. He and the woman behind the camera wore hideous rubber masks, the kind that are used in spas to smooth wrinkles."

"You're sure the photographer was a woman?"

"Yes. She never spoke a word, her entire head and face were covered by the mask, and she wore a long, flowing caftan so I couldn't see her body, but she was definitely female. And before you ask, there is no way I can prove what happened to me."

"I don't need proof, Mrs. Merryweather. I believe every word you're saying."

"You've received a ransom note, I assume?"

"No," Luther said. "There have been no demands, and that's what worries me the most. Talk to me, Mrs. Merryweather. Tell me everything you know, and regardless of the outcome, I will be in your debt. You can call in the favor anytime."

"I don't need your money, Mr. Pell. Bradley married me for my trust fund, but I am the only one who can access it. If I leave, the money goes with me."

"I have connections on both sides of the law, and sometimes those can be more useful than money."

"I do not doubt that. But you don't have to offer me an incentive, Mr. Pell. The only thing I ask is that if you are successful you will destroy the people who kidnapped your friend and me."

"You have my word on it."

The words were a solemn vow, Angela thought. A tiny spark of hope flared inside her.

"Thank you," she said. "I will tell you what I can, but I don't know if I can help you. I never saw anything except the actual room where I was held. They used drugs and blindfolds when they kidnapped me. I was blindfolded again when I was taken to the train station."

"Let's start with the drugs. How were they administered?"

"I've thought about that a lot," Angela

said. "There were no pills. No injections.
The drugs must have been in the tea."

CHAPTER 33

Lyra found herself fighting an exhilarating battle across the sitting room. It was almost five o'clock in the morning and she'd had no sleep but she was on fire. So was Simon. They struggled to get rid of their clothes and hang on to each other at the same time. Her shoes and her blouse were already on the carpet. So was his shirt. She was curiously light-headed. An intoxicating sense of anticipation and certainty heated her blood.

She was aroused and excited to a degree that was beyond anything she had ever experienced. Her panties were damp and Simon had not yet done anything more than kiss her.

By the time they got through the doorway her fingers were shivering so badly it was all she could do to tug his undershirt off over his head.

For a moment she was mesmerized by the sight of his bare, sleekly muscled chest. She flattened her palms on his warm skin and stroked slowly down to the waist of his trousers, savoring the heat and strength of him.

"You are amazing," she whispered.

He gave a hoarse crack of bemused laughter. "No, you're the amazing one. Unique. Fascinating. There are no words. I've never met anyone like you, Lyra Brazier." He reached behind her and undid the fastening of her silky bra. When it fell to the floor he closed his palms over her breasts. "And you're beautiful. Perfect."

"Obviously you need your glasses, but you do make me feel beautiful." She could have sworn that some of the energy in the room was coming from her. She wondered if she was glowing. "You make me feel like a goddess."

He caught her face between his hands. "You *are* a goddess."

She unbuckled his leather belt, got his trousers undone, and pushed them down to his ankles. He kicked the pants out of the way. His snug briefs did little to conceal the size of his erection. She stared down at the evidence of his arousal, shocked.

A flicker of uncertainty whispered through her. She wondered if she was in over her head. She considered herself a modern,

315

sophisticated woman. She had seen her share of naked and scantily dressed men. But this was . . . unexpected.

"Lyra?"

She recovered in a heartbeat. She was not about to stop now. She took a shaky breath and cupped him in one hand. He was heavy, thick, full, and absolutely rigid.

He groaned at the intimate touch. His mouth came down on hers again in a deep, wet kiss that made her feel deliciously scandalous. His palms slipped down her hips, stripping off her panties.

He scooped her up, carried her across the shadowed room, and settled her on the bed.

"I'll be back in a minute," he promised. "Don't go anywhere."

She levered herself up on one elbow and watched him disappear through the doorway. A few seconds later he reappeared, carrying his briefcase. The laughter bubbled up inside her.

"What?" he said, aggrieved. "You've never seen a naked man with a briefcase?"

"Nope. This is a first."

He set the briefcase on the floor beside the bed and unlatched it. "I like to keep it close at hand."

"Right. Your gun is inside."

"That is not the only reason I want it

316

handy tonight."

He reached into the briefcase and took out a small tin.

"You brought prophylactics?" she said. "I'm impressed. But you and I didn't exactly get off to a warm start. What on earth made you think that we would wind up in bed together? Oh, wait. You were hoping to meet up with a reckless divorcée in Burning Cove. That's why you happen to have that tin in your briefcase."

"The original plan was derailed, but I like to think I'm adaptable."

He sheathed himself, got into bed, and came down on top of her, caging her between his arms. He took her mouth in another scorching kiss. She sank her nails into his muscled back and abandoned herself to the demands of the urgent hunger that was building inside her.

He moved his lips to her throat and then he was using his tongue on her nipples. She was so sensitive now she gave a tiny, muffled yelp. She reached down between them and wrapped her fingers around his erection.

He sucked in a harsh breath. "Better not do that. I won't be able to last."

"I don't want you to last," she whispered. "I need you to finish this soon or I'll scream."

"Wouldn't want that. It would scare the other guests on this floor."

"Exactly." She tightened her fingers around him and tugged gently.

In response, he drew his palm down over her belly and lower still. The tension deep inside her ratcheted up several more notches. Her breath tightened in her chest. The small muscles at her core began to clench and unclench. She tightened her grip on him.

When he began to stroke the aching bud between her thighs, she levitated partway off the bed.

"You are so hot," he rasped. "So wet. I can't take any more of this."

"Good. Neither can I. Finish it."

He settled himself between her legs and thrust into her, going deep and hard.

Pain ripped through her. The thrilling tension dissolved in an instant, leaving her gasping, outraged.

Simon froze. "What the hell?"

"It's not supposed to hurt this much the first time, damn it. Vivian lied to me. *A mere pinch,* she said. *You'll hardly notice,* she said."

Simon's eyes were blazing, but she could not tell if he was stunned or furious or both.

"Why didn't you tell me?" he grated. "You should have warned me."

"What business was it of yours? Did you tell your partner the first time you had sex?"

"That was different."

"I don't see why."

"You let me think you were experienced."

"I *am* experienced. I've been out on more dates than I can count, and I was engaged for a while. I've kissed a lot of men and I've seen a fair number of nude males because occasionally I help my sister with her art photography. I just never went all the way."

He narrowed his eyes. "Why? Saving yourself for marriage?"

"No. There were other reasons."

"Such as?"

"I just wanted it to happen with the right man."

"And you picked me to run your grand experiment?"

She gripped his shoulders. "Yes, I chose you. Because you are the right man. In fact, you're perfect. Just what I wanted. Don't panic. I don't expect you to propose because of what happened. I thought I made it clear I don't plan to marry."

"I am not in a panic," Simon said through set teeth. "I'm annoyed. Irritated. Angry. There's a difference."

"I think you're in a panic. It's the only explanation for this sudden mood swing."

"That is not true. Being mad accounts for my current mood."

"All right," she said, trying for a soothing tone. "Why are you angry?"

"Because you used me, damn it."

She stared up at him, shocked. "No."

"Yes, you did. You were curious, admit it. You wanted to experience sex and you used me to get that experience."

"That is not true. If I wanted to have sex just for the sake of experience, I've had plenty of other opportunities. I was engaged, remember?"

"Why didn't you carry out your big experiment with him?"

She felt herself flush. "He told me he didn't want to risk getting me pregnant. He said there would be gossip if we suddenly had to move the wedding date forward. I realize now that he was trying to figure out how to avoid marrying me."

"He panicked."

"Yep. I seem to have that effect on men."

"I am not panic-stricken, damn it."

"I thought you wanted me as badly as I wanted you," she whispered. "Was I mistaken?"

"No."

"Do you regret having sex with me?"

"That is not the point, Lyra, and you

know it."

"You wanted a reckless, fast, modern woman. Preferably a divorcée. Okay, I failed to meet the last requirement, but you have to admit I fit all your other criteria."

"I can't believe we're having this argument."

"Are you going to finish this? Because, if not, you should remove yourself from me and my bed."

His eyes got a little hotter. This time the fire was unmistakably sensual.

"That sounds like a dare," he said.

She framed his face in her hands. "Don't worry, I'll make sure it's good for you."

"Is that so?"

"My mother explained to me that it's easy for a woman to fake an orgasm. She said sometimes a wife does it just to make sure her husband doesn't feel that he failed. My sister, Vivian, assured me that there was no real trick to it. Just a few gasps and a moan or two. Men fall for it every time, she says."

Simon clamped a hand over her mouth. "Don't say another word. I don't think my nerves can take it."

She nodded quickly to show she understood. With his hand firmly plastered across her mouth, he started to move deep inside her. His eyes locked with hers.

"Don't even think of faking it," Simon warned.

She nodded again and considered her situation. She was still uncomfortable, but some of the exciting urgency and tension she had been experiencing earlier began to return. Pain and urgency blurred and then tension became the dominant sensation. Once again everything inside her got tight. Intuitively she started to clench and unclench around him.

Simon groaned. His jaw could have been carved from stone. His eyes were fierce now. She knew he was fighting to hold on to his control. He took his hand away from her mouth.

In the next moment she had to squeeze her eyes shut because she could no longer focus on anything except the growing tightness in her lower body. It was once again becoming unbearable. She dug her fingers into Simon's shoulders and fought him for the release she sensed was almost upon her.

The rippling waves of the climax cascaded through her. She was still trying to cope with the flood of sensations when Simon began moving faster, driving deep in long, urgent thrusts. His back arched. His mouth opened on a low roar. He looked like a man facing heaven or hell. She felt his release crash through him.

She held him close until he collapsed on top of her.

There was a long moment of silence while Simon caught his breath. Then he rolled off to one side.

"Please tell me you didn't fake it," he said.

"I didn't fake it. Please tell me you're not still mad at me."

"I'm exhausted," Simon said. "I don't have enough energy left to be mad. Ask me again in the morning."

"It is morning." She stretched her arms over her head and smiled up at the ceiling. "I wonder if this is how lovers usually talk after having sex."

"Can't speak for anyone else, but I can tell you I've never had a conversation like this in my entire life."

The phone rang.

Simon rolled out of bed. "That will be a message from Pell. For once his timing is excellent."

CHAPTER 34

"Your theory is right," Luther said. "It's a kidnapping ring that targets women connected to wealthy families. The bastards take compromising pictures to use as insurance that no one goes to the police."

"In other words, the ransom isn't the end of it," Simon said.

He was in a public phone booth near the tennis courts. He had arranged a stack of coins on the shelf beneath the phone. He had his story ready in the event someone wondered why he was using a phone that was probably meant for the employees, but luckily there was no one else around at that hour.

"Angela Merryweather's husband has political ambitions," Luther said. "Every indication is that he is headed for the Senate. If he makes it, those photos will give the kidnappers a hell of a lot of leverage over him."

"How bad are the photos?"

"Mrs. Merryweather says they were taken shortly after she was kidnapped. She was awake but still under the effects of the drug they used to knock her out before they grabbed her. In the pictures she is nude and chained to a four-poster bed. She is not wearing a blindfold. There is one man visible, the bastard who assaulted her. He's naked, too, but he wore a rubber mask. Mrs. Merryweather says it's the kind that are used for facial treatments in spas. It was violet colored."

"Which means it came from Guppy's House of Beauty."

"Presumably. There was a woman behind the camera. She wore a spa mask and a shapeless gown. No distinguishing features except her perfume. The house brand. Violet."

"Mrs. Merryweather was raped."

"She says the bastard was never able to penetrate her, which evidently infuriated him. She was afraid he might strangle her on the spot, but the woman behind the camera grabbed his arm and pushed him toward the door. He left the room. The woman picked up the photo equipment and followed him. Mrs. Merryweather never saw either one of them again."

"If Mrs. Merryweather wasn't able to see the faces of either person, she probably couldn't give you much of a description."

"Mrs. Merryweather," Luther said evenly, "is a very angry woman. She is also a very observant lady. She said that, although she couldn't see the man's face, she did notice a large birthmark on his upper right chest. She told me his chest and pubic hair are dark brown. He was athletically built."

"Anything else? A ring, maybe?"

"No ring. She was very sure of that. She looked for one."

"What about his voice?"

"He never spoke. Just grunted a few times. The woman behind the camera didn't say a word, either. Mrs. Merryweather got the feeling that as far as the woman was concerned it was all business. But the man with the birthmark was definitely unbalanced."

Simon thought about that. "They didn't speak because they were afraid she might recognize their voices. That indicates they were people she might have come in contact with at the hotel. What did she tell you about the bedroom where she was held?"

"The linens were scented with Guppy's signature scent."

"Violet," Simon said.

"Right. She said the towels in the bathroom also came from the hotel. She got a plate of cold breakfast rolls and a pot of herbal tea once a day. All of it was served on hotel dishes. She stopped drinking the tea and eating the rolls, because they were all poisoned with some sort of drug that made her hallucinate and eventually fall into a heavy sleep."

"Someone is driving to and from the location every day to deliver the food and the tea. The place where they kept her can't be that far away from the hotel."

"I agree," Luther said. "She felt the driving time back to the location where Draper picked her up and took her to the train station was about half an hour."

"And according to Draper, another half hour or forty minutes into town," Simon said. "But the kidnappers might have used a circuitous route to confuse their captives. What did Mrs. Merryweather recall about the room besides the four-poster bed?"

"Nice furniture but dated. She said the tile work and the bath fixtures looked like they had been designed for a wealthy individual about a decade ago — shortly before the crash."

"Someone in ill health who moved to the desert in hopes of benefitting from the mineral springs," Simon said.

"Mrs. Merryweather also remembers that she was forced to walk up one flight of stairs to get to the bedroom, so we know the house is at least two stories. The windows in the bedroom and bath were boarded up, so she never saw the landscape outside, but she was certain that on the way to the pickup location she was driven downhill for a ways."

"The cabin is in the foothills," Simon said. "Sounds like the house is, too. That gives us a lot to work with. Meanwhile, Lyra and I have made some progress here."

In short, efficient sentences he filled Luther in on the discovery of the murder in the paraffin bath.

"We're waiting for the body to be found so that we can get a positive ID, but Lyra thinks the victim is one of the treatment ladies, Miss Frampton. She gave Miss Kirk a facial and appears to have been involved in the kidnapping ring."

"If that's true, and she's dead, it probably means she knew too much and had become a liability," Luther said. "It's also possible that she tried to blackmail him."

"Or maybe someone is closing down the business. Did Mrs. Merryweather know if there was a guard posted at the house where they kept her?"

"She said she was chained to the wall and there was a heavy bolt on the other side of the door, but for the most part the house felt empty. With the exception of the man who assaulted her and the photographer, the only other person she came in contact with was the person who brought the food each day. He wore a mask, too, never stayed long, and never spoke."

"So we're looking for a large home in the foothills that was probably built in the twenties and is now at least partially boarded up. There can't be that many houses fitting the description. Where are you? I'll call you as soon as I have more information."

"Don't bother. I'm on my way to Labyrinth Springs."

Simon hesitated. "I'm not sure that's a good idea."

"I'll be there in two hours. Where shall I meet you?"

Simon abandoned the argument. There was no point. Nothing he could say would stop Luther. Besides, if they were getting close to finding Raina, it would be good to have someone else with a gun handy.

"On the way into town you'll see a gas station," he said. "There's a diner next door to it. It's a little after five now. It will be open by the time you arrive. Lyra and I will meet you there."

"Right."

"Wait, before you hang up, did Irene Ward find out anything about those newspaper clippings that might help us?"

"Just that the story was true, as far as it went. A woman took a sailboat out, apparently got caught in a storm, and was never seen again. The husband moved back to Boston and became a recluse until he died. But there was one new detail. The husband was rumored to have been confined to an asylum for the insane."

"You think the woman who vanished at sea was Miss Kirk, don't you?"

"I think there's a very high probability that the wife who found herself married to a dangerous madman and risked her neck to escape was Raina, yes."

Simon heard the receiver slam into the cradle on the other end of the line. The phone went dead.

CHAPTER 35

Simon came through the door of the suite just as the young man from room service finished setting up the breakfast Lyra had ordered.

"Oh, there you are, dear," she said. "I hope you had a nice early-morning walk. This is Ted. He was just telling me there's a rumor going around that the spa will be closed today. They say a body was found in the paraffin bath room. Can you imagine? It gives one cold chills just to think about it. The police have been summoned, of course."

"I'm shocked." Simon closed the door and glared at Ted. "Another accident, I suppose? Mrs. Cage had a very close call in the steam room yesterday. Obviously the spa is a dangerous place. I've forbidden my wife to take any more treatments there."

Lyra shot him a sharp, quelling glare, but she decided to let the *I've forbidden my wife*

331

comment go. Simon was staying in character, playing the part of an outraged husband.

"Mr. Billingsley, the owner of the hotel, and Madam Guppy are very concerned," Ted said quickly. "They have instructed the staff to assure the guests that it was an accident, but the spa has been closed while the police investigate."

"Were you acquainted with the victim?" Simon asked. "Was it one of the guests?"

"No, sir. It was Miss Frampton, a treatment lady. But she did facials. No one knows why she would have gone into the paraffin bath room in the middle of the night. It's very strange. The other treatment ladies are afraid to go back to work now."

Lyra picked up the coffeepot and poured two cups. "Ted told me management is trying to keep things quiet but some of the staff think the death was the work of a madman. A fiend."

"That's right," Ted said. He lowered his voice. "Sally, the treatment lady who sets up the paraffin bath every morning, is the one who found the body. She says Miss Frampton was in the tub and covered head to toe in paraffin. She looked like a wax statue, Sally said. They had to peel the stuff off her face to see who it was."

"Poor Sally must be very upset," Lyra

remarked, not without genuine sympathy. The memory of Miss Frampton shrouded in wax would haunt her dreams for a long time to come; maybe for the rest of her life.

"Yes, ma'am," Ted said. "It was a real shock to her nerves."

Lyra shuddered and handed Ted a hefty tip. "A perfectly reasonable reaction, if you ask me. Thank you so much for the prompt service this morning, Ted. Mr. Cage and I appreciate it. We're early risers, as you can see."

"Anytime, ma'am." Ted gave her a grateful smile and pocketed the money. "Call room service when you're finished and I'll pick up the tray."

"I will do that," Lyra assured him.

Ted crossed the room with a jaunty stride and let himself out into the hall. When he was gone Simon sat down at the table, removed the lid of a silver dish, and helped himself to a large portion of scrambled eggs. He shook his head, bemused.

"I can't get over how you can get anyone to talk," he said around a mouthful of eggs.

Lyra sat down, deliberately moving her body in a subtle, gliding twist that caused the silk dressing gown to swirl around her. She watched covertly, but as far as she could tell, Simon did not notice the glimpse of bare thigh that she had allowed to be revealed. He was too busy wolfing down the scrambled eggs and bacon and biscuits she had ordered for him.

She stifled a small sigh and reminded herself that he was working now, doing his job. Conducting an investigation. Clearly he had set aside all thoughts of the passionate interlude they had shared only a short time ago.

Or perhaps he was trying to forget the episode entirely.

That possibility cast a shadow over an otherwise lovely desert morning. She reminded herself that she had no right to be in good spirits anyway. A woman had been brutally murdered during the night and Raina was still missing. This was no time to be indulging romantic memories; no time to dream of a future with a man who was annoyed because she hadn't met all of his requirements in a lover.

She put down her cup and buttered a bite of biscuit.

"I do now," she announced.

Simon snapped off a piece of bacon with his teeth and chewed with the determination of a man who is worried about where his next meal will come from.

"What?" he said.

She popped the little chunk of buttered biscuit into her mouth, munched, swallowed, and then dabbed at her lips with her napkin. She smiled.

"Oh, nothing important," she said. "I merely remarked that I now meet all the requirements you demand in a lover. Okay, I'm not a divorcée, but aside from that —"

Simon turned red. "This is not the time to discuss that."

She raised her brows. "Our relationship? All right, we'll save the chat for later. Back to business. You heard what Ted from room service said. The hotel management is going to try to pass off the murder of Miss Frampton as a dreadful accident."

Simon went back to his eggs and bacon, clearly relieved by the change of subject.

"It won't work," he said. "I doubt the police will go along with it. But even if they do, the hotel and spa staff won't be able to keep their mouths shut. This is a small town. I can see the headlines already: *Fiend Buries Woman in Hot Wax at Local Spa.*"

"No doubt."

"The murderous-fiend-on-the-loose angle will work better for the killer or killers, anyway. It will distract the public and the police."

"I agree." Lyra picked up her coffee cup.

"Well? Don't keep me in suspense. What did Luther Pell tell you?"

Simon's eyes heated with a familiar intensity. "We're looking for a nice house in the foothills about thirty minutes from the cabin where we found Miss Kirk's notebook. Mrs. Merryweather told Luther she was held in an upstairs bedroom, chained to the wall. Food came from the hotel kitchen."

"This hotel?"

"Yes. Her captors always wore spa masks that covered their faces and heads. And yes, the kidnapping was done for the usual reasons — money and blackmail."

"Blackmail?"

"Photos were taken."

"Those bastards. They not only kidnapped her, they raped her?"

"She was assaulted, and the photos appear graphic, but she said the man who did it was unable to get an erection. He was never able to penetrate her but in the photos it appears that he succeeded. The man wore a spa mask, but he had a distinguishing birthmark on his upper chest."

"Anything else?"

"Dark hair on his chest and . . . elsewhere. Athletically built. The ransom demand was telephoned to Mr. Merryweather within

336

hours after they grabbed her."

"But there has been no ransom demand in Raina's case. It's exactly as Kevin Draper told us — they took her for a different reason."

"Pell is convinced this is connected to Miss Kirk's past."

"He thinks Raina may have been the woman in those clippings, doesn't he?" Lyra said. "The one in Bar Harbor who disappeared on a sailboat."

"Yes. Pell told me that Irene Ward dug up some new information. There were rumors in Bar Harbor that the marriage was unhappy. Mr. Whitlock kept his wife a virtual prisoner. A lot of people in town suspected that he somehow murdered Mrs. Whitlock and made it look as if she had been lost at sea."

"But he died about eighteen months later."

Simon finished the eggs and put down his fork. "The rumor in Boston is that he died in an asylum, not at home. Suicide."

Lyra tapped her fingers on the side of her cup. "What if the husband isn't dead? Maybe his family made him disappear inside a psychiatric institution and told everyone he fell down the stairs. Maybe he escaped."

Simon's eyes tightened at the corners. "And came looking for Raina? It's a possibility. But that would mean he knew Guppy was in the kidnapping business out here in California."

"Don't forget she had a long history in New York before she moved her spa to Labyrinth Springs. From the outset she catered to the social world. That's a small one. She and Whitlock may have known each other."

"Very true. It's interesting that Guppy suddenly closed down her New York business and opened up on the other side of the country."

Lyra considered briefly for a moment. "There's another possibility. Raina told me she worked for a small but exclusive law firm in New York. It handled a lot of confidential business for its clients. Secretaries know all the secrets. Maybe someone thinks she knows too much, tracked her down to Burning Cove, and arranged to lure her to Labyrinth Springs so that she could be kidnapped without drawing Luther Pell's attention."

"If that was the plan, it failed," Simon said. "I agree, it's on the list of possible motives, but, again, we don't have time to investigate that angle. Our priority this morning is to find the house where they're holding Miss Kirk."

The cup in Lyra's fingers trembled. She put it down very carefully.

"If Raina is still alive," she said.

"We keep going until we find her, regardless. Pell needs to know what happened to her."

"So do I, but I was hoping you would offer a more optimistic scenario."

"You want optimism? Here's what I've got — Mrs. Merryweather's description of the house where she was held. It's called a lead, Lyra. We run it down."

"Right." Lyra straightened in her chair. She had a job to do. "How do we set about looking for it? There are private homes scattered around Labyrinth Springs. Most are miles apart. It could take days to locate them all and try to figure out which one the kidnappers are using."

"Not if you call in an expert," Simon said.

"Who in the world — ?"

"An ambitious real estate agent who knows the local market well."

"That," Lyra said slowly, "is a brilliant idea."

"Thank you. As I believe I've mentioned, I've been doing this sort of work for a while now."

"I have so much to learn."

"You're getting a crash course in the investigation business." Simon tossed his napkin down on the table and got to his feet. "Let's move. Pell's on his way here. We're going to meet him on the outskirts of town in about two hours. That gives us time to wake up a local real estate agent and see if we can pinpoint the property."

She shot to her feet. "I'll get dressed." She rushed toward the bedroom doorway, pausing at the entrance to look back. "It occurs to me that we may know more about the house than we think."

"What's that?"

"We know the kidnappers are linked to the hotel and the spa. The new owner purchased the resort about two years ago and opened it a year later, the same time that Guppy moved her spa here. The kidnappings started soon afterward. I'll bet the house where the captives are held was probably acquired at about the same time. Every real estate agent remembers sales, especially in a small community like Labyrinth Springs."

Simon's brows rose. "You're a fast learner."

His praise sent a little burst of pleasure through her. She hurried into the bedroom and pulled on a pair of rust-brown trousers and a long-sleeved, cream-colored blouse. She was tying the laces on her sport shoes when Simon appeared in the doorway. He had his briefcase in one hand. He looked at the bed.

"What is the housekeeper going to think?" he asked.

Lyra glanced at the tumbled bedding and the telltale stains on the once-pristine white sheets.

"The housekeeper will assume the obvious," she said, pulling a scarf out of the drawer. "We're a couple of honeymooners who couldn't figure it out the first night but managed to get it right on the second night."

Simon shook his head. Reluctant amusement lit his eyes. "You've got an answer for everything, don't you?"

"No, I don't, but that's okay. It's the stuff I don't know that keeps life interesting."

CHAPTER 36

The sound of a heavy bolt being slid aside brought her out of the restless, nightmare-laced sleep that had finally overtaken her. Raina sat up on the edge of the four-poster bed. She glanced at her watch and saw that it was six fifteen. There was no way to know if it was morning or night; no way to know how much time she had lost.

The door opened. A man in a violet-colored rubber mask entered, a tray in his hands. He was silhouetted against a murky daylight emanating from windows elsewhere in the house.

That answered one question: It was morning.

"What day is it?" she said. She was startled by how thick the words sounded.

The man in the rubber mask did not answer. He set the tray down and left. She caught a glimpse of the heavy bolt on the other side of the door. Despair threatened to overwhelm her. With luck and the proper tool she might be able to pick the lock on the manacle, but she didn't stand a chance against the bolt. It could be unlocked only from outside the room.

She pushed herself to her feet and looked at the tray. More hotel breakfast rolls and another pitcher of tea. This was the third food delivery so it was most likely the third morning of her captivity. It was hard to keep track of time because the drugs had left her confused and disoriented. She was hungry because yesterday, in addition to dumping the tea down the sink, she had crumbled the poisoned rolls and flushed them down the toilet. But the drug had exacted a heavy toll. It had been difficult to think clearly, and in the end she had slept for most of the day and night. The result was that she had not been able to put together a coherent escape plan.

This morning she was a little light-headed from lack of food but she could finally focus. She disposed of the food and the tea, drank a couple of glasses of water, and tried to take stock of her situation.

She was still properly dressed, although her clothes were badly rumpled. Her hair had been in a chignon when she had collapsed in the hotel room. Now it hung in

343

tendrils. There were, however, a few pins left. She removed them carefully and gripped them as if they were more precious than gold.

She went back into the bedroom and studied it carefully, noting details and filing each piece of furniture, every architectural feature, and every object under one of two categories — useful or not useful.

The furniture was expensive, heavy, traditional. The patterns on the faded wallpaper and curtains were at least a decade out of date. There were a couple of elaborately framed but decidedly insipid paintings featuring bowls of flowers. A handful of items was scattered on the small dressing table. An empty perfume bottle — not Violet — and an old hairbrush.

She clanked her way to the dressing table. Methodically she opened drawers. There wasn't much left inside. She found a couple of tubes of used lipstick. The shades were out of date. There were an empty pack of cigarettes and a book of matches in the center drawer. The matchbook was violet. LABYRINTH SPRINGS HOTEL & SPA was stamped on the cover.

For the first time it occurred to her to wonder what had happened to her clothes and toiletries. The kidnappers must have packed them up. They could hardly afford to leave them in room two twenty-one for the housekeeper to find.

There was a closet at the far end of the bedroom. The doors were closed. There was no way to know if her things were inside.

She sat down on the bed, propped her chained ankle on the opposite knee, and went to work on the manacle with one of the hairpins.

CHAPTER 37

The rumble of a vehicle in the drive shattered the oppressive silence of the big, empty house. Raina stopped pacing and checked her watch. Panic sparked. It was mid-morning. The drugged food had been delivered hours ago. Why would the kidnappers return now?

The pattern that had been established yesterday had been broken. That was not a good sign. Her plan, such as it was, had been built around what she assumed to be the food delivery schedule.

She heard the door open on the ground floor. Voices. Two men, not one. Another break in the pattern. Yesterday and today the man who had delivered the food had arrived alone and never spoken.

"I'll get her," one of the men said. "With luck she'll be semiconscious or maybe asleep by now because of the rolls and the tea."

"Hurry," the other man said. "The boss says they're looking for her. We can't take the chance that they'll find her. We have to get rid of her."

"No one was supposed to get hurt," the first man said.

"People have already gotten hurt, in case you haven't noticed. You think Frampton got into that paraffin bath all by herself? Plans change."

Yes, they do, Raina thought. She double-checked her preparations. She had freed herself from the manacle. The chain was now arranged on the floor so that it led from the wall ring into the bathroom. She had closed the door as far as possible. The objective was to make it appear that she was making use of the facilities.

She had found her suitcase and handbag in the closet, but of course the pistol and the box of ammunition were gone. The original plan had been to use one of the heavy, gilded picture frames on the delivery-man's head, grab his keys, and use his car to get as far away as possible.

But now that she knew there was another man downstairs, things were not going to be simple. She needed a distraction.

Footsteps thudded on the stairs.

She went to the dressing table, picked up

the matchbook, and struck a light. Her hand was trembling. The match went out almost immediately. She struck another one. The flame steadied.

She touched the burning match to the thin material of the lace sheers on the window. The old fabric caught instantly.

She struck another match and set a different section of the lace alight.

The footsteps were in the hall now.

She picked up the heavy wooden picture frame that she had taken down earlier and flattened herself against the wall behind the door.

The bolt slid aside. The door opened partway. A man moved into the room. He was not wearing a spa mask. Another bad sign. It signaled that he didn't care if she could identify him.

He paused briefly, focusing on the chain that led into the bathroom. He did not notice the small fire on the other side of the room.

"Come on out of there," he said. "You're going home today."

He started toward the door of the bath. On the far side of the room the curtains abruptly flared. Smoke billowed.

"What the fuck?" His voice rose. "Pete, there's a fire. Get up here. I need help."

Raina stepped out from behind the door, raised the picture frame, and slammed the sharp corner against the man's skull. He went down without so much as a grunt, but the floorboards shuddered. She knew his companion downstairs must have heard the sound.

"Joe? What's going on up there?" Pete shouted.

Raina crouched beside Joe. He groaned. She debated whether to use the picture frame on him again but quickly decided she couldn't spare the time.

Footsteps pounded on the staircase. Pete ran down the hall.

"Shit, Joe, there's smoke. We gotta get out of here."

The old, sun-faded curtains were going up fast now. The smoke was thickening. Behind the door, Raina waited, clutching the picture frame.

Joe stirred. His eyes opened partway. He struggled to sit up.

"Pete, you gotta help me," he gasped.

Pete finally moved. He lurched out of the doorway and went toward Joe.

"What about the woman?" Pete said.

"Never mind her. Just get me out of here. This old house is a tinderbox."

Raina did not hesitate. This was as good

as it was going to get. With luck the men had left the keys in their vehicle.

She used both hands to hurl the picture frame in the general direction of Pete and Joe and then she bolted out from behind the door and ran into the hall. She paused to glance right and left, spotted the staircase, and rushed toward it.

She was halfway down the stairs, moving so fast she had to keep one hand on the railing to ensure that she did not fall, when a third man appeared. He wasn't wearing a mask, either. He had a gun in his hand.

Billingsley. The owner of the hotel. He had come out of his office to welcome her and hand her the key to room two twenty-one.

"You've ruined everything, Kirk," he said. "I should never have agreed to the deal. Guppy and I had such a sweet game going. But thanks to you and that bitch, I've got a fucking disaster on my hands."

She froze. He knew her real name, the one she had been using since she had stopped being Mrs. Malcolm Whitlock.

"Boss." Pete appeared at the top of the stairs, half dragging the barely conscious Joe. "She set the fucking house on fire."

"What's wrong with Joe?" Billingsley said.

"I think she hit him with a picture frame." Pete started down the stairs, his movements hampered by his burden. "Let's move. This house is old. A lot of the wood is rotten."

"Leave Joe," Billingsley ordered. "Get the woman."

"What?" Pete looked confused. "Why? She's the one who set the fire."

"She's our ticket out of town if someone tries to stop us," Billingsley said. He motioned at Raina. "Get down here. Move or I'll kill you where you are and leave you behind with Joe. In fact, now that I think about it, maybe killing you here and now is the best way out of this thing. The fire will take care of your body. They might never find it, and if they do, they won't be able to identify you."

"Wait, don't shoot her, not yet," Pete yelped. "You might hit me."

There was a thump on the stairs. Raina glanced back and saw that Pete had abandoned Joe and was leaping down the stairs to get to the bottom before Billingsley pulled the trigger.

Even if she reversed course and made her way back up the stairs, she would be trapped by the fire.

That left only one reasonable option. She would try to fake a stumble at the bottom of the stairs. If she managed to collide with Billingsley, she might get another chance to get out the front door.

"Don't shoot," she said. "I'm coming down."

"Hurry," Billingsley snapped. "You'll live as long as you cooperate."

Pete plunged past Raina. When he reached the bottom of the stairs he headed toward the front door. Billingsley ignored him. He motioned with the gun.

"Move, you stupid woman," he roared.

Luther spoke from the shadows of the downstairs hall beneath the stairs.

"Freeze, Billingsley. You *might* live, but only if you drop the pistol."

"Fuck." Billingsley whirled toward the sound of Luther's voice and fired three shots in rapid succession.

A single shot came from the shadows of the hallway. Billingsley jerked violently. He stared down at the bloodstain that was blossoming on the front of his shirt, stupefied.

"Who?" he said. He sank to his knees. The gun clattered on the floor. "Fuck. You're Pell."

"Yes." Luther walked out of the shadows and kicked the gun aside. "You took the wrong woman, Billingsley."

"Guppy warned me you were dangerous. Didn't believe her. Told her . . . told her you were just a small-time crime boss."

Blood gushed out of Billingsley's mouth. He fell facedown at the foot of the stairs.

Luther looked up at Raina. His eyes burned with a cold fire.

"Are you all right?" he asked.

"Yes." She gripped the railing with both hands to steady herself. "I'm okay."

Simon appeared in the doorway. He was not alone. He had Pete. There was a lot of blood on Pete's face.

"What happened to him?" Luther asked.

"Fell over a briefcase," Simon said.

Lyra rushed up to peer over Simon's shoulder.

"I heard shots," Lyra said. "Looks like everyone I care about is still standing, so let's get out of here. In case you hadn't noticed, this house is on fire and the flames are spreading fast."

"Get out of here," Luther said to Raina. He crouched and started unfastening Billingsley's shirt. "Simon and I will handle this."

"Right."

Raina went down the rest of the stairs on trembling legs.

By the time she got to the bottom, Luther had the dead man's shirt off. Her first thought was that he was trying to determine if Billingsley was still alive. Then she realized he was studying a mark on Billingsley's upper chest.

"He had a birthmark?" she said. "Is that important?"

"Very important. Go with Lyra and get the car. Simon and I will haul these three out of here."

"They're not worth bothering with," Raina said.

"They have information," Luther said.

"Including the dead man?"

"Sometimes the dead tell the most interesting stories."

CHAPTER 38

Billingsley's suite was on the third floor. It was easy to identify. In addition to the PRIVATE sign on the door, the lock was more impressive than those on the guest suite doors.

And then there was the unwholesome energy radiating from the door handle. Simon grimaced and jerked his hand off the metal knob.

"Bad?" Luther asked.

"Very."

"Let's move. It won't be long before the police get here. If they find those blackmail photos there won't be any way to keep them from falling into the wrong hands. Someone will realize they are worth a fortune."

Simon shoved the key they had found in Billingsley's pocket into the lock.

"Don't worry," he said. "Raina is a witness with a story to tell and Lyra has a talent for making conversation. They know we need time to find those files. They'll keep the police busy as long as necessary."

He opened the door and moved into the room. Luther followed, closing the door. Simon crossed the space and quickly drew the curtains closed. When he was sure they would not be noticed from the outside, he turned on a couple of lamps.

"I suggest you do a standard search," he said. "I'll try a sweep and see if I can pick up anything interesting."

Luther went to the sofa and started removing cushions. "These are — were — Billingsley's personal quarters. Won't everything in here have the same vibe as the doorknob?"

"Yes," Simon said. He walked slowly around the room, his senses open. "But we're talking about a man who liked to have pictures of himself taken while he was trying to get an erection in front of a woman who was chained to a bed. I'm betting there will be a lot of additional heat around the place where he stored those photos."

"Because they are important to him."

"Yes," Simon said.

He began in the bedroom. It was the place most people stashed their secrets. He went to the doorway and stopped short when he saw the bookcase. It was crammed with volumes.

Luther joined him. "See something?"

"Books." Simon crossed the room and pulled a couple of volumes off the shelf. "A complete set of the Encyclopedia Britannica. No home should be without this invaluable educational tool. You owe it to your children to make this investment. Just ask any door-to-door encyclopedia salesman."

"Let me take a wild guess here," Luther said. "You don't think Billingsley spent his evenings browsing the encyclopedia?"

"No, I don't. None of these books have been handled in a very long time. They're covered in dust." Simon ran his fingertips along the edge of the bookcase. "Here we go."

He tugged on the bookcase. It opened on hinges, revealing the door of a wall safe.

"We're in luck," he said. "Combination lock."

He set his briefcase on the floor, unlatched it, took out the stethoscope, and went to work.

A short time later he opened the safe.

Luther moved into the room. "Anything inside?"

"Some cash," Simon said. "A small bottle and a couple of envelopes." He took out the bottle, removed the top, and sniffed cautiously. The acrid bite of strong herbs made him grimace. "I think this is the stuff that was used to drug Raina and Lyra and the others."

"Leave it in the safe," Luther said. "And the money as well."

Simon replaced the chemical bottle and picked up the envelopes. He opened the first one and removed a legal document.

"It's the deed to the house where we found Raina," he said.

He tossed it aside, opened the second envelope, and dumped several photos onto a table. Each picture showed a nude woman chained to a bed. There was a man in each photo. He wore a rubber spa face mask, but in the images that showed his chest, the birthmark was visible.

"That bastard," Luther said quietly.

Simon sensed the sick heat coming off the pictures. He picked one up and took a closer look. "Shit." He picked up another photo and shook his head. "This is worse than we thought."

"What is it?" Luther asked.

"Take a look." Simon handed him one of the photos. "Billingsley used a blade to cut the throat of each of these women. He fantasized about murdering them."

"We'll burn these immediately."

"That won't protect the victims," Simon said.

"I know. We need to find the negatives, too. As long as they exist, someone can make more prints."

Simon glanced at the open safe. "They should have been in there with the photos. There's no other secure place in this suite."

Luther surveyed the room again. "He must have hidden them somewhere else."

"Pete and Joe told us that Billingsley was the boss, and maybe he was, as far as they were concerned. But Raina is convinced that Guppy was involved in the kidnappings. We assumed she was an accomplice like Frampton, the treatment lady who was murdered. But what if she was more than that? Maybe she was a full partner in the kidnapping operation."

Luther got a thoughtful expression. "Or maybe the one in charge. She's the one who knows the formulas for the drugs. She reigns supreme at the spa. It's her reputation that draws potential victims here to the resort."

"If that's true, she's the one who has the negatives," Simon said. "There's a safe in her office. I opened it last night. There were some financial records and bundles of cash, but no photographs or negatives."

"A safe in a business like Guppy's spa is often opened several times a day. There's a big risk that sooner or later one of the staff — the cashier or the bookkeeper, for example — will discover the combination. If those photos had been found, it would have been the end of Guppy's House of Beauty. If Guppy is the ringleader, I don't think she would keep blackmail negatives in her office safe. More likely they're hidden in her home."

"She lives here at the hotel," Simon said. "But there aren't that many places to hide something as dangerous as those photos in one of these rooms. The spa is her world. She created it and she controls it. From what I saw of the interior there are a lot of places she could conceal half a dozen photographs and negatives. I might be able to find the location."

Luther raised his brows. "The way you found those photos in this suite?"

"It's what I do, Luther. Why you hire me."

"I know." Luther gave him an odd look. "Are you aware that something changes in the atmosphere when you do whatever it is that you do?"

Simon did not move. "I know some people get nervous when they watch me work. It's one of the reasons I rarely work with a partner. Does the shift of energy in the atmosphere bother you?"

"No. I've got other people working for me who radiate some sort of energy when they use their talent. I have no problem with the concept of the paranormal. All I care about are results, and you always come through with those. Do you mind if I ask you a personal question, though?"

"Depends on the question."

"Has Lyra seen you work?"

"Yes."

"She doesn't appear to be nervous or anxious around you."

"No." Simon exhaled slowly. "But she asks a lot questions. She wants to know everything — how it feels when I pick up the heat. If there was anyone else in my family who could do what I do. How I turn my extra senses on and off."

"So? Sounds like she's interested in you. Is that a problem?"

"I'm a new experience for her."

"I repeat, is that a problem?"

"The woman is insatiably curious, Luther. When she starts asking questions, people talk to her."

"Including you?"

"Including me. I swear, it's almost like

mesmerism, except you know what's happening when you start answering her questions. Later you look back and you say, *What the hell was I thinking?*"

Luther's eyes gleamed with a flash of amusement. "I think I'm beginning to understand the problem here."

"We haven't got time for an analysis of my personal life." Simon collected the photos, stuffed them back into the envelope, and slipped the envelope inside his jacket.

"Let's go take a look around Guppy's room," Luther said. "I doubt we'll find another wall safe, but we need to check. After that we'll try the spa."

Simon glanced at the open safe. "What about the money and the bottle of chemicals?"

"Leave both for the cops to find. Make them look good."

There was only one object of interest in Guppy's suite: a large walk-in closet that had been converted into a darkroom.

"She's the one who took the photos and developed them," Luther said.

CHAPTER 39

Simon checked his watch. It was mid-afternoon, but there was no one hanging around the service entrance of the spa. He set his briefcase down in front of the door.

"I don't think anyone is going to interrupt us," Luther said. "The question is, where is Guppy?"

"She's nothing if not a good business-woman," Simon said. "She probably realized things were going downhill fast and took off for L.A."

"If that's true we won't stand a chance of finding the negatives in the spa. She'll have them with her."

"We'll find her," Simon said. "But we need to search the spa first."

The local police had concluded the investigation of the Frampton murder — the special afternoon edition of the *Labyrinth Springs Gazette* had gone with a headline that closely echoed the one he had envi-

sioned at breakfast that morning. FIEND AT-
TACKS WOMAN IN LOCAL SPA, BURIES
HER IN WAX.

Beneath that article had been another
sensational headline: OWNER OF LOCAL
RESORT SHOT DEAD. POLICE SUSPECT
DRUG DEALING.

He gripped the doorknob. A ghostly howl
of violence and rage roared across his
senses. The back of his right hand burned.
His pulse thudded and he started to sweat.

"Shit," he said.

Luther reached inside his jacket and
slipped his gun out of his shoulder holster.
"Hot, I take it?"

"Very. Something bad happened in here."

"The paraffin bath murder?"

"No, this heat is new."

"I don't suppose you can tell who went
through that door last?"

"No," Simon said. "Only that whoever did
was enraged — ready to murder. Not in full
control."

"Bad combination. Billingsley?"

"Maybe. Or Guppy."

Simon tightened his hand around the
doorknob again and tested it. The door was
unlocked. He opened it, picked up his
briefcase, and moved into the storage room.
Luther followed and closed the door.

They both stood quietly for a time, letting their eyes adjust to the gloom and listening for indications that they were not alone.

"What's that smell?" Luther asked.

"Violet perfume," Simon said. "It's a little on the heavy side."

"I'll say. Smells like a funeral parlor." Luther looked around. "Feels empty in here."

"I agree." Simon started forward. "Guppy's office is close to the front entrance, but as I told you, I didn't find anything in the safe except money and some financial records relating to the spa business."

"I like financial records," Luther said. "They are always useful. We'll grab those first. After that we'll search the place and see if you can find any hot spots."

"Right."

They walked slowly past several closed treatment rooms. Simon methodically brushed his fingertips across the doorknobs, each time bracing himself for a jolt.

The paraffin bath room was still hot, but the energy was not as intense as it had been hours earlier.

"That's where Frampton was murdered," he explained to Luther.

"The local paper is declaring it the work of a fiend."

"A fiend, maybe, but not some random killer who happened to target the woman."

"No coincidences in a murder investigation."

"No."

Simon stopped at Guppy's office. The door was locked. He took out the lockpick and went to work. Thirty seconds later they were inside.

He crossed the room to the safe, set his briefcase down on the floor, and crouched next to it. Luther watched the hallway, gun in hand.

"There's some hot energy on the combination lock," Simon said. "It was opened recently. Whoever did it was anxious. Tense. In a rush. But it's not what I felt on the service door."

He opened the safe. Luther swept the beam of the flashlight around the interior. The only thing inside was a stack of receipts.

"This is interesting," Simon said. "The last time I opened it there was a lot of cash inside. A couple thousand bucks, maybe."

"Let's check out the rest of this place. Where do you suggest we start?"

"The steam chamber," Simon said.

He led the way down another hallway and opened the door of the dressing room where he had found Lyra in the shower. There had been no time to repair the window in the door that separated the dressing room from the steam chamber. He tested the handle. The scars on his hand burned. The energy was fading, but there was enough left to tell him that the person who had tried to murder Lyra was not the same individual who had opened the back door of the spa earlier that day.

He had to exert more than the usual amount of control to suppress his fierce response. The effort must have been etched on his face, because Luther looked at him with a curious expression.

"Are you okay?" Luther asked.

"I'm fine."

"Just asking. You don't have to bite my head off."

"Sorry. I can feel the energy of the person who tried to kill Lyra."

"I understand."

Simon remembered the cold fire in Luther's eyes when he had shot Billingsley.

"I know you do," Simon said.

He opened the door, turned on the lights, and made himself walk through the steam chamber with his senses heightened. It was difficult to focus, because there were plenty of hot spots in the room — relatively fresh pools of energy — but they were tinged with panic, fear, and desperation. Usually he could only identify strong emotions, not the individual who had laid down the energy of those emotions. But he realized with a deep sense of certainty that he would know Lyra's energy anywhere. There was a bond between them now. He'd never experienced anything like it.

"Simon?" Luther said quietly.

"Sorry. Got distracted. Lot of energy in here."

He moved on, circling and crisscrossing the steam chamber. When he was finished he went back to the door where Luther stood.

"Nothing out of the ordinary," he said. "Let's try the gym. A lot of possible hiding places in a gym."

They went down the hall to the gymnasium. The door was unlocked. Simon touched the handle and got hit with a flash of rage. There was something else, as well. An overlay of the anxiety and excitement.

"Hot," he said. "And the energy is fairly fresh. Two different people, I think."

Luther took out his gun. "Someone inside?"

"Maybe." Simon peered through the opaque glass set into the door. The room on the other side was cloaked in gloom. "No way to know for sure until I'm inside."

"In my experience, that is usually too late."

"Yeah, that's been my experience, too. Let's see if we can make whoever is in there panic and run."

Simon opened the briefcase and took out his pistol. He and Luther flattened themselves against the wall. Simon opened the door.

Silence. But not the silence of an empty space.

A heartbeat later the shooting started. The glass in the door exploded. Bullets zinged off metal and thudded into the hallway wall.

Footsteps thudded inside the room. A few seconds later a figure rushed out of the gym.

And tripped over the briefcase that Simon had positioned on the threshold of the door. Luther switched on his flashlight.

A man in a hotel uniform sprawled on the tiles. It took a beat for Simon to recognize him.

"The night clerk," he said. "Hiram."

"I didn't do it," Hiram whimpered. "I swear I didn't do it. Nobody was supposed to get hurt."

Luther looked at Simon. "Someone, probably half the guests in the hotel, will have heard the shots. The front desk is probably calling the police right now."

"We'll have to come back later," Simon said. He studied Hiram. "You're the one who takes care of the paperwork needed to cover up the middle-of-the-night checkouts. Did you make up room two twenty-one after the guests were kidnapped?"

Hiram groaned. "Yeah. But I had nothing to do with what happened to those women. All I know is that they were all okay. Draper put them on the train. Nobody got hurt."

"A lot of people did get hurt," Luther said. "But lucky for you we don't have time to go into the details. We'll leave that for the police."

"Fuck," Hiram muttered. "I just came here for the money. Janet Frampton and I were seeing each other. I found out she had the combination of Guppy's safe. She wrote it down and kept it in a drawer in her bedroom. After I heard what happened to Janet I figured I might have a shot at opening the safe. I got the combination, but I had to wait for the cops to leave. When Billingsley took off, I decided to make my play."

"You got the money," Simon said. "Why go into the gym?"

"Janet said she was almost positive Guppy kept the drugs in there. She'd seen Guppy coming out of the gym at odd hours when no one else was around. Janet searched the place several times, but she was never able to find the stuff."

"You're talking about the drugs used to keep the victims in a semiconscious state?" Luther asked.

"Yeah. Guppy gave the drugs to Janet to put into the women's food and tea. After I got the money out of the safe I decided to take a quick look around the gym to see if I could find the stuff. Figured I could sell it on the street in L.A. Lot of drugs in that town. That's when I saw her. I knew I had to get out. Next thing I know, you two are coming through the door."

"Your day is going downhill from here," Luther said. "In a few minutes you'll be talking to the police."

"I didn't kill her," Hiram whimpered. "I swear it. It must have been Billingsley."

"Who is dead in there?" Simon asked.

"You'll see." Hiram shook his head. "I didn't do it."

Sirens wailed in the distance.

Luther hauled Hiram to his feet and turned to Simon. "Let's go take a look."

Simon flipped on the lights. The overhead fixtures illuminated a metal forest of gleaming machines. Some of the equipment was familiar. He recognized the treadmills and

371

weight-lifting apparatus, but many of the devices were nothing short of bizarre.

There were steel cages that had clearly been designed to accommodate a female body. Several machines were equipped with electrically driven rollers. Others featured ominous-looking leather straps. A number of tables had pulleys and cables attached at all four corners.

"Lyra is right," Simon said. "The place looks like a modern version of a medieval torture chamber."

"She's over there," Hiram muttered.

Simon turned around. So did Luther.

There was a woman locked inside one of the humanoid metal cages. She stared out through the bars with unseeing eyes. Her elaborate makeup could not disguise the fact that her features were frozen in a mask of rage and horror.

Luther reached through the bars of the cage to check for a pulse.

"Dead," he announced. "A few hours, I think. Judging by the marks around her throat, she was strangled."

"Edith Guppy," Simon said. "I never met her, but I recognize her because her face is on all the hotel brochures."

"Billingsley killed her, I tell you," Hiram insisted. "It must have been him."

"He realized we were closing in, so he murdered his partner before he went to the house to grab Raina," Luther said quietly. "Or else he was just insane."

"Or both," Simon said.

He walked closer to the steel cage and touched one of the bars. "Same energy I felt in the paraffin bath room where Frampton was murdered. Same stuff that's on the door handle of this room and the door we used to get into the spa tonight. It was on the door of the house where we found Miss Kirk today."

Hiram stared at Simon and then at Luther. "What the hell are you two talking about?"

They ignored him.

"Billingsley killed Frampton and Guppy and tried to murder Raina," Simon said.

"Judging by those photos we found in his safe, Billingsley was mentally unstable," Luther said. "He obviously hated women. Hell, the press got it right. He *was* a fiend."

"The question is, did he come here only to murder Guppy? Or was he searching for the negatives, too?"

"What negatives?" Hiram yelped.

The sirens screamed one last time and stopped somewhere just outside the spa.

"The cops are here," Luther said. "We'll have to deal with this later."

"Nobody was supposed to get hurt," Hiram wailed.

CHAPTER 40

Three hours later Simon threaded a path through the maze of machines, touching each one lightly. He and Luther were alone. The cops were gone now. They had taken Guppy's body and Hiram with them.

Luther had impressed the police with some official-looking identification and assured them they would get all the credit for destroying a major drug ring. Simon had explained that some of the evidence was in plain sight in the form of the chemicals itemized in Guppy's desk calendar. Any chemist would recognize the components of powerful drugs that could induce visions, sleep, and even death. Luther had also suggested that the police search Billingsley's quarters, as he suspected there might be a hidden safe.

Neither of them mentioned the kidnappings. It was unlikely Hiram or Pete or Joe would bring up the subject, either. There was no evidence and it was doubtful that any of the victims would come forward.

"There's a lot of energy in here," Simon said. "Gyms are difficult because people give off a lot of stress and emotional energy when they work out. If someone hasn't touched the hiding place recently and left some very hot prints, I may not be able to get a good read on this room."

He stopped when he saw the large, circular machine in the corner. It looked like a human-sized gyroscope equipped with wrist and ankle attachments. It was mounted on a heavy platform made of steel.

Luther moved to stand beside him. He studied the gyroscope. "I think the idea is to get inside that thing. They strap you in place so you won't fall out. The gyroscope spins you around every which way. Probably makes a person dizzy and nauseous."

"Lyra mentioned this machine," Simon said. "She told me it was the one piece of equipment she really wanted to try, because it looked like a carnival ride. She thought it would be an *interesting experience.*"

Luther's mouth twitched a little at one corner. "Got a problem with curious women?"

"One in particular. Let's just say she definitely qualifies as an *interesting experi-*

ence, herself."

Luther cleared his throat. "Right. Getting back to business. Why are you interested in the gyroscope?"

"Lyra was told it was out of order, so she didn't get the opportunity to use it. She was told it hasn't functioned for quite a while."

"So?"

"It strikes me the device looks like it weighs several hundred pounds."

"No one could walk off with it, that's for sure," Luther said.

"The base of it would make an excellent safe."

Simon walked toward the big gyroscope and touched the metal rings. There was very little energy on the device. It had not been used in a long time.

The heavy metal base, however, gave him a flash of heat. It was not the wild, erratic rage that Billingsley had left on the doors.

"This feels like the vibe I picked up in Guppy's office," he said. "She's been here on a number of occasions."

The combination lock was hidden beneath a steel plate that opened easily once he found the slight indentation that activated the spring mechanism. He pulled his stethoscope out of his briefcase.

"You know, you could have been a successful burglar," Luther remarked.

"I *am* a successful burglar. The only difference between me and my competition is that I work for you."

"That is one way of looking at it."

Simon got the safe open. There were a large envelope and a handful of small jars of chemicals inside. He took out the envelope and gave it to Luther, who opened it.

"Prints and negatives," Luther said. He sounded satisfied. "Same photos we found in Billingsley's suite."

"Guppy gave Billingsley a set of prints to keep him satisfied. She kept the negatives. I'm sure she knew Billingsley was unstable."

"We've got what we came for. Let's get out of here. It's been a long day. I think we all need a drink."

CHAPTER 41

Raina took a sip of her martini and set the glass down with exquisite care. She had to move cautiously, because the occasional bouts of shivering came out of nowhere and washed through her in unpredictable waves.

Luther was sitting close beside her. Evidently sensing her tension, he touched her knee under the table in a silent attempt to reassure her. She raised her chin, took a steadying breath, and looked at the three people who were sharing the booth with her. Luther and Simon and Lyra were waiting for an explanation, but she literally did not know where to begin. Words failed her.

As usual, however, words did not fail Lyra. She swallowed some of her sidecar and cast a disgusted glare around the bar of the Labyrinth Springs Hotel.

"I can't believe we're going to spend another night in this horrid place," she said. "All because of that storm. Gerald was right. It would have been very dangerous to try to get out of this valley and through the mountain pass tonight."

The heavy rains had arrived that afternoon, churning up mud and creating flash floods that made driving next to impossible.

Luther raised his brows. "Who is Gerald?"

Simon answered, his tone very dry, "The waiter who just brought us our drinks. I told you, everyone talks to Lyra."

"He was also kind enough to warn us against the soup," Lyra added. "Apparently the fish that was going bad the other night ended up in it."

"None of us is in any condition to drive, anyway," Luther pointed out. "We all need rest."

"I was afraid the hotel might shut down suddenly, stranding us and the rest of the guests," Lyra said. "But Gerald told me that the front desk got a phone call from the law firm in New York that handles the Billingsley estate. The lawyer instructed everyone to remain on duty until they could get someone out here to assess the situation. He said the staff will receive regular wages until a decision has been made. That is very good news for Gerald and the others who work here. They still have jobs."

"If they're smart, they will all start looking for other jobs tomorrow," Luther said. "I predict the resort won't last long now that the spa is closed."

Lyra made a face. "You're probably right."

Raina began to relax a little as the easy conversation flowed around her. She was among friends.

She finally found her voice.

"I owe the three of you more than I can ever repay," she said.

"You don't owe me anything," Luther said, his voice a little too cold and flat.

She realized he was offended; no, more than offended. He was hurt.

"I'm sorry," she whispered. "I don't know what else to say. What happened is my fault. Everything is my fault. I put all of you at risk."

"Just doing our job, ma'am," Simon said, mockingly serious. "You know, investigating."

"Right," Lyra said. "And speaking for myself, I can tell you that this case has been a real learning experience for me."

Raina looked at her. "You and me both."

Luther's eyes narrowed. "No more taking off on your own without an explanation or a proper good-bye. You do owe me that much."

"Yes," she said. "I do."

She grabbed the cocktail napkin and dabbed at the tears leaking from her eyes. Luther put an arm around her and pulled her close against him.

"Sorry," he muttered. "It's just that I've been so damned scared."

"I know." She dried her eyes and straightened, recovering her composure. "You may not want my gratitude, but you have a right to an explanation, and I intend to provide it."

The others went quiet, giving her time to gather her thoughts and tell her story. It wasn't easy, because her emotions and her nerves were in chaos. She could not even identify exactly what she was feeling. There was overwhelming relief at having been set free, but there was also the knowledge that she had failed to protect Luther and the others from the long tentacles of her past.

Now she had to deal with the fact that if it hadn't been for the three of them she would be dead. Luther had explained that others had also played a part in rescuing her — Irene and Oliver Ward; Ward's secretary, Elena Torres; and a brave and very angry woman in Pasadena whom she had never met. Luther had explained that without the information from Angela Merryweather they might not have discovered the prison house in time.

A small community of people had worked to save her. Ever since Bar Harbor she had thought of herself as a loner, afraid to let anyone get close. Terrified to reveal her secrets. In Burning Cove she believed she had finally found a haven. She had just begun to dream of a different future when she had received the phone call from the Ghost Lady.

"In another life I had a different name," she said, feeling her way slowly into the past. "I lost my parents when I was eighteen. After their deaths I discovered my father had died bankrupt. I was alone in the world. A year later a man named Malcolm Whitlock appeared. I thought he was perfect — charming, caring, handsome, and wealthy. Attentive. He was descended from a distinguished Boston family. His relatives made it clear from the outset that they did not approve of me or the marriage. They did not encourage us to live in Boston. We moved into what Malcolm called the summer cottage in Bar Harbor. There was a trust fund for Malcolm, so he did not have to work. We spent a lot of time on the water. He taught me how to sail because he enjoyed giving me orders and hurting me when I didn't do things right."

"Bastard," Lyra muttered.

"It didn't take me long to find out why the Whitlocks did not want us around in Boston, why they pretended that we did not exist," Raina said. "While they did not approve of me, they were absolutely terrified of their son."

"He was violent?" Simon asked.

"Yes, but his moods were unpredictable. It was as if he had two personalities. He could appear perfectly normal for weeks on end and then, in a heartbeat, he would turn into a monster. I never knew which man I was going to get when I woke up in the morning. He must have realized I was working up the nerve to leave him, because he began to lock me up at night. During the days he controlled my every move. I could not even shop on my own. I had no friends."

"You escaped," Lyra said. "We found the newspaper clippings in that shoebox. You faked your own death on that sailboat."

"Yes. But I knew he would never stop searching for me and if he ever found me he would murder me. I had to invent a new identity. I managed to get to New York. I stayed in a charity house and found a job as a waitress. There were other women in the house who'd had experiences similar to mine. We heard rumors, little more than whispers, really, of a wealthy woman who had the money and connections to help women like me disappear entirely and reinvent themselves under new names and new identities. They called her the Ghost Lady."

Lyra's eyes widened with excitement. "You found her?"

"Yes. It wasn't easy. I never actually met her. She takes precautions, of course. She moves in society. She can't risk having her work with desperate women exposed. At the very least it would destroy her ability to protect her *clients*, as she calls them. She herself would be in danger from some obsessive man who wanted revenge. She must stay in the shadows."

Luther was about to take another sip of his martini. He paused. "What did this Ghost Lady do for you?"

"She gave me a new identity as Raina Kirk and she paid my tuition at an elite secretarial academy. When I graduated I had a career and a future. I started out working as a private secretary. I was good. I got excellent recommendations from my employers. Eventually I ended up at the law firm of Enright and Enright. When the owner and his son both died, I moved to Burning Cove. I truly believed that my past was three thousand miles behind me."

"But deep down you were always afraid that your husband might someday show up," Lyra said.

Raina sighed. "The news that he had died in a fall at his home in Boston appeared in the papers, of course. The family was prominent socially. But I didn't dare to believe it. I knew him too well, you see. I knew what an accomplished liar he was."

"Irene Ward told me that the rumor in Boston was that the family had him committed to a private asylum for the insane," Luther said. "That's where he died. Suicide."

"Eventually I heard that rumor, too," Raina said. "It made more sense than the fall down the stairs, but I've always been afraid to believe he's really dead."

"So you kept your new identity and pursued your new career," Lyra said. "And you wound up in Burning Cove."

"Yes. But the other morning I got a phone call."

Luther went dangerously still. "From Whitlock?"

"No. The call was from the Ghost Lady, or at least I believed it was her. It was just a low whisper on the phone. I could tell it was a woman, but that was all."

"You didn't question the identity of the caller?" Simon asked.

Raina hesitated and then shook her head. "I was too terrified by her message to ask questions."

"Of course," Lyra said. "You had no reason to suspect that someone would pose as the Ghost Lady."

"There are rules in the investigation business," Luther said. "One of them is question everything."

Lyra glared at him. "That advice is not particularly helpful at this moment."

Luther blinked.

Raina almost smiled. She saw a flash of amusement in Simon's eyes and knew that they were both thinking the same thing: It required considerable nerve to take a stern tone with Luther Pell.

"You're right," Luther said. "I'll save it for later."

"That won't be necessary, believe me," Raina said. She cleared her throat, determined to finish her story. "I was surprised the Ghost Lady had managed to track me down in Burning Cove, but I wasn't suspicious. After all, it's not as if I changed my name when I moved to California. So, no, I never questioned the identity of the caller."

"What did she say in the phone call that

sent you to Labyrinth Springs?" Simon asked.

"She told me that Malcolm Whitlock was alive, that he had escaped the asylum and was looking for me. She said he had vowed to murder everyone around me and make me realize that my new friends were dying because of me. In the end he would kill me, too. She said she knew where to find him. She would send someone to meet me in Labyrinth Springs, one of her messengers. The woman would have the information I needed to locate Whitlock before he started murdering my friends."

"And after you got here you were booked into room two twenty-one, given a schedule of treatments for the afternoon, and instructed to request Janet Frampton for your facial," Lyra said.

"Yes. When Frampton gave me the facial treatment, she said I would receive a visit from the Ghost Lady's messenger in my room that night. I was told to order room service. I didn't eat much, but later a tea tray was delivered. I did drink the tea. Not long afterward I began feeling dizzy and disoriented. Then I started hallucinating. I didn't know what was happening. I was terrified, but I couldn't even call for help. I collapsed on the bed."

"You were poisoned," Lyra said.

"I was never completely unconscious. When those two men came for me I tried to fight, but in the end I was overwhelmed."

"Not so overwhelmed that you couldn't leave us a clue when you were taken to the cabin," Simon said. "That reminds me." He reached down, opened his briefcase, and took out a notebook. "I believe this belongs to you. We got the message that Guppy was involved."

Raina took the notebook. "I didn't know what was going on but I was certain she had to be part of it. Frampton wasn't in a position to run a sophisticated kidnapping operation out of a famous spa."

"Guppy and Billingsley were obviously partners," Luther said. "They were definitely running a kidnapping ring, but it was the usual ransom-and-extortion scheme until you. Taking you broke the pattern. We still don't know why. The people who could give us the answers are dead."

"Everything points to the fact that Guppy was in business for the money," Simon said. "Billingsley didn't need money, but he was playing out some sick sexual fantasies. On the surface it looks like neither of them had a strong motive to grab you.

"We need to know why they changed their

business model," Simon said. "Someone must have convinced them it was worth the risk."

Lyra had been about to take another sip of her cocktail. She paused. "Or threatened them with something that forced them to do it."

Raina looked at her. "That is a very interesting theory."

Simon nodded. "It would explain things. But what kind of threat would make them risk drawing the attention of Luther Pell?"

Raina felt the onset of another attack of the terrible shivering. She could not control the panicky response. Hastily she set down her glass before she spilled the drink.

"Malcolm Whitlock," she whispered. "It must have been him. He's alive and he's out for revenge. He won't stop coming after me. If any of you get in the way —"

"Oh, we'll get in his way, all right," Luther said.

Chapter 42

After dinner Luther took her back to the suite they were sharing. There had been no question of separate rooms. Luther had made it clear he was not going to leave her alone. She was not certain of his mood. He had slipped into his private shadow zone. It was impossible to tell if he was still angry or hurt. The one thing she was certain of was that he would not welcome any more apologies.

It was going to be a long night.

He took off his evening jacket and tossed it over the back of a chair, loosened his tie, unbuttoned the collar of his shirt, and crossed to the drinks cart. He poured two brandies and carried one back to her.

"I know you did what you felt you had to do to protect your friends and me," he said. "But you should know by now that I can take care of myself, and you, as well."

She tossed back a healthy swallow of the

brandy and glared. "Okay, so I panicked."

"Yes," Luther said. His hard features softened. "But I understand."

"You do?" She took a moment to absorb that. "Thanks. I think."

"I understand because if the situation was reversed — if one of the ghosts from my past came back to haunt me and threatened you — I would panic, too."

"It's hard — no, it's impossible to imagine you in a panic."

"I would do exactly what you did — disappear and try to take care of the problem on my own."

"To protect me."

Luther's eyes burned. "It would be the only thing I cared about."

"For the first day I was lost in a dream world."

"Because they were drugging you."

"But at some point you showed up."

"In your dream world?"

"Yes." Raina did not take her eyes off him. "I could barely see you at first but I knew you were there, searching for me. You saw me falling into a whirlpool and you reached down to grab my hand, but I kept falling. After a while I realized you were the one thing that was real in that place. Somehow I *knew* you were looking for me. I managed to surface long enough to realize I was being drugged. I poured the tea down the sink the first morning. But I made the mistake of eating the breakfast rolls. The next day I flushed them down the toilet."

Luther smiled appreciatively. "And then you figured out how to escape. Setting the fire as a distraction was a brilliant idea."

"I wouldn't have made it out of that house if you hadn't shown up when you did."

"Don't bet on that." Luther used his fingers to sweep the few strands of hair that had escaped her chignon back behind her ears. "I sure as hell would never bet against you, and I used to be in the gambling business. You could say I'm a professional when it comes to estimating the odds."

She set the unfinished brandy aside. "Just before I got that phone call from the woman I thought was the Ghost Lady, I was drinking coffee at the breakfast table and thinking that it would be very pleasant if you were there with me."

"I would like that very much."

She smiled and touched the side of his jaw. "Tomorrow morning you and I will be having breakfast together for the first time. Pity we had to go through so much trouble to get to that stage of our relationship."

"You aren't the only one with ghosts in

the past," Luther warned. "Sometimes mine wake me up at night."

"Sometimes mine do, too. On the nights when that happens we will get out of bed, pour a little brandy, and talk about our future."

"Are you saying you want a future with me?"

"Yes, but it won't work unless you want the same future."

He put his glass down and gathered her close. "I love you, Raina. I would kill for a future with you."

"Yes, I know. You did exactly that this afternoon."

He wrapped his arms around her and kissed her with the fierce passion of a man who had been alone for far too long. She returned the kiss with the same intensity and for a similar reason. She had been alone for far too long.

The last wisps of fog that had shrouded her future for so many years evaporated. The precise details of what lay ahead were not revealed, but that didn't matter, because the most important thing was now crystal clear — she would never again face the future alone.

"I can't wait to go home to Burning Cove," she said.

"We have one stop to make on the way," Luther said.

"Where?"

"Pasadena."

Raina smiled. "Yes, of course."

"We have one stop to make on the way," Luther said.

"Where?"

"Pasadena."

Haina smiled. "Yes, of course."

CHAPTER 43

Lyra emerged from the bedroom tying the sash of her silk dressing gown. She stopped short at the sight of the small mountain of violet boxes sitting on the table in the center of the honeymoon suite.

"I never did like that fragrance," she said.

Simon finished pouring two brandies and handed one to her. "Does that mean we don't have to fit all that stuff into the trunk of my car in the morning?"

She smiled, enjoying the sight of him. He had discarded his evening jacket, loosened his tie, and rolled up the sleeves of his white shirt.

"Don't worry, I'm definitely not taking any of the Guppy's House of Beauty products home with me," she said.

"What about me?" Simon asked. "Think you might want to take me home with you?"

A little thrill of hope sparked through her.

"Aren't you worried that I might be using you?"

"You don't use people, Lyra. You're curious about them and you're interested in them but you do not use them. I know that. Deep down I've always known it."

The spark of hope became a glorious flame. "Yes. Yes, I'd very much like to take you home with me. Are you talking about staying in Burning Cove for a while?"

"I realize that even though you hold very modern views, it wouldn't look right if I moved in with you. Burning Cove is a small town, after all. But I could rent a cottage on the beach next to yours."

She sipped some of the brandy and thought about that.

"Convenient," she said.

He drank some of his own brandy and lowered the glass. Energy whispered in the atmosphere.

His eyes heated. "Very convenient."

Hope mingled with anxiety. She was surprised by the tension. This was what she wanted. The thought of an affair with Simon was exciting. Thrilling. So why was she hesitating?

It took her a couple of heartbeats to acknowledge that she wasn't sure how she felt about being convenient. Yes, it would be exciting for a while. A passionate adventure. But what would happen when the situation was no longer *convenient*? What if she lost her heart?

What if she had already lost it?

A tiny flare of panic arced through her.

She gulped some more brandy, fortifying herself, and took a little stroll around the room. A thought struck her. She stopped near a wall and turned to face him.

"There's your bookshop to consider," she said, trying to buy a little time. "You can't just walk away from it."

"Don't worry about the bookshop." He set his half-finished brandy on the table and came toward her, halting inches away. He flattened one hand on the wall behind her head. "I'll figure it out."

She caught her breath.

"How long do you think you might want to stay in Burning Cove?" she whispered.

"That depends."

"On what?"

"You."

"Oh."

The most fascinating man she had ever met was offering her an affair — a *convenient* affair.

"Does that arrangement work for you?" Simon asked.

"Yes." She took the plunge. "Yes, that will work for me."

"Good. We have an understanding, then."

He took her brandy glass, set it on the end table, and flattened his other hand on the wall behind her, effectively trapping her.

He leaned in close and kissed her.

She stopped trying to analyze the word *convenient* and put her arms around his neck.

The kiss was different. It wasn't the scorching embrace that had swept her away last night. This kiss was slower, deeper; somehow more intimate. Last night had been a wild storm of heat and energy. Tonight they were testing the new boundaries that defined their relationship.

Simon's hands settled around her waist and then moved to cradle her rear. He lifted her up against him. She was intensely aware of his heavily aroused body. It was gloriously exciting to know that she had such an effect on him. He wanted her and she wanted him. They were both free to explore the depths of their desire for each other.

The future would take care of itself.

CHAPTER 44

Simon sensed the precise instant when Lyra threw herself into the kiss. The woman never did anything in a halfhearted or hesitant manner. He had been hard a moment ago but now he was beyond aroused. He craved her as he had never craved any other woman. The need was not just sexual. It was far more powerful. He had no words. He only knew that he wanted her in his life, no matter the cost.

From the outset he had been aware that she had the power to upend his carefully controlled and lonely world. He had been right. Nothing would ever be the same now that he had known her. The trick was to hang on to her.

He set her back on her feet and undid the sash of the dressing gown. The silk wings fell open, leaving her in a peach-colored satin nightgown. The luminous fabric slipped gracefully over her breasts and hips.

400

He eased the dressing gown off her shoulders and let it fall to the carpet, a pool of floral silk.

Her fingers moved to the buttons of his shirt. He let her push it off. When it was gone he took the time to hoist his undershirt over his head and toss it aside.

He took her hand and drew her into the shadowed bedroom.

The lovemaking was different tonight. He was not sure why. The passion was soul-stirring and, ultimately, explosive. But there was another element involved this time. It was as if they were both participating in a sacred ceremony, forging a bond that was not meant to be severed.

When it was over and they lay spent and damp and satisfied in each other's arms he tried and failed to find the words. As usual, Lyra did not experience the same problem.

"That was weird," she mumbled into the pillow.

So much for enjoying the postcoital glow.

He sat up and rolled her onto her side so that she had to face him.

"What the hell is that supposed to mean?" he asked.

"Nothing." She smiled a dreamy smile and threaded her fingers through his hair. "It just felt different, that's all."

"Different good or different not good?" he asked, deeply wary now.

"It felt like a real wedding night."

He stared at her, floored. "How would you know what a real wedding night is supposed to feel like?"

"Turns out you know it when you see it."

"But we're not married," he pointed out.

"No." She yawned and cuddled against him. "That may turn out to be a problem."

"Uh."

"Go to sleep, Simon. We've got a long drive ahead of us tomorrow."

Chapter 45

Angela Merryweather took one look at the couple standing on her doorstep and knew that Luther Pell had kept his promise. She opened the door.

"Come in, Mr. Pell," she said. "It is very good to see you again."

"Thank you," Luther said. "This is Raina Kirk, the lady I was searching for when I spoke with you."

Angela smiled. "I'm so glad you are safe, Miss Kirk. Will you come in and have coffee? My housekeeper doesn't come in until the afternoon, but I made a fresh pot a few minutes ago."

"Please call me Raina. Coffee sounds lovely. It's been a long drive from Labyrinth Springs, and we have another two hours on the road ahead of us. We are on our way home to Burning Cove."

The warmth in her voice when she said the words *We are on our way home* told

403

Angela everything she needed to know about the relationship between Luther Pell and Raina Kirk.

It's time for me to find a home of my own, Angela thought.

She led the way into the living room and went into the kitchen to get the coffee things. She carried the silver tray back into the other room and set it on the low table in front of the sofa.

"The Labyrinth Springs news made the morning papers here in Pasadena and, I'm sure, everywhere else in the Los Angeles area," she said. "It was on the radio, too." She poured three cups of coffee and handed one to Raina. "Something about special agents of the FBI working undercover to help the local police break up a drug ring operating out of the hotel and spa. There was no mention of the kidnappings or the victims. I don't mind telling you that I feel as if I can breathe again."

"We can both breathe again," Raina said. She smiled. "Luther has a gift for you."

Angela looked at Luther, hardly daring to hope. "You found the photos?"

"And the negatives," Luther said. He handed her an envelope. "I destroyed the others but I thought you might like to burn these yourself."

404

Angela took the envelope. Tears burned in her eyes. "I don't know how to thank you."

"You don't owe me any thanks," Luther said. "I am in your debt. The information you gave me helped us find Miss Kirk in time. They were preparing to kill her. The last time I was here I told you that if you ever need a favor of the sort that I can provide, you have only to ask. That offer stands."

Angela gave him a tremulous smile. "Thank you."

They drank coffee together while Luther and Raina gave her the details of the events in Labyrinth Springs.

Forty minutes later Angela stood on the doorstep and watched Luther get into one of the two speedsters parked at the curb. Raina got into the other vehicle. Both cars pulled away and drove off down the street.

Going home to Burning Cove.

When the cars disappeared around the corner Angela went back inside the cold mansion and headed for the kitchen. She dumped the negatives and the two sets of prints into the sink and went back into the living room to get Bradley's gold-plated cigarette lighter.

She returned to the kitchen and set fire to each print. Then she burned the negatives.

When the ashes cooled she collected them and took them into the bathroom to flush down the toilet.

Afterward she went into her bedroom and packed up the essentials. She ignored the clothes and shoes that had been purchased with the goal of entertaining Bradley's business associates and political friends.

She was hoisting the last suitcase into the trunk of her car when Bradley pulled into the driveway. He climbed out of his speedster and started toward the front door.

"I just came home to change clothes," he said over his shoulder. "Got an important meeting at the L.A. office."

"Take your time," Angela said. "I won't be here when you get back."

"What?" Startled, he turned around in time to see her shut the lid of the trunk on the four suitcases inside. "Where do you think you're going?"

"Reno. Six weeks from now I'll be a single, legally divorced woman. I'll be out of your life forever. You can finance your own political campaign."

Bradley stared at her, stricken. "What the fuck?"

"Oh, and there's no need to worry about the photos or the negatives. I burned them a couple of hours ago. In case you didn't see the morning papers, the kidnappers are dead. They won't be bothering you."

"You can't just leave like this," Bradley said.

"Watch me."

She got behind the wheel of the car, turned the key in the ignition, and drove away from the cold house. She glanced into the rearview mirror and saw Bradley standing, slack-jawed, in the driveway. The look of shock on his face made her smile. She turned the corner.

Time to find a real home.

CHAPTER 46

"I borrowed these from the library," Irene said. She put copies of two popular fashion magazines on Raina's desk and opened each one to a feature article about Guppy's House of Beauty. "Edith Guppy showed up in New York toward the end of the Great War and opened Guppy's House of Beauty less than a year later. She told everyone she was originally from Paris, but she was also fluent in German and English. She seemed to have plenty of money and implied she was connected to one of the old royal families."

"Very cosmopolitan," Raina said. "She was an attractive woman who must have been stunningly beautiful in her younger days. Her looks combined with her sense of style and a sophisticated continental accent no doubt made it easy for her to attract an upper-class clientele in New York."

The small crowd gathered around her

desk included Luther, Simon, and Irene and Oliver Ward. The only one missing was Lyra. She had left shortly before Irene and the others arrived. Personal business. Raina understood. She knew how it felt to live with unanswered questions.

"She had more than looks and a fancy accent," Irene said. She flipped through her notebook. "According to a couple of newspaper interviews, she concocted her own perfumes, face creams, and other products."

"Products like that damned poisoned tea that Frampton gave to Lyra," Simon said.

Raina glanced at him. His eyes were unreadable, but something in the atmosphere around him sent a chill down her spine.

"Apparently she had some training at a pharmaceutical lab before she went into the beauty business," Irene said.

Luther leaned forward, planted both hands on the desk, and took a closer look at the photos. "Huh."

That got everyone's attention.

"What?" Raina asked.

"Nothing. Yet." Luther glanced at Irene. "Go on. Have you got anything else on Guppy?"

"Such as why she closed down her apparently successful business in New York and moved to California?" Simon asked.

"Good question," Irene said. She turned another page in her notebook. "According to my newspaper source there were rumors of a scandal that reached into the highest levels of society. It involved drugs, rape, and blackmail. The entire affair was hushed up because some of the most distinguished men in the city were said to be involved, including several politicians. There were rumors of a little book filled with names."

Simon opened his briefcase and took out a leather-bound volume. "A book like this one? Luther and I found it when we discovered the photos of the kidnap victims. It's a very precise record of names, dates, addresses, and the ransom amounts. Each entry has a number that corresponds to the numbers on the back of the pictures of each victim."

"Simon and I burned most of the photos and the negatives," Luther said. "I let Mrs. Merryweather deal with those that involved her, but it's safe to say they have been destroyed, as well. We can't guarantee there aren't any more copies of the photos, but I think the odds are good that, aside from the set she made for Billingsley, Guppy would not have allowed another set to be made. They were too valuable."

"And she was nothing if not an excellent businesswoman," Simon said.

Raina looked at Irene. "What about Billingsley?"

"He's not nearly as much of a mystery," Irene said. "He was born into wealth and had all the advantages, but he was dismissed from a series of private schools for unspecified reasons. In his twenties he was considered an extremely eligible bachelor and man-about-town, but he never married. There were rumors that he frequented houses of prostitution that catered to those with what my informant referred to as *eccentric tastes.*"

"Define *eccentric* in this case," Raina said.

Irene looked up from her notes. "He was apparently unable to complete the act in the normal manner. He could only find physical satisfaction if the woman was chained to a bed and pretended to be terrified of him. Then he would stand over them and, ah, finish the business. He blamed the women for his problems. Apparently he had a habit of taking out his rage on the prostitutes. After two ended up in the hospital, most of the houses refused to let him through the doors. He probably turned to the streets but there is no way to know."

"The women who are forced to work on

the streets have no protection," Raina said. "A violent man could literally get away with murder. I wonder if Guppy was aware of just how dangerous her business partner was."

"She knew," Simon said. "That's why she tried to placate him by letting him have a set of photos. There's no doubt that she was the real boss of the kidnapping ring. The question is, why did she get involved with an unstable business partner?"

"I can think of one reason," Irene said. "My source tells me that she was rumored to be facing bankruptcy a few years ago. Billingsley was very rich. I imagine she needed his money. She needed it again when she had to close down the New York spa and move west."

"He bought an entire hotel and added a spectacular spa just so he could pursue his desire to hunt and humiliate women," Simon said.

"For Guppy, there was more than money involved," Luther said. "Simon and I went through the names in her book. Her victims were not just the wives and daughters of wealthy men. She chose women who are closely connected to politicians, government officials, and successful industrialists."

Simon looked at him. "Men who are in

power or will be soon."

"Men who would have access to government secrets during a war," Luther said.

"But the Great War ended twenty years ago," Irene pointed out. She stopped as understanding struck. "Oh. You mean the next war."

"The world will soon be on fire again," Luther said with grim resignation. "And the U.S. will be drawn into it. There will be no avoiding that abyss. When war comes, Guppy's book of blackmail targets would have been extremely valuable to certain parties."

Raina took a sharp breath. "You think she was collecting blackmail material on powerful people so she could sell the information to a foreign government?"

"That's the pattern that I see," Luther said. "What's more is that I recognize it because I've seen it before. Guppy's age, her background, the photography, the pharmaceutical training, the poison, it all fits."

"What do you mean?" Raina asked.

He took his hands off the desk and straightened. "People, including professional spies, rarely change their style. If a strategy worked in the past they'll continue to use it."

Simon watched him intently. "You think Edith Guppy was working for a foreign power?"

"I think she worked for a foreign power during the Great War and was probably positioning herself to be an independent contractor in the next one."

"Who was Guppy?" Oliver asked.

Luther walked to the window and looked out at the street. "The spy world is a small one. I'm not saying we all knew each other personally during and after the war, but we were certainly aware of each other, especially those who were particularly effective. I and the members of my department studied their styles, their techniques, their strategies. Some were more obvious than others. Some were brilliant when it came to concealing their identities. But once you knew their patterns you could create a file and assign a code name to the person."

"You're telling us you had a file on an agent who fit Edith Guppy's pattern?" Raina said.

"Yes." Luther turned around. "Janus. We were sure of very few things about her, but one thing we assumed, based on her skill with poisons, was that she'd had some pharmaceutical or medical training."

"Guppy concocted all her signature formulas," Irene said.

"Janus was also thought to be beautiful

and seductive, because she managed to get close to powerful men," Luther continued. "She was suspected in the deaths of some highly placed individuals, but she preferred to get them into compromising situations and obtain proof that could be used to blackmail them."

Oliver looked at him. "You're going to tell us that Janus was one of the many agents who vanished after the war, aren't you?"

"Yes," Luther said. "We kept an eye out for her for a few years, but if she was alive there was no indication she was still in business — at least, not as a spy. But now I'm wondering if she reinvented herself in New York."

"Interesting," Raina said. "But that brings us back to the start of this thing. Why grab me? I'm not in a position to be of use to a foreign power. And there were no compromising photos taken."

Simon looked at her. "We agree that you don't fit the pattern."

"Which means this is personal," Luther said.

"You can forget Malcolm Whitlock," Irene said. "I was able to confirm that he really is dead. My source is a reporter in Boston who covered the funeral because the family is an important one in the city. He told me he saw the body and said it definitely matched photos of Malcolm Whitlock that had been published over the years in the society sections of the papers. He also said that everyone who attended the funeral appeared relieved, not distraught."

Luther looked at Raina. "That leaves us with your connection to the law firm of Enright and Enright."

Raina shook her head. "Both Enrights are dead. There was no other close family. Who would care enough to come after me?"

"Someone who thinks you have some valuable information," Luther said.

"We've been focusing on the possibility that your husband was still alive, Raina," Simon said. "But now that Irene has confirmed his death, we need to come up with another angle."

Raina froze. "The files."

Everyone looked at her.

"What files?" Irene said.

Raina cleared her throat. "I took a few with me when I, ah, closed down the offices of Enright and Enright. I grabbed them because I knew Graham Enright considered them particularly important. At the time I didn't know what I had. There wasn't time to go through them. But somewhere along Route 66 I finally got a chance to examine the files."

"Blackmail materials?" Simon suggested.

"In most cases, yes," Raina said. "I hate blackmailers. I burned almost all the files that night. But one folder contained a list. It was meaningless to me but I knew it had to be important. I saved it."

"What happened to it?" Irene asked.

Raina hesitated.

"She gave it to me," Luther said. "It's a list of names, but none of the people involved in this case are on it."

"Names get changed," Simon said.

"I know," Luther said. "But it's going to take a lot of time to track down every name on the list and try to find out if that person hired Guppy to kidnap Raina."

"Sounds more likely that Guppy was Janus," Oliver said. "Maybe she thought Enright had a file on her and that Raina had it."

"She was afraid Raina knew too much and grabbed her to silence her," Irene offered. "If that's what happened, the case is closed. Guppy is dead."

Luther's jaw tightened. "There is one other detail I remember about that particular agent. She was given the code name Janus for a reason."

"Because she was two-faced?" Raina

asked. "That's the definition of a spy, isn't it?"

"Not in this case," Luther said. "She was named Janus because we suspected she worked with a partner."

A disturbing intensity heated Simon's eyes. "We need to go back to the beginning of this thing."

"The phone call from Guppy that sent me to Labyrinth Springs?" Raina suggested.

"That wasn't the beginning," Simon said. "You told us Lyra had some personal business to take care of this morning."

"That's right." Raina glanced at her watch. "She should be back soon."

"Do you know where she went?" Simon asked.

"Yes," Raina said.

She told them where Lyra had gone. Even as she said the words out loud she felt the tiny hairs on the back of her neck stir.

"We've been ignoring the very big coincidence at the start of this case," Simon said.

He headed swiftly for the door. Raina and the others followed.

CHAPTER 47

Lyra brought her little speedster to a stop in the front drive of the Adlington villa. She sat behind the wheel for a moment, recalling her first visit to the big house. The memory of the sickening crunch she had heard and felt when the golf club struck Charles Adlington's head shivered through her.

And then she thought about the terrible shock that had hit her when she led Detective Brandon and his officers around the house to the pool and saw the bloody golf club lying in a different position on the patio.

She'd had another nightmare about the scene during the night and had awakened, pulse pounding, in the midst of an anxiety attack. Simon had held her close, offering comfort and common sense. Raina's words had whispered through her. *You did what you had to do to save yourself and Marcella*

Adlington.

But neither of them could answer the question that haunted her. *Was I the one who killed him? Or was it you, Marcella? Did you hit him again and again with that club because he showed signs of life? I just need to know the truth.*

She opened the car door, got out, and reached back to pick up her handbag. She was not dressed in the severe business suit she had worn the first time she had come to the house. Today she had on a pair of light gray, high-waisted trousers, a tailored, long-sleeved white shirt, and lace-up shoes. This was not a meet-the-client visit. This was about getting some answers.

She walked to the front door, paused a moment to collect her nerve, and clanged the big brass door knocker. Twice.

She heard crisp footsteps in the hall. The door opened. Marcella Adlington smiled at her.

"Come in, Miss Brazier."

"Thank you for agreeing to see me on such short notice," Lyra said. She moved into a formal foyer covered in terra-cotta-colored tiles. "I won't take up much of your time. I realize you're leaving Burning Cove today."

"Yes. My suitcases are in the trunk of my

420

car. I sent my housekeeper home after she packed my things. I prefer to close up the house myself, to make sure all the doors and windows are locked."

"I understand."

"Let's go into the living room. I've made tea."

Marcella led the way into a high-ceilinged room furnished in the Spanish Colonial style that was so popular in Burning Cove. A pair of saddle-brown leather sofas sat on either side of a carved wooden coffee table. A large red lacquer liquor cabinet was conveniently positioned near the sofas. Cocktail, wine, and cordial glasses sparkled behind the glass doors. A handsome silver corkscrew occupied a place of honor in the center of the open shelf.

There were colorful throw pillows and gleaming tiles everywhere, but the rich Mediterranean hues did little to warm and brighten the house. It was infused with shadows.

Well, there had been a death in the family, Lyra thought. Gloom was expected.

"Please sit down, Miss Brazier," Marcella said, gesturing toward one of a pair of sofas.

A porcelain teapot, cups and saucers, dainty spoons, and a sugar bowl were neatly arranged on the silver tray that sat on the coffee table between the sofas.

Lyra perched on the edge of one of the sofas. She had not slept after the nightmare, and a low-level tension had been rattling her all morning. The cold chills on the back of her neck had gotten worse after she had made the decision to call Marcella Adlington and request the meeting. She told herself her nerves would settle down after she got the answers she needed.

Marcella sat on the facing sofa, picked up the pot, and poured tea into the two cups. "Sugar?"

"No, thank you," Lyra said.

Marcella set the cup and saucer on the coffee table in front of Lyra, positioned her own cup in front of herself, and smiled a cool smile.

"Now, what is it you want to ask?" she asked.

"I will come straight to the point," Lyra said. "I know you used the golf club to strike Mr. Adlington at least a couple of times after I left the patio to greet the police. Did you strike him because he moved? Were you afraid he might awaken and perhaps try to attack you again?"

"In other words, you want to know which one of us killed Charles."

"Yes."

"He did not regain consciousness, but I went close to see if he was still breathing. I had to know, you see. I had to be sure. I touched his wrist. He still had a pulse. I grabbed the golf club and struck him again. Three times. I was in an absolute panic. Terrified that he might survive. And if that happened I knew he would come after me and he would not stop until he murdered me."

"I see," Lyra said.

She had her answer. It was the one she had hoped would give her some peace of mind, but for some reason it failed to do that. The opposite, in fact. She was more unnerved than ever. The frissons that had whispered through her on so many occasions during the past few days had not diminished.

She remembered the first time she had experienced the disturbing sensation. It was the day she had walked into the Adlingtons' garden and discovered Charles Adlington attempting to drown Marcella.

She wondered if she had been permanently traumatized by the act of violence she had engaged in that day. It had been followed by several more days filled with danger and violence. Odd to think that the brush with death she had experienced here on the Adlington property had been followed immediately by Raina's disappearance and more death.

Simon's words rang in her head: *There are no coincidences in a murder investigation.* Damn.

She needed to leave. Now. She had to talk to Simon and Raina about the theory that had just struck her with such force she could hardly breathe. Maybe she was wrong. Maybe her imagination had gone wild. Maybe all the stress of the past few days had rattled her nerves so badly she could no longer think clearly.

"Your tea is getting cold," Marcella said.

"Yes, of course." Lyra picked up her cup and saucer.

"I am sorry you have been so upset by what happened the day you came to see me," Marcella said. "But I also hope you know that I am very grateful to you. If you had not arrived for our appointment on time, Charles would have killed me. He was a large, strong man, and he was quite insane. He could easily have held me underwater until I drowned. My death would have appeared accidental."

No, Lyra thought, *you knew what you were doing. You set me up so that you would have an excuse to murder your husband. You didn't care if Charles killed me in the process.*

424

Maybe you expected him to do that, because it would have justified your use of the gun.

It had all worked out well for Marcella Adlington, but it hadn't gone entirely according to plan.

One thing had gone very wrong: Marcella had expected Raina to show up for the client interview.

"No need to thank me," Lyra said. She set the cup and saucer down on the coffee table and got to her feet. "I appreciate the answer to my question. I'll be going now. I don't want to delay you any longer. I'll see myself out."

She grabbed her purse and headed for the door. Her intuition was screaming at her now, telling her to get out of the dark, shadowed house.

She took only three steps before Marcella spoke behind her.

"Stop or I will pull the trigger of this gun," Marcella said.

Lyra froze beside the large liquor cabinet. She took a breath and turned around very slowly. Marcella was on her feet, a pistol in her hand. She appeared to know exactly what she was doing with the weapon.

"You figured it out, didn't you?" Marcella sighed. "I was afraid of that. Everything that could go wrong did go wrong, right from the beginning. But thanks to you coming here today I might have one last chance to end this the way it was supposed to end."

"With Raina dead? That's what you intended, isn't it?"

"Yes, I wanted her dead, but I did not want to draw the attention of Luther Pell."

"In that case, you miscalculated. Badly. Pell would have walked into hell to find the person who murdered Raina."

"But the beauty of my original plan was that he would have had the killer handed to him on a platter," Marcella said. "Charles Adlington."

"Who would also have been conveniently dead because you would have shot him in what would have looked like a desperate but doomed effort to protect Raina."

"But you showed up instead, and the next thing I knew, that fool Charles was on the ground and probably dying because you hit him with a golf club."

"But you had to be sure. And now you're going to murder me because you know I figured it out."

"You leave me no choice. I'll find another way to deal with Raina Kirk."

"Why do you want her dead?"

"Because she murdered Graham Enright and stole my file. I have no idea where she hid it, so killing her is the next best thing to recovering it. It will be easier to search for it once she's gone."

The sound of the front door opening had an electrifying effect on Marcella. Panic flashed in her eyes.

"Who is it?" she shouted. "Who's there? Go away or I'll call the police."

"I doubt that," Raina said.

She appeared at the arched entrance of the living room. Lyra marveled at her cool, businesslike demeanor, as if this were just another meeting with a client. She was carrying Simon's briefcase in her arms. It was positioned like a shield across the front of her body.

Marcella moved quickly to put the barrel of her pistol against Lyra's head.

"If either of you move, Miss Brazier is a dead woman," she said.

"I'm Raina Kirk," Raina said, ignoring the threat. "I believe you've been trying to get hold of me, Mrs. Adlington. Or should I call you the other face of Janus?"

"So you do have my file."

"Yes," Raina said. "It was obviously very special to Enright."

"The bastard. We were lovers for a time. I don't know why I allowed myself to trust him. I suppose it was because I thought of

427

him as a kindred spirit. I believed that Graham and I understood each other, that he viewed me as his equal. I convinced myself that there was a bond between us. That we would make a good team."

"Enright had a talent for molding himself into whoever he wanted you to think he was," Raina said.

"I didn't realize he had created a file on me until shortly before his death. He asked me to do him a favor. He wanted me to steal some secrets from a powerful man. It was too dangerous. I refused. That was when he told me about the file. He threatened to turn it over to the FBI. I knew I had to get rid of him and destroy the file. But killing a man like Enright is not a simple matter. I had to be careful."

"Then you heard that he had taken cyanide."

"I was immediately suspicious," Marcella said. "It just wasn't in Graham's nature to take his own life. You're the one who put the cyanide in his coffee, aren't you?"

Raina did not even blink at the accusation.

"Graham Enright was a monster," she said. "And so was his son. They were also very good at pretending to be normal, upright citizens. It took me several months to realize I was working for a couple of cold-blooded killers. What made you conclude I was the one who took the file?"

"You were not at the top of my list of suspects, not at first," Marcella said. "You were, after all, just the secretary. It didn't occur to me that you would have had the guts to poison Enright and steal the file. But after I checked out all the other possibilities I finally realized you were the only one who could have taken it. Then I had to find you. That wasn't easy. You left no forwarding address, Miss Kirk. You just disappeared."

"Apparently I didn't do a very good job of vanishing," Raina said.

"Don't blame yourself. My skills may be a bit rusty, but I am a professional."

"And the Ghost Lady?" Raina asked. "How did you find that connection?"

"I owe Graham Enright for that bit of information. He researched you very thoroughly before he hired you. He discussed the matter with me. He always made certain his secretaries had no immediate family, no one who would notice if they suddenly went missing."

"Because eventually Enright's secretaries always went missing," Raina said.

Marcella shrugged. "Eventually they

learned too much about Enright's business affairs. Where is the file? Hand it over and I won't have any reason to kill you and Miss Brazier."

Lyra looked at Raina. "We both know she's lying. She plans to kill us once she has the file."

"Now, why would I do that?" Marcella said. "I told you, I'm a professional. I prefer not to leave dead bodies around. They attract far too much attention."

"One more question," Raina said. "How did you persuade your old partner to help you?"

"Guppy understood that if that file ever fell into the wrong hands she would be in as much danger as me," Marcella said.

"Too bad she got involved with Billingsley," Raina said.

"The man was unstable. I warned her she would regret using him to finance her spa and carry out the extortion schemes. She insisted she could manage him."

"Your husband was also mentally unstable," Raina pointed out. "What made you think you could manipulate Charles Adlington?"

"My plan would have worked just fine if you had shown up that day," Marcella said. "Instead Lyra was the one who came through that gate and killed Charles."

"You know how it is," Lyra said. "My first real case. I wanted to show initiative."

Raina cleared her throat. "About your file, Marcella."

That got Marcella's attention. "Where is it?"

"It's in this briefcase. That's what you really want. You can have it if you let Lyra go."

"Show me the file," Marcella said.

"Let Lyra go."

"Not until I have the file."

"If you insist," Raina said.

She looked as if she was about to set the briefcase on the floor. But she stopped when a fist-sized metal ball flew across the room and landed on the floor.

Marcella stared at the ball. Shock flashed across her face. It was followed by panic. *"Grenade."*

She turned to run but stopped short when she saw the figure moving into the room from the conservatory.

"Put the gun down," Simon ordered.

"No." Marcella raised the pistol.

Lyra grabbed the silver corkscrew off the shelf of the liquor cabinet. She swung around and stabbed with all of her strength. She did not have time to aim. The tip of the steel screw speared through the fabric of Marcella's blouse and into the soft flesh of her upper shoulder.

Marcella yelled and staggered back a couple of frantic steps. Lyra kept her grip on the handle of the corkscrew, pulling it free of Marcella's shoulder. Blood flowed, saturating the blouse.

"The grenade," Marcella gasped, wild-eyed. *"The grenade."*

"Isn't live," Simon said. He snapped the gun out of Marcella's slackened grasp. "I find it useful as a distraction from time to time. It's amazing how people panic when a grenade lands in front of them."

Luther emerged from the foyer. "Especially those who were in the war."

Irene and Oliver Ward followed Luther into the living room. Irene yanked a notebook and a pencil out of her handbag.

Marcella looked at Lyra. "You stupid amateur. You ruined everything."

"Beginner's luck," Lyra said.

CHAPTER 48

Raina put the phone down and looked at Lyra. "That was the doctor. He said that, barring serious infection, Marcella Adlington will be fine."

"I can't tell you how happy I am to hear that," Lyra said.

They were in the office of Kirk Investigations, just the two of them. Simon was with Luther in Luther's private quarters above the Paradise Club. They were composing a carefully worded report for the FBI and a certain clandestine government agency.

In the end everyone had concluded that the only thing that required an explanation was the kidnapping of Raina. Luther had decreed that they would stick with the simplest story — the kidnappers had believed he could be persuaded to pay the ransom. Instead, he and some of his associates had organized a rescue mission. There was no need to mention Raina's connection to the now-defunct firm of Enright & Enright.

Lyra slumped against the back of her desk chair and blew out a sigh. She had spent another sleepless night wondering if dawn would bring the news that Marcella Adlington had died of her wound. Now that it looked like Adlington would live, there was another, possibly bigger problem.

"What happens if Marcella talks?" she said. "She might tell the police that she suspects you were, uh, responsible for Graham Enright's death."

"She has absolutely no proof," Raina said. "And why would anyone take the word of a former spy who worked for a hostile power in the Great War over that of an innocent secretary who was on vacation when her boss died? Trust me, Luther will take care of any problems from that direction."

"Good point," Lyra said.

"Don't worry, no one questioned Enright's death at the time. By then his only son was dead in a car crash. There was no other close family. His estate went to distant relatives who certainly won't want anyone to open up an investigation that might bring other would-be heirs out of the woodwork."

"I don't see any way they can connect her to the so-called drug ring that was operating out of the Labyrinth Springs resort, either," Lyra said. "That doesn't leave much except attempted murder."

"Which is enough to ensure that she does prison time," Raina said. "However, I doubt it will come to that. Luther is going to see to it that she is turned over to the FBI. The Bureau will want to question her about her previous career as a spy. There will be a lot of juicy headlines in the press. When all is said and done she will be notorious. That is not a particularly useful status for a professional spy or a socialite."

Encouraged, Lyra sat forward. "I wonder what will happen to her?"

There was a short silence from the other desk.

"You seem to be a woman of boundless curiosity," Raina said.

"Character flaw."

"In view of that particular flaw I can't help but notice that you haven't asked me if Marcella Adlington's assumptions concerning Graham Enright's death are right."

"You mean, I haven't asked you if you killed your old boss? Nope."

"Why not?"

"If you did give him the cyanide, you did what you had to do to save yourself. The same reason I used the golf club on Charles

435

Adlington."

"But aren't you curious to know for sure if you're working for a woman who —"

Lyra looked at her. "I know the truth, Raina. You and everyone else seem to think I'm naïve, but I'm very good when it comes to reading people. If you ever need to talk about what happened in New York, I'll listen. But I think you should talk to Luther Pell first. He loves you and I'm sure he knows the truth about you."

"Yes," Raina said. "He knows."

"He doesn't care. Neither do I. I am curious about Marcella's file, however. Does it exist?"

"If it did and if it's one that I took when I closed the office, it no longer exists. I burned all the blackmail files somewhere along Route 66. The names were all coded. Enright is the only one who could have identified them."

"Marcella would have had no way to know that you destroyed her file."

"No." Raina looked out the window at the sun-dappled street. "When I came to Burning Cove I was hoping to find a new life but I never expected to discover something else."

"What have you found here?"

"A man I can trust enough to love. Good

436

friends. A place where I feel like I belong."

"It's called *home,* Raina."

Raina smiled. "I'm starting to realize that."

"You know, it occurs to me that you have been through a lot of stress lately."

Raina's brows rose. "So have you."

"We both survived. I suggest we do what successful investigators do when they close a case — celebrate with a dinner at the Burning Cove Hotel and then hit the hottest nightclub in town."

For a few seconds Raina looked as if she was going to cry. The sheen of tears glittered briefly in her eyes.

But this was Raina, so of course she didn't do anything so unsophisticated and emotional.

"That sounds like an excellent plan," she said. "Does this mean you've decided to remain here at Kirk Investigations?"

"If you'll have me. I learned a lot about myself in the past few days, Raina. I realize I need this kind of work. I want to search for answers for people who need those answers, even if it brings pain. I feel I was born to open or close doors for those who can't sleep because they can't open or close those doors themselves."

"What about your dreams of taking over your family's business?"

"I've closed that door, and I don't have any desire to open it again. I wasted a lot of years trying to prove to my father that I could take control of Brazier Shipping. I did my best to be the good daughter to make up for my sister's wild, independent ways. But now I know I wouldn't have been happy as the head of Brazier Shipping. Oh, I'm sure it would have provided lots of interesting problems to solve, but I wouldn't have taken much satisfaction in finding the answers."

"Why not?"

"Because dealing with financial matters, logistics, and construction problems, to say nothing of the internal politics that is always a part of large business operations, would never have given me the satisfaction I got from finding you and watching Simon and Luther destroy those horrible photos and negatives."

"Not all cases end in a satisfying way," Raina warned. "Sometimes it's too late to save anyone. Sometimes you won't find all the answers. Sometimes there is no justice."

"I know. But I can live with the uncertainty as long as I have a friend and colleague to share a drink with afterward."

Raina smiled. "You definitely have that."

"Thanks. I suggest we also invite a couple

of very interesting men to join us — the kind of men who don't have a problem with fast women."

"An even better plan," Raina said. "Do you know, it's only here in Burning Cove that I have been able to enjoy one of life's most amazing pleasures."

"What is that?"

"An evening with good friends."

CHAPTER 49

Simon heard the soft sounds of women's footsteps on the carpeted staircase that led up to the mezzanine floor of the Paradise. Luther heard them, too. They both rose from the private booth.

Lyra and Raina appeared at the top of the stairs and came toward them. Both women smiled.

"We are a couple of extraordinarily lucky men," Luther said quietly.

"Yes," Simon said. "We are."

When Lyra and Raina were seated and their cocktails delivered, Simon raised his glass in a toast.

"To good friends," he said.

The words were echoed around the table.

It dawned on Simon that it was the first time he had ever felt the need to toast anyone, let alone good friends. Lyra smiled. He knew she sensed what he was thinking.

"You two gentlemen might be interested

to know that Lyra made a couple of phone calls this afternoon and cleared up one more detail that has been bothering us about the Adlington case," Raina said.

"What was that?" Luther asked.

"It was obvious that Marcella married Charles Adlington for his money, because immediately after the wedding she arranged to have him committed to an asylum," Lyra said. "The situation was extremely convenient for her, because she had complete control of his fortune. The question was how did Adlington get out of the asylum, and why did Marcella take the risk of trying to use him to murder Raina?"

"I'm assuming you found out it was not a convenient coincidence that he was in the pool trying to drown Marcella when you walked in that day," Simon said.

"No, it was not." Lyra picked up her glass. "I spoke with the director of the asylum. He said Mrs. Adlington had signed papers to have her husband discharged against professional advice. Said he tried to talk her out of it but she was adamant."

"She obviously thought she could manipulate and control him long enough to carry out her plan," Raina said. "She was trying to kill two birds with one stone. She didn't intend for him to survive the afternoon."

"And she made certain that he didn't," Lyra said. "But that was the only thing that went right for her that day. After the police left she must have gotten on the phone to Guppy and told her they needed another plan and they needed to implement it quickly."

"Marcella didn't dare risk another attempt to kill me here in Burning Cove," Raina said. "She was convinced she could get away with murder by proxy — using her insane ex-husband to kill me. That would have given her the perfect reason to shoot him. But when things went wrong she knew that a second attack on me, even if it looked like an accident, was certain to get Luther's full attention. She did not dare do that."

Lyra smiled and raised her glass toward Luther. "Marcella may not have known you personally, but she knew the legend."

Luther waved that aside. "I told you, the world of spies is a small one. Terrible gossips, spies."

"I wonder what happened to Kevin Draper," Lyra mused.

"All I can tell you is that he never showed up here in Burning Cove," Luther said.

"I'll bet he heard the news about Labyrinth Springs on the radio and concluded that he didn't need protection after all,"

Simon said.

Luther's mouth kicked up at the corners. "Which means I still owe you a favor."

Lyra brightened with curiosity. "Why do you owe Simon?"

"He saved my life a while back," Luther said. "The McGruder case."

Raina looked surprised. "The poisoner who was killing people with his fake cure for lung diseases?"

"Simon and I worked together on that project," Luther said. "At the end McGruder surprised me with a vial of acid. He was about to toss it into my face. It would have blinded me. But he was so focused on me he didn't hear Simon come up behind him. Simon grabbed his arm and twisted it. McGruder dropped the vial of acid. Some of it splashed on the back of Simon's right hand. McGruder was maddened. He grabbed the letter opener off his desk and charged Simon. There was a struggle. It was over in a few seconds. At the end, the blade of the letter opener was in McGruder, not Simon."

Simon exhaled a long-suffering sigh. "Sooner or later everybody talks."

Lyra glared at him. "No more odd jobs of that sort. Stick to the book business."

"Mostly I do," Simon said. He smiled. "It

pays better."

Raina looked at Simon. "Lyra tells me you plan to move your bookshop to Burning Cove."

"That's right," Simon said. "I'm going to close down Cage Antiquarian Books in L.A. and open Cage Books here in town."

Luther's brows quirked. "Not Cage *Antiquarian* Books?"

"No," Simon said. "I'll continue with the consulting side of the business — there's too much money in antiquarian books to ignore it. Besides, I like the feel of the old books."

"It certainly makes a great cover for the odd jobs you do for Failure Analysis," Luther said. "Not to put pressure on you."

"Don't worry, I'm not getting out of the odd-job business, not entirely. But my new bookshop will focus on current titles. The past will always be there, but the future is rushing toward us at a hundred miles an hour. The goal of my new bookshop is to keep up with it."

Raina raised her glass. "To the future. It's good to know we will be facing it with friends."

CHAPTER 50

"I like him," Vivian said. "Not that my opinion ought to matter. But I think he's perfect for you."

"You are my sister," Lyra said. "Of course your opinion is important. You tried to warn me off Hamilton, and you were absolutely correct. I'm not saying your feelings about Simon would be decisive, but I'm very glad you approve of the man I'm planning to marry."

Vivian smiled in a knowing way. "I have the feeling he doesn't know you're planning to marry him."

"I'm giving him time to adjust to the relationship."

"He seems to think the two of you can live happily in side-by-side cottages on the beach for the foreseeable future."

"I consider myself a lady with a past now, but Simon is right. This is still a small town. Living together without the benefit of marriage would cause talk. I don't want to generate any unfortunate gossip that might impact Raina's business. Kirk Investigations enjoys an impeccable reputation."

"It strikes me that Raina and Luther are going to have to figure out their own relationship sooner or later."

"I'm sure they will," Lyra said. "It's obvious they love each other."

"Yes. Well, if it helps, Nick likes Simon, too, and so does Rex. Both of them have good instincts when it comes to judging people. I think it's safe to say that you have the approval of my side of the family."

"Excellent," Lyra said. She sat back, satisfied, and picked up her coffee cup.

They were sitting on the patio of a café in the heart of Burning Cove's picturesque shopping district. In addition to the coffee there was a tray of delicate sandwiches and scones on the table.

It was another golden day in Burning Cove, Lyra reflected. Palms shaded the streets. People strolled the sidewalks, glancing into windows filled with fashionable clothes. Art galleries were scattered about. One of them, the Ashwood Gallery, had the latest photograph from Vivian's Men series displayed in the window. A bowl of flowers had been discreetly arranged in front of the more revealing portions of the nude male in the picture. The price tag was also concealed, because the figure was quite high. *If you have to ask,* Lyra thought, smiling to herself. Vivian was a swiftly rising star in the world of art photography.

Simon and Vivian's new husband, Nick, were in a nearby hardware store, shopping for whatever oddities men somehow never failed to discover in hardware stores. Nick's impressively dangerous-looking dog, Rex, was with them.

"I can tell from the way he looks at you that Simon really cares for you," Vivian said. "I think Mom and Dad will like him but I must admit I'm sorry Dad won't be gaining the son-in-law he hoped for, the man who would take over Brazier Shipping. Still, it's his own fault. He should have made you the heir to his business. I suppose that when he's ready to retire he'll have to sell the company."

"Don't worry, I've got a plan to keep Brazier Shipping in the family," Lyra said.

Vivian had been about to take another sip of coffee. She put the cup down, startled. "I thought you liked your new career as a private investigator."

"I do. One of these days I'm hoping Raina will make me a full partner in the firm. She says I am no longer an apprentice. I am now a full-fledged investigator."

"How is that going to keep Brazier Shipping in the family?"

Lyra smiled, pleased with her own brilliance. "Dad is in his early fifties, and he's in excellent health. I'm sure he will be running Brazier Shipping for the next couple of decades, by which time both of us will have no doubt provided him with a few potential heirs to the throne. He can take his pick."

Vivian stared at her. "Grandchildren? How do you know — ?"

"That you and I will both have children?" Lyra winked. "Call me psychic."

Vivian started to laugh. Lyra joined her.

Simon and Nick appeared and pulled up chairs. Rex greeted Vivian and Lyra with lavish enthusiasm and then took up a position under the table, where he waited expectantly for food to magically appear.

Nick eyed Lyra warily and then switched his attention to Vivian. "Are we missing something?"

"Don't worry about it," Lyra said. "Just a little sisterly chat."

Nick looked skeptical. "Uh-huh."

"Lyra has a plan to keep Brazier Shipping in the family," Vivian explained.

"How?" Nick asked.

"Isn't it obvious?" Simon said. He popped a tiny sandwich into his mouth. "Grand-children. That's where you and I come in. I suspect it's been her master plan all along."

Lyra had just taken a sip of coffee. She tried to swallow and failed. She sputtered, spewed some coffee, grabbed her napkin, and went into a violent coughing fit.

Simon leaned over and thumped her lightly on the back. He smiled at the others. "She has an answer for everything."

CHAPTER 51

Simon brought the speedster to a stop at the front entrance of the Hidden Beach Inn. He contemplated the mansion with a sense of doom. *Just call me psychic.*

"This is not a good idea," he said.

Half an hour ago he had been blissfully savoring a cup of coffee and the scrambled eggs he had prepared in the cast iron skillet that Lyra claimed she had no idea how to use. It had been amusing trying to teach her how to cook eggs.

Lyra had answered the phone. The instant he saw her eyes light up with the all-too-familiar gleam of curiosity, he had known trouble was coming.

"It's for you," she said, holding out the phone. "Dr. Otto Tinsley. He says he's here in Burning Cove."

It was the perfect way to ruin what had been the start of a perfect day.

"You should not come in with me," he

said. "It would be better if I deal with Otto alone."

"I'm looking forward to meeting him," Lyra said. "I've never met a professional psychic researcher."

"He's a con artist, Lyra. A fraud."

"Wouldn't you say he's more of a showman?"

"No. I would not say that. With a professional showman you know you're watching a performer at work. It's an act. Tinsley pretends to be the real deal, a prestigious researcher."

"From what you told me he didn't claim to have paranormal powers — he says his machine can detect them."

"The machine is a fake. Every time he hooked me up to it onstage a green light glowed on the front of the damned thing. He told the audience it was detecting my paranormal ability."

"Well, you do have some sort of extra-sensory perception," Lyra said.

"The green light came on because he switched it on every time we went onstage, Lyra. The act was a complete con. He *used* me."

"Got news for you, Simon. Everyone gets used occasionally."

"Is that right? When was the last time

anyone used you?"

"Gosh, let me think," Lyra said. "Oh, right, there was the time Marcella Adlington used me as an excuse to kill her husband and try to murder Raina."

Simon groaned. "Why do I bother arguing with you? You've got an answer for everything."

"And then there was the time you planned to use me to amuse yourself while you vacationed in Burning Cove."

"That's different. I wasn't going to use you, damn it. I just wanted to share my vacation with someone."

"You wanted a no-strings-attached affair with a reckless, fun-loving divorcée, a lady with a past. A fast woman."

"Are you going to hold that over my head forever?"

"Probably," Lyra said. "I like to watch you turn red."

"Okay, I admit I miscalculated. I wanted to keep things light."

"Superficial."

"Superficial," he said through set teeth. "Whatever. But I had my reasons. I've got a lousy track record when it comes to relationships."

"So do I."

He narrowed his eyes. "Your record isn't

nearly as bad as mine."

Lyra turned to face him. She rested her arm along the back of the seat and appeared to give his comment some serious consideration.

"I'll grant you that point," she said. "I suppose I could work on my track record by going through a few more lousy relationships. But I think it would be a waste of time."

"Why do I have the feeling that I'm not winning this argument?"

"Probably because you don't stand a chance. I've got an answer for everything, remember?"

"Sarcasm is beneath you."

"No, it's not. What do you say we go meet Dr. Otto Tinsley?"

"He's not a real doctor of anything."

"Lots of people use honorary titles."

"Fake titles."

"I'm through with this quarrel." Lyra opened her door and put one foot on the ground. "I can't wait to meet Dr. Tinsley."

"We are not going anywhere until I finish what I started here," Simon said.

"Oh, all right." She turned halfway around to face him. "I'm listening."

"I'm trying to tell you that I thought it would be better for both of us if things didn't get serious. But then they did. I no longer want a fling. I want more — a lot more. I love you, damn it. I realize you've decided that you never want to marry, but —"

"I've changed my mind."

"But I think you feel something for me," he said, determined to finish what he had started. "I'm hoping it's enough to convince you to continue our relationship. I know you're committed to your new career at Kirk Investigations. That's not a problem —"

He broke off as her words finally hit him. "What?"

She smiled. "I said I've changed my mind about marriage. I love you."

"What the hell? Why didn't you tell me?"

"I just did. I was biding my time, waiting until I thought you were ready for the truth."

"I didn't think a close relationship would ever work for me."

"You hadn't met me."

"That is so damn right." He wrapped a hand around the back of her neck and drew her toward him. "Will you marry me?"

"Yes." She brushed her mouth against his and then pulled away. "Now let's go meet Dr. Tinsley, expert in parapsychology."

"We're talking about marriage and you want to go meet a con artist. You're moving a little too fast for me."

"You wanted a fast woman. That's what you've got." She opened the car door, got out, and paused to look back at him. "Try to keep up."

He laughed. It was the very last thing he had anticipated doing after the phone call from Tinsley. But the laughter roared up from a wellspring somewhere deep inside and crashed through him. He was suddenly euphoric. Joyous.

He opened his door, climbed out from behind the wheel, and followed Lyra through the front door of the Hidden Beach Inn.

CHAPTER 52

"Welcome to the Hidden Beach Inn. I'm Amalie Jones, the proprietor. How can I help you?"

"Lyra Brazier, an agent with Kirk Investigations," Lyra said. "And this is Mr. Simon Cage. We're here to see Dr. Otto Tinsley. I believe we are expected."

Simon glanced at Lyra, noting the smooth note of professionalism in her voice. He realized she enjoyed introducing herself as an employee of Kirk Investigations. Her obvious delight in having found a career reminded him of his own reaction to being sent out on his first case for Luther Pell. He knew he had grown jaded over the past few years, but the work still had a hold on him. He was no longer obsessed with the thrill of the hunt, but he had a feeling he would always get a little rush of excitement and anticipation whenever Pell presented him with an intriguing opportunity.

456

But now there was room in his life for something else, something that would bring him a deeper sense of satisfaction and commitment. There was room for a woman to love; room to create a family — a real family. He wanted a home, a place where he belonged, and his dream was at long last within reach.

But if there was anyone on the face of the earth who could destroy his bright new future, it was Otto Tinsley.

"Dr. Tinsley told me he was expecting Mr. Cage," Amalie said. She gave Simon a vivacious smile. "I'll be happy to show you to his room. Miss Brazier, will you be accompanying Mr. Cage? Or would you prefer a cup of tea while you wait?"

"Call me Lyra. And yes, I'll be going upstairs with Simon. Wouldn't miss this for the world. I understand Dr. Tinsley is a renowned expert in the paranormal."

Amalie was amused. "That's what he tells me. When he checked in last night he insisted on walking through the Hidden Beach with an instrument he calls a paranormal energy detector. He claims he was able to detect deposits of the stuff in several locations, including my front desk."

"That sounds like Tinsley," Simon said.

Both women looked at him.

He gave them a polite smile. "Dr. Tinsley knows how to put on a show."

Amalie nodded agreeably. "So do I. I used to be a flyer in a circus. Dr. Tinsley and I had a lovely chat about how to read an audience. If you will follow me, I'll take you upstairs."

Amalie slipped out from behind the counter with a dancer's grace and led the way through the grand lobby to the staircase.

Simon took in the high ceilings with their distinctive wooden beams, the sun-splashed Mediterranean colors, the massive fireplace, and the beautiful tile work. The Hidden Beach Inn wasn't the Burning Cove Hotel, but it looked and felt expensive.

"Nice place," Simon said. "Evidently Tinsley is doing well with his new act."

Lyra gave him a quelling glare. Amalie pretended not to hear him. She went lightly up the stairs.

"It's a pleasure to meet both of you," she said over her shoulder. "I've been following your exciting exploits in the *Herald.*"

"Raina Kirk tells me that you've had your own adventures recently here at the Hidden Beach," Lyra said. "Something about your first guest being murdered by his own robot?"

"It was not the best way to go into business, I can tell you that," Amalie said.

And just like that she was off and chatting comfortably with Lyra. Simon shook his head in silent wonder.

Amalie did not stop talking until they reached a room at the end of the hall. She broke off in mid-sentence — something about rumors of a ghost at the inn — and rapped smartly on the door.

"Your guests are here, Dr. Tinsley."

The door opened, and Simon's past came rushing back with the force of a runaway train. The usual swirl of emotions struck hard. Affection, anger, despair, loss. He had to fight to suppress the storm.

With his mane of silver hair, short, elegantly trimmed beard, and gold spectacles, Otto managed to appear both distinguished and fashionable. He wore a hand-tailored light blue jacket, trousers, and a pristine white shirt. The collar of the shirt was crisply starched and pressed. His striped silk tie was elegantly knotted.

Simon saw that exact same knot in the mirror whenever he put on a tie. A memory flashed through him — Otto standing behind him, patiently guiding him through the process of tying a sophisticated knot. Giving him fatherly advice. *The knot says everything about you. It signals your back-*

ground, your financial worth, and your educa-
tion. It conveys power and control. If you want
to command an audience, you must first
control the knot of your tie.

"Thank you for showing my guests to my room, Mrs. Jones," Otto said in his deep, resonant voice.

"Of course." Amalie stepped back. "Shall I have tea sent up?"

Otto looked uncertain. He glanced uneasily at Simon. "I —"

"A tea tray would be lovely," Lyra said.

"Right away," Amalie said.

She half glided, half levitated back down the hall, heading toward the stairs.

Otto closed the door behind her and turned to smile at Simon. "Good to see you again, son."

"I'm not your son," Simon said.

But he said it the way he always said it — without any expectation of making Otto acknowledge the reality of their relationship. It was part of the pointless ritual they went through every time they met. Otto deliberately reminded him of their connection, and Simon tried to deny it. Neither could win the battle of wills yet both of them engaged in it every time they encountered each other.

True to form, Otto acted as if he had not

heard the denial. He switched his attention to Lyra. "You must introduce me to this lovely lady, Simon."

Lyra smiled her golden smile and held out a gloved hand. She spoke before Simon could make the introductions.

"Lyra Brazier of Kirk Investigations," she said.

"A lady private investigator," Otto marveled. "Fascinating. Are you here in a professional capacity?"

Lyra laughed. "No. This is a personal matter. I'm very keen to see this paranormal energy-sensing machine of yours. I have always been intrigued by the possibilities of extrasensory perception. I've attended a few demonstrations purporting to prove the existence of ESP, but they were not particularly convincing."

Otto narrowed his eyes. "Who staged the demonstrations?"

"One was provided by Dr. Roland Hodges," Lyra said. "The other was given by Dr. Charles Montgomery."

"Bah. Charlatans, both of them. You are welcome to examine my machine, Miss Brazier. It's over there on the table. I admit it is a work in progress. I have been perfecting it for years. But it is the real thing, I assure you."

Lyra gave him another charming smile and enthusiastically crossed the room to take a close look at the strange machine sitting on the table.

Otto looked at Simon.

"Thank you for coming here this morning," he said.

"The last time we saw each other you borrowed five hundred bucks that you swore you would pay back within six months," Simon said. He walked through the doorway and into the room. "I'm still waiting for my money."

Otto chuckled. "You will have it soon. That is precisely why I am here today."

"To repay me?" Simon did not bother to conceal his disbelief.

"In due time," Otto said. "Today I want to tell you more about the amazing opportunity that has come my way." He gestured toward the table. "Behold, the new and improved Tinsley Paranormal Energy Detector."

Simon was forced to admit he was reluctantly intrigued. There had been a time when he had believed in Tinsley's device; a time when he was convinced Otto really was on the way to making a serious contribution to research that would prove that the Simon Cages of the world did not belong in asylums.

Against his better judgment, he crossed the room to join Lyra. Together they contemplated the impressive-looking machine.

The detector looked as if it had been designed for the set of a Frankenstein movie or perhaps copied from the cover of *Popular Mechanics.* It was a bit larger than a typewriter, made of metal, and covered with dials, gauges, and a couple of small light bulbs, both of which were dark. A couple of long cables dangled from one end.

"Looks like the old Tinsley Paranormal Energy Detector," Simon said.

"Just the exterior," Otto said. "I assure you the mechanism inside has been greatly improved. It is far more sensitive now."

Lyra picked up one of the cables and examined it. "How does the detector work?"

Before Otto could respond, one of the bulbs began to glow with a green light. The needle on the dial moved.

"Huh." Otto hurried forward to check the gauges and dials. "This is very interesting."

"What?" Lyra said.

Otto frowned. "It's indicating that it senses some paranormal energy."

"Wow, what an amazing surprise," Simon said.

Lyra and Otto ignored him.

"Is it emanating from Simon?" Lyra asked.

"No, he's not the one holding the cable." Otto looked up, excitement heating his eyes. "I believe it's coming from you, Miss Brazier."

"Another astonishing surprise," Simon remarked.

Again he was ignored.

"Really?" Lyra said, her eyes sparkling.

"Let go of the sensor and we'll see what happens," Otto said.

Lyra set the cable on the table. The green light faded and disappeared.

"Yes, it's definitely indicating that you have a perceptible level of paranormal talent," Otto said. "My theory is that all humans have a degree of extrasensory perception but we usually dismiss it as intuition."

"So your device is merely indicating I've got some intuition?"

"If so, it's a good deal more than average intuition," Otto said. He got an expression of intense concentration. "I have a lot of work to do to enhance the detector. The problem is that, although it can sense stronger-than-average paranormal currents, it can't give me any clue to the exact nature of the energy or what type of abilities might be associated with those particular wavelengths."

"I trust you're not hoping to reach the Other Side," Lyra said.

Otto was outraged. "Don't be ridiculous. There's no such thing as talking to the spirit world. Anyone who claims to be a medium is a fraud."

"I agree," Lyra said. "I just wanted to be sure you weren't pursuing that goal."

"Absolutely not. The scientific research into the paranormal has been badly muddled by the fakery of those who claim to be able to speak to the dead. Thankfully, some reputable academic institutions are starting to take a serious interest in paranormal research."

Lyra nodded. "I know that Duke University has a facility dedicated to parapsychology and the study of extrasensory perception. There are other institutes around that are investigating paranormal phenomena. I doubt it will be long before the government takes an interest in the field."

Simon glanced at her, clearly impressed. "You're aware of all that?"

She shrugged. "I told you, I have always been interested in psychic phenomena."

"We don't have all day," Simon said. He looked at Otto. "Why did you track me down here in Burning Cove?"

Otto started to answer but a crisp knock on the door interrupted him.

"Room service," a woman sang out.

"I'll get it," Simon said.

At least it gave him something to do.

He opened the door. A perky young woman stood in the hall. She held a large platter laden with the usual tea paraphernalia.

"I'm Willa," she said. She gave Simon a cheerful smile. "Amalie said to bring you a tea tray. I added some freshly baked shortbread. It's my specialty."

"Please set the tray on the coffee table," Simon said.

"Yes, sir."

Willa whisked into the room. She set the tray down and arranged the cups and saucers. When she straightened she saw the detector.

"Is that your paranormal energy detector, Dr. Tinsley?" she asked.

"Yes, it is," Otto said.

"Amalie said you found all sorts of paranormal energy here at the inn."

"An unusual amount, yes," Otto said.

Willa brightened. "That is very exciting and quite helpful."

Simon eyed her warily. "How is it helpful?"

466

"We can use Dr. Tinsley's findings for marketing purposes," Willa explained. "People will love the notion of staying at an inn that has been scientifically proven to have a lot of paranormal energy in the atmosphere. It's even better than the ghost. Excuse me. I've got to run. Got another batch of shortbread in the oven."

Willa vanished out into the hall. Simon closed the door behind her and looked at Otto.

"You've always been right about one thing, Otto," he said. "People are fascinated with the paranormal."

Lyra sat down on the couch and picked up the teapot. "I think the widespread curiosity about the paranormal stems from the fact that everyone dreams and everyone has had a flash or two of inexplicable intuition. Neither can be easily explained, so we are forced to consider the notion that there is a great deal about the natural world that we do not know, let alone comprehend."

Otto lowered himself into a chair, crossed his legs, and accepted a teacup. "I congratulate you on your sophisticated approach to the subject, Miss Brazier."

Simon began to prowl the room. "Get to

the point, Otto. What do you want from me?"

Otto contrived to look hurt. "Why must you always leap to the conclusion that I only visit when I want something from you?"

"Isn't that the way it is?"

Otto sniffed in a pathetic manner. "If that is the case it is because I don't feel terribly welcome when I do visit." He looked at Lyra. "Simon is like a son to me. He was an orphan, you see. He was about to turn thirteen and they were going to toss him into an asylum. They said he was delusional."

"She knows about my past," Simon said evenly. "There's no need to explain that I owe you a debt I can apparently never repay. So let's just skip to the end game. From the looks of your clothes and your choice of hotels, it seems you did well for yourself on your East Coast tour. Have you gone through all the money you made?"

Anger and something else — something that might have been pain — sparked in Otto's eyes. He got the strong emotions under control in a matter of seconds but Simon was oddly flummoxed by the small revelation. Otto rarely displayed any genuine emotions. He was always, *always* under control.

468

In search of enlightenment, Simon glanced at Lyra. She had just popped a small slice of shortbread into her mouth.

"Now I know why you're so hard to read, Simon," she said around a mouthful of shortbread. She dusted crumbs off her hands, picked up the plate of shortbread, and offered it to him. "You learned from a master, didn't you?"

Simon glared at her and then at the tray of cookies. Unable to think of anything else to do, he picked up a slice of shortbread and took a bite. It was excellent.

Otto smiled at Lyra. "Are you implying he learned that trick from me?"

Lyra set the plate on the table and gave him a serene smile. "Simon is very good at concealing his emotions. I believe you taught him that skill, didn't you?"

Otto raised one shoulder in an elegant, modest shrug. "The ability to project a certain image is vital if one hopes to control —"

"The audience," Simon concluded. "You taught me that a long time ago, and I will admit that it has proven useful from time to time. Now if you would just tell me what the hell you want —"

"As it happens, I don't need to borrow any money from you," Otto said. "Not this time. I'm still flush from the tour."

Simon stopped by the coffee table long enough to pick up another slice of short-bread. "Don't keep me in suspense. There must be something you think I can do for you."

Otto exhaled heavily and appeared to brace himself for rejection. "I want you to assist me with the demonstration I am scheduled to give to the members of the Department of Parapsychology at the college where I hope to obtain a position. I need someone I *know* has some strong talent. If I advertise for volunteers I'll get fakes and people who are delusional. I must have someone with at least some proven ability."

"Forget it," Simon said. "I told you, I'm never going onstage again."

"I'm not asking you to go in front of an audience," Otto said. "The only people who will be present aside from you and me are the faculty members who will vote on whether to accept me as a researcher."

"That's an audience," Simon said. "I'm no longer in show business."

Otto gave a bleak nod and picked up his teacup. "I was afraid you would refuse, but I had to try."

Lyra set her cup down on the saucer.

"How about me? You said I had some talent."

"What the hell?" Simon said.

"It would be an interesting experience," Lyra said. "I've always been curious about the theories of paranormal energy. It's exciting to know that some serious research is going on. I would love to assist Dr. Tinsley."

"Can't you see that Otto is trying to take advantage of what he thinks will be a money-making opportunity?" Simon growled.

"No," Lyra said. "I don't believe that. I think Dr. Tinsley sincerely believes in the paranormal and he wants a chance to prove that there is such a thing as extrasensory perception. What better way to go about it than by engaging in serious research in a properly equipped laboratory?"

"What makes you so sure Otto isn't a fraud?" Simon said.

Lyra smiled. "Simple. He found you and identified you as someone with genuine talent."

"He used me."

"No, that's not true." Otto slammed his cup and saucer down with enough force to send tea sloshing over the side. He paid no attention. He shot to his feet. "I didn't use you. We worked together. We were a team."

"You needed me to make money," Simon said. "Admit it."

"You needed me to take you out of that orphanage before they decided to lock you up in an institution."

Lyra sipped tea calmly and lowered the cup. "Sounds like you needed each other. No, I take that back. I'd say you rescued each other."

Simon and Otto swung around to face her.

"Do you mind if I ask why your act broke up?" Lyra said.

"Ask Simon, not me," Otto muttered. "He's the ungrateful wretch who walked out. Never bothered to tell me why, either. Just packed his bags and said he was going to try another career."

"Where were you when Simon decided to leave?" Lyra asked.

"Seattle," Otto said. He glared at Simon. "It was at the end of a one-week engagement. We sold out the theater every night. Why did you leave? And don't tell me it's because you decided we were a couple of con artists. We gave legitimate demonstrations to audiences who were interested in the paranormal. Yes, we made money doing it, but we were not charlatans, damn it. Your talent is real. Your readings were real. Everything about the show was real."

Simon stalked across the room and stopped in front of the window. He clasped his hands behind his back and looked out at the view of the sun-splashed Pacific.

"Not real enough," he said. "I finally figured that out in Seattle."

A charged silence gripped the room.

"I don't understand," Otto said. "You have a genuine talent. Hell, you're using it to make a living now as an investigator."

"I'm not talking about my ability," Simon said. "It was in Seattle that I realized I could never be what you wanted me to be when you took me out of the orphanage."

"What did you think Otto wanted you to be?" Lyra asked gently.

"A replacement for his son — his *real* son. The heroic one who survived the Great War only to come home and die of the flu in Seattle."

"Simon," Otto whispered. He sounded stricken. "No. It wasn't like that. Where did you get the idea I saw you as a replacement for Edward?"

"I knew Seattle was difficult for you," Simon said, "but I didn't know why until I followed you one afternoon. I knew you had lived in Seattle during the war. I told myself you were going to see an old friend, maybe a woman. But something didn't feel right. I

473

thought maybe you had gotten into trouble with a loan shark. I was worried."

"So you followed me to Edward's grave."

"You wept, Otto. It was pouring rain, and you cried. I had never seen you cry. You were always so controlled. But you broke down in tears at that grave and I knew there was nothing I could do to console you because I could never be Edward. I was just a poor kid from an orphanage who happened to have a little useful talent."

A cup and saucer clattered on the coffee table. Simon heard Otto get to his feet. A moment later the man he had once thought of as his father was standing beside him at the window. Together they looked out at the Pacific.

"I never realized you felt I was trying to use you as a replacement for Edward," he said softly. "The two of you are so very different. Your personalities, your tastes, your interests. No, I never saw you as a stand-in for my first son. But I do see you as my other son. That is who you will always be for me."

Simon's throat tightened. "You saved me from the asylum. You made me the man I am today. Those are things that a good father does. I walked away from you and the act that night in Seattle because I was afraid I could never live up to the standard Edward had established."

"Miss Brazier was right, you know. We rescued each other. You came into my life when I was in despair. I had no one, and I was unable to prove a damn thing with my machine. I was thinking of ending things, if you want to know the truth. When I heard about the boy in an orphanage who was delusional because he believed he sensed ghosts in certain objects, I assumed the doctors were right. I was sure you probably were unstable, like so many others I had tested. But I took one look at you and I saw a boy who needed a family, not an institution. I would have taken you out of that place even if you hadn't had a lick of paranormal talent. You brought something alive inside me, something I thought had died. You gave me a reason to go on."

The door of the room opened and closed very quietly. Simon turned quickly. So did Otto.

Lyra was gone.

CHAPTER 53

Amalie was behind the front desk working on some papers. She looked up when Lyra came downstairs alone.

"Everything okay up there?" she asked.

"I think so," Lyra said. She reached the bottom step and crossed the lobby to the front desk. "Dr. Tinsley and Simon have a long history together. First time they've seen each other in months. I got the feeling they need to have a private conversation, so I thought I'd leave them to it."

Amalie raised her brows. "Men aren't always very good at those sorts of conversations."

"Well, I'm very good at getting those sorts of conversations started. It's up to them to finish this one."

"I had a feeling that this meeting was more than just a routine business discussion. Dr. Tinsley has been very anxious ever since he arrived. He called the Burning

476

Cove Hotel first. When he was told that Mr. Cage had checked out, he looked so lost and forlorn that I felt I had to point him in your direction. I had a hunch Mr. Cage might be eating breakfast at your place."

Lyra smiled. "Because everyone knows he spent the night with me?"

"Burning Cove is a small town. When it comes to gossip it can hold its own with small towns everywhere."

"I've learned that."

"Between you and me, I think Dr. Tinsley was afraid Mr. Cage wouldn't show up for the appointment this morning."

Lyra glanced at the stairs that led up to the floor above. "They have a few things to work out, but I'm almost positive it will go reasonably well."

Amalie's eyes flashed with amusement. "You're that good when it comes to getting people to talk?"

"Some would say it's a talent."

"Everyone has one. Sometimes it just takes a while to figure out what it is. Can I interest you in another cup of tea while you wait for the men to finish that private conversation?"

"Sounds great, thank you."

Amalie floated out from behind the desk. "Let's go into the tearoom."

477

Lyra followed her. "Is it true that Dr. Tinsley's detector picked up a lot of paranormal energy here in your inn?"

"So he claims. A lot of it was probably laid down by my husband."

"Mr. Jones?"

"He's literally a human lie detector. It's a very disconcerting talent."

"Really? I would think it would be quite useful."

"Matthias tells me the problem is that everyone lies. As far as he's concerned, it's intent that matters."

"That's very interesting. Simon has an ability to sense emotions infused into objects."

"He can do that?"

"If the energy is strong enough."

Amalie walked into the small tearoom. "I think you and I have a lot to talk about."

"I believe we do," Lyra said.

She and Amalie were deep into a conversation about their new careers when Simon appeared in the doorway of the tearoom.

"Am I interrupting anything?" he asked.

"No, I should be getting back to the office," Lyra said.

"And I've got some work to do," Amalie said. "Lyra, it's been a pleasure. We must get together again soon. Perhaps the four of

us — you and Mr. Cage, Matthias and I —
could meet for drinks at the Paradise soon?"

"That would be lovely," Lyra said. "We'll
look forward to it, won't we, Simon?"

He gave her a bemused smile. "Sure." He
turned to Amalie. "Do you think your cook
might be willing to give me the recipe for
her shortbread cookies?"

Amalie laughed. "Of course."

A few minutes later Lyra and Simon walked
out the front door of the inn and got into
the Cord.

"Out of curiosity, do you happen to have
read Dale Carnegie's *How to Win Friends
and Influence People?*" Simon asked.

"No," Lyra said. "Why do you ask?"

Simon laughed and fired up the big engine. "Never mind."

"How did things go with Dr. Tinsley? Are
you going to help him with his demonstration?"

"Yes." Simon put the car in gear and drove
down the long drive toward Ocean View
Lane. "I don't think he and the others in
that new laboratory will get far with their
paranormal research but I do agree that
Otto is serious about studying extrasensory
perception. He's too old to be on the road
all the time. It will be good for him to settle

down and devote himself to what he sees as his life's work. The college he hopes will employ him is in L.A."

"Not far away." Lyra smiled. "That's good. Let's invite him to join us for dinner at the Burning Cove Hotel tonight."

"You know, people used to accuse me of being a recluse, but lately my social calendar seems to be filling up fast."

"That happens when you've got friends and family."

"I seem to have acquired a lot of both recently."

"And you haven't even met my parents," Lyra said.

"Trying to scare me?"

"Nope. Wouldn't be possible. You're an agent of Luther Pell's Failure Analysis, Inc. You catch bad guys for a living and you've got serious paranormal talent. Nothing scares you."

"You're wrong," Simon said. "One thing scares the hell out of me."

"What?"

"The possibility that I might have misunderstood you earlier when you said you loved me and that you'd marry me."

"Don't worry, your hearing is just fine. I've been waiting a very long time for you to show up, Simon Cage. Now that you've

The employees of Thorndike Press hope you have enjoyed this Large Print book. All our Thorndike, Wheeler, and Kennebec Large Print titles are designed for easy reading, and all our books are made to last. Other Thorndike Press Large Print books are available at your library, through selected bookstores, or directly from us.

For information about titles, please call:
    (800) 223-1244

or visit our website at:
    gale.com/thorndike

To share your comments, please write:
    Publisher
    Thorndike Press
    10 Water St., Suite 310
    Waterville, ME 04901

arrived I'm not about to let you get away. We can make things legal with a courthouse ceremony this week. When my parents get home from London they'll insist on a big reception in San Francisco, but I'll convince them to combine it with the one they plan to give Vivian and Nick."

Simon smiled. "You move fast, lady."

"I seem to recall that was the kind of woman you were hoping to find here in Burning Cove."

"Yes," he said. "I got the lady I was looking for."

She smiled. "One with a past."

"And a future," he said. "With me."

He drove down Ocean View Lane and made a left onto Cliff Road, heading back toward town. The pavement followed the cliffs above the sparkling Pacific. Lyra savored the warm, golden light of the California sun and thought about the future. A joyful sense of wonder welled up from somewhere deep inside. For a moment she was too dazzled to speak. When she found her voice, she turned in the seat.

"We're home, Simon," she said.

"Yes, we are," he said. "Wasn't sure what it would look like if I ever found it. Turns out you know it when you see it."

ABOUT THE AUTHOR

Amanda Quick is a pseudonym for Jayne Ann Krentz, the author, under various pen names, of more than fifty *New York Times* bestsellers. There are more than 35 million copies of her books in print. She is also the author of the Ladies of Lantern Street novels and the Arcane Society series.